Also by L. E. Smith

Novels
The Consequence of Gesture
Travers' Inferno

Stories
Views Cost Extra

ISBN-978-1-944388-31-7
Library of Congress Control Number: 2017959427

Fomite
58 Peru Street
Burlington, VT

Untimely RIPped

L. E. Smith

Fomite
Burlington, VT

For Calvin D. Smith

BEFORE I START, I JUST WANT TO SAY, this is not a book. Books smell like old people. Think of this as a sad song in a major key, what country songs do all the time. Tonal brighteners added to heartache. Such as the Dad singing Merle Haggard out from the shower when he lived at home. Think of this as my brain singing while iPhone cameras flash in the hands of dorm proctors because Marvin Herkimer hangs from a school tie fastened to the top bunk. I rolled out of bed and it was over. Laxed out you might think. Or desperation drunk. My lacrosse bros of Poncy Prep will think a hardcorebadass whittled to suicide by some babe putdown. But no. None of those. It was just easy.

I know about Holden Caulfield and about Gene Forrester. SparkNotes pretty much covers those two. Mental breakdowns and suicide clubs. Idgaf! to that! is what I say and which, if you don't know, is the textese way of saying those two don't rate. Because, I'm none of those delicate ones. My parents paid tuition to find that out. For one thing, I'm dead. I dressed in school colors, blues and grays, which is what Poncy Prep wants for special occasions. I think my suicide is special enough.

Poncy is what the locals call it, an all boys' school in Sapperstown, New Jersey, a couple hours ride from Philadelphia and so deep in corn you'd think Jersey has no shore. Pontificate Preparatory School is where you find it on Google, which is a Benedictine name because some bishop broke a chalice of Christ's blood on a corner stone somewhere to launch the place. Then lost his job for resisting the perverty priest round up. This school taught me about irony.

This song comes to you from the afterlife. It's the mourner's gathering first weekend after my embarrassing intentional. Teachers and trustees, they all get down and party, all the significant adults, the big farewell. But, like, really more a clever move by Headmaster Langly to detour my parents lawyering up. I swear I can see myself reflected in the chrome sheen of the Mom's jewelry. Me standing there ghostly dead at the Headmaster's campus digs. She accepting gracefully drunken teacher condolences, some with tears for other reasons than my suicide. There's Mr. Ralph, by example, my English teacher, who is unwelcome here, a neglect circle of side-looks forming around him because he's been fired by Headmaster Langly. He's crashed this scene deliberately to lean into the Mom saying poetry in his emoticon voice, something about an athlete dying young. Mr. Ralph dressed in a beige suit with a red scarf to bragcast his red hair and beard, a chunky smorg from Maine that always thinks he's right. But he's mostly smart even if he over-thinks. My death needs to fit into a cubby of ideas where it will masticulate awhile in the acid juices of his over-revved brain and then expel a diarrhea bomb. Which is what he's directing at the Mom.

"Your son may have run a short race," says Mr. Ralph, "but as the poets say, in sunshine and on the fields of glory. There was no reason for his death beyond life's sometimes short fuse. Do you see? No one is to blame."

"He was a runaway, doing stupid things, and the drugs...," says the Mom.

"Oh, I didn't know. Drug problems? Were there drugs in his system?"

"I don't know. Probably. It was after that party. A pharm party is what they call it."

"They would know," says Mr. Ralph. "But so unlike your son. He was an athlete, and a scholar in the making. I would suggest, the way you want to remember him ...

"Yes thanks, Mr...?"

"Just call me Ralph. Didn't I say? I was your son's English teacher. I'm not a teacher anymore. At least not in the formal way. Change is good, right?"

"Well, Ralph, had you seen my son blue and rigid lying in a morgue, you might not still have him trotting the Elysian Fields, you might not think change is so good. Bryn Mawyr taught me to do my own thinking. Thanks for your kind words."

△

THAT'S THE MOM. Mr. Ralph doesn't know she trained as a lawyer but only uses it in her personal life. She's pretty tough now the Dad's out of the house. She's good at slinging the sideball insult. But she doesn't need to try so hard. Mr. Ralph will soon be told by Headmaster Langly to leave or be escorted out by campus security. This is his due, many think, per his role helping engineer one of my last public appearances. They think shame on Mr. Ralph, and good riddance. But no. He's still an influence for reasons that you'll learn of later.

The Mom shifts off, taps the shoulder of Maria Petra, a hotty

Mexican babe Langly's banging. Petra's in a tight push-up bra and black ominattractive wear serving drinks from a tray. The Mom snags a glass of Chablis, her third. Theresa Whitley is tapping Petra's shoulder from the other side. Whitley's our art teacher. She has been all night eyeballing Petra and wiping the menopause sweat from her upper lip with a cocktail napkin. When Petra ignores her, Whitley moves into the Mom's lane to shortcut her escape and begins telling the Mom of all the family that has died. Her older sister recently of cancer which becomes excrementally detailed in her monologue. That's a Shakespeare term, "monologue," which means someone goes excess on mouthy. I'm pretty educated for a young, expired dude.

Anyway, there's Whitley saying, "So tempting to blame God, isn't it. He's a bastard isn't he? Most male deities are. But I suppose it depends if you're Old Testament or New. So, death is either payback for bad choices or a way to Heaven, right? My sister, she suffered something awful. At least your son went quick. Well, that is, unless to live is to suffer, in which case he suffered what... 18 years? 19?"

"Almost nineteen."

"Right, so my sister died of ovarian cancer, a stromal tumor, just a month ago. I mean, to have your own estrogen turn on you, when your ovaries go malignant, believe me, Mrs..."

"Herkimer."

"Right, it's not a kind world, and her treatment another torture before death. Let me tell you ..." and blah, blah, blah.

Anyway, the Mom is being polite. She's mostly good at being polite. She should say to Whitley, "Don't talk to me you jejemonster," which is a texter with really bad word warping. She should text-sing this little finger ditty –iT'z bEtTaH to0 SzAy GuDBai 2U.

Because Whitley is the last person still on Friendster blogging to no one in medical speak. Which is too much for the Mom who swings her jewelry such as a car bumper into the face of another mourner, turning her back on the hormonal Theresa Whitley, hoping those feet have pattered away. But Whitley's not like that. She teaches paint between the lines. She claims a spot and grows there. Doing art with her is mechanical drawing – all perspective and proportion. No feeling. Nothing out of place which is the place where feelings live. Kind of the way she presents her hogly self to the world – hair all braided and pinned, teeth capped, stomach tucked into a wide belt to jimmy the appropriate profile, and so a kind of breathless voice and jowls she can't do much about that fall from her cheekbones to her chin and shake when she talks. The bros try not to look at her when she talks and she's talking all the time. She doesn't trust the silences between words and so has stockpiled repeat wisdom nuggets such as "Boys, must to remember, art holds the mirror to our lives." Which makes you wonder if she owns one herself. Not a life. I mean a mirror. Or maybe both. Hasn't she ever heard of plastic surgery? Bradley Turcotte says, "She needs to get laid by a blindfolded Samaritan dude." Bradley is my best friend at Poncy, or was, or still is. This gets confusing.

△

THE MOM USED TO GET TUCKS AND NIPS at Christmas, gifts from the Dad. All covered on insurance under a mental anguish clause. But I'm guessing Theresa Whitley's teacher's insurance is not so generous. If it was, she would be getting counseling for teaching shits like me and Dennis Higgins with the unstoppable talkhole and Bradley Turcotte with all his diss-talk genderalities. I'm guessing those jowls of Whitley are one thing that fall outside her concept of the ideal form. Hard for her to ignore. I feel sorry for her. I really do. Chicks have it hard. Dudes are pricks. Chicks have to walk through a forest of aggrasive pricks in the beforelife, which is what us expired dudes call the pre-transformation condition.

But even the Mom has about excessed on Whitley. I can tell. She's picking at her watch band. Never a good sign. The Dad admires his x-wife from a distance, the shag auburn hair with minimal gray, her stair-step tonality and spray-on tan. The Dad steps in and takes Whitley by the elbow, says, "Headmaster Langly tells me you're the art teacher." The Dad's a suave dude for his age, manages sales at a Jeep dealership so has learned to value presentation.

Whitley is always up for a little flirtmance. She says, "Yes, that's right and who's this handsome man?" She leans into the Dad, checks her breath with a cough to the back of her hand to detect dragon-mouth fumes, thinks good-to-go, leans closer in.

"I'm Marvin's father," says the Dad leading her to an ignored corner of the room nearby the fireplace which is about burned to ash.

"Oh, right. Sorry."

"I was never much for the arts when I was a kid. I liked math. What's it like as a woman teaching art to the boys?"

"Oh, well, my brothers are boys."

"That's how you got the job?"

"Oh, no. I'm a good artist."

"What's your style?"

Whitley takes a closer look at the Dad's smile, wonders if this could be a deflection bounce off a Teflon wife. She says, "That's getting sort of naughty personal isn't it, Mr. Herkimer?"

"How well did you know my son?"

"Not very. I had him first semester. I don't really remember Marvin in my class, but that's a good thing. Believe me. Most of these boys are shits. Well, pardon my French but you don't mind me being frank. You're name's not Frank is it? I'm not saying I'm you."

"No, I'm not Frank."

"That's good. Well, the ones I remember best are the shits. But not much different from girls their age if you ask me – they're all hiffie over Gen Y secrets they share with complete strangers when cranked on Facebook sprees."

"Sorry. I don't know what you just said."

"Gen Y? The new lost generation? Facebook addiction? Oh, well, no matter. You want their respect, you learn their language. Same as any foreign culture. Ever been to Paris?"

"Only in the movies."

"Well, that's a shame. I could show you some things ... if you ever want to ... (the Dad's fading smile is a non-starter, easy to read; Whitley gets it, walks back the talk). These boys, they think all landscape is leafy trees. They're big on leafy trees. They think art is trees. Sissy images. Do you see? I teach the boys life's hard edges, the art of geometrics. I help them to become men. Do you see..." and blah, blah, blah.

If they were still married, the Dad would get a BJ from the Mom tonight for his kindness in detouring Whitley. Too bad for him. His third wife, the trophy, she has become less generous with the mouth organ since she has got to feel secure in her upkeep. But just imagine what the suits have to say about my suicide – Headmaster Langly and trustees – in those calculator brains of theirs. They're all worried over lawsuits. Dude! They should be. My parents could own this place if they want. The suits are so scared. They're having calculasms of the brain.

△

HERE IN THE AFTERLIFE we laugh at you beforelifers that orient with GPS. Earthly compass points, you know, latitude and longitude, satellite positioning. Supposing you know where you're at and where you're going, which we don't have to worry about here in the afterlife. But it's comfy. Anyway,there are, like, no rules! Which is a kind of Heaven after Poncy. And I see patterns everywhere. Which makes me dizzy. Takes getting used to. I mean, imagine seeing everyone of you beforelifers as snowflakes, so there's your special pattern, but, hey, even so, you're all snowflakes! It's the ultimate spyware. I mean, I get it. I get who you are. I hadn't realized what a fucked up zombie Googleheimer I was in the beforelife before. But I'm getting it now. All us beforelifers stuck in patterns I hadn't noticed. There's Headmaster Langly, for one. Flynt Thrush Langly. Now that's a lavish name. He has the habitude of a toady to rich parents and disrespects us ones of lesser googlical proportions.

"How's it hanging, Langly?" is what Dennis Higgins says to him before expelled for excessive mouthyness and a general hipster unconformity to everything, especially the dress code. Dennis likes his clothes used and his hair uncombed and when dressed in Poncy blues and grays, he wears them inside out. But Dennis tells it, because Langly wears very tight pants that crowd his junk so you can see which thigh his dick is chaffing. He's dangling a big one, of which he is proudful. He points it such as a factbomb at all the faculty wives and secretaries and cleaning help.

As I speak to you from the ashes of my mourners' session, as the remaining guests put in more effort because more visible, Langly has left the party goodbyes to his wifeopotamus with the sticky hors d'oeuvres fingers. He's upstairs giving it to cleaning lady Petra whose first name is Maria who has put down her tray of drinks. She is one of our mexinvasion lackeys, but she's hot if bottom heavy and bent over Langly's desk in the study. As the shitfaced teachers say goodbye to the Mom and the Dad and shake on their coats and enter the bleak hours of dorm supervision, Petra is taking it from behind in the enforced quiet of evening study hours during which all my bros of the beforelife are in their dorm rooms pretending to study but really Skyping to see their girlfriends naked, or streaming movies, or maybe stalking their exes on Facebook.

So there's Petra. She's become pretty good deflecting advances from Whitley. But with Langly, it's this – she's in his study upstairs, the last of the mourners to leave are downstairs tipping their drinks and Petra's saying in a husky kind of whisper, "Oh, master, oh, master," which gives me a whole other outlook on the job – I mean, try this: "Care for a little head ... master?"

You can imagine the sex talk. I don't feel I'm missing anything being dead when I look at those two. She has the bottom of a ripe pomegranate, seeds and all, which if we call it what it is is zits. And Langly has the squared-off skull of a battering ram. He thinks himself another Socrates because bald with only just swatches of gray hair behind the ears such as the plaster bust of the old bald, Greek fudge packer that shares his office.

Langly was a philosophy major in college. Which to his squared-off thinking makes him Socrates at the Lyceum, which was an all boys' school such as Poncy only for homos entirely. When Langly puts his arm around a Poncy dude, in advance of our formal blues and grays dinners, and asks him to "square the quad with him," he means walk a path around the school's green, what Langly calls "the peripatetics." Which is a philosophy word from Socrates of walking and talking. The ones chosen to square the quad are usually Langly's tadpole dorm proctors. Such as who found me dead and which is a lacrosse reference you might not have picked out, tadpole that is, a little guy with a big stick. The tadpole being the dorm proctor and, well, you know which is the big stick.

But sometimes Langly is tickling the ears with his quad talk one of us regular dudes whose behavior needs modification. So one time he has Dennis Higgins under his flabby arm, their breath smogging the air in lamplight, and he's saying something like this:

"Dennis, I know this can't be easy for you. Being away from home. Making new friends. Challenging classes. We have made allowances for this, believe me (here Langly double-squeezes Dennis's shoulder, smiles, adjusts his voice to peek out with authority from behind comfort words). But this language of yours, I mean, the rudeness, it has to stop."

Dennis shrugs his shoulder beneath Langly's arm, says, "What rudeness?"

Langly doesn't know for sure where to go with this. He thinks be cool, make friends, but underneath he wants to step on this kid, exterminate the turd ass, wipe the shit off his shoes and get on with his day. There's a trustee waiting at dinner. But he decides on the Socratic method. Let the kid discover for himself what Langly already knows. So he says, "Well, Dennis, if you don't know you've been rude here at Pontificate, tell me how you talk to your parents at home."

Dennis smells the trap. He's been here before. He puts on the brakes so his skinny frame bends with the recoil, pushes a lock of curly hair off his forehead, looks Langly full in the eyes with his own spaniel weepy ones, says, "My parents beat me."

Langly tenses, knows he's been bested at the game, removes his arm from Dennis' shoulder and says, "I'm sorry to hear that," while thinking Parents know best. I'd beat this one too.

Langly's gray hairs at the base of his neck, they stick out in a ring of chicken feathers. He's a little afraid of Dennis Higgins. He should be. Langly leaves behind Dennis to preen his victory and modes into the springy trot of a satyr toward dinner. No kidding! Dude, I've studied mythology. He trots on goat legs, all hairy and skinny and bowed and a permanent hard on. He is definitely a horny old satyr goat. Like I said, I learned a lot at Poncy before I became dead.

△

I WAS BACK WHEN ALIVE one of the tribe of "bros" that carry lacrosse sticks everywhere with us such as a bishop carries a crozier, which is what my Catholitic bro Bradley Turcotte says. He's a baller, he really is, which is a lacrosse term but applies otherwise too is what he thinks. Anyway, he calls his stick sometimes a crozier or a dye-job because he often changes the color of the webbing of the head. All the bros, they pretend to mourn my death when they really want to be excused for it. Well, not so much Brad. He wasn't there. He was on his dad's tax-shelter island squeezing the fruit. And, yes, there were pills, someone's parents' prescription high Xanax and others mixed together in a bowl and vodka to swallow it down, a pharm party. Which is a good term for this farmer's paradise where the school has taken root. If not for those pills, you might think, I would still be here. Or maybe not. It's not that simple. I never took those pills. I don't give a shit if jacks and jills need pills or booze or weed to feel good. I needed something else.

I think of Bradley Turcotte as I watch Theresa Whitley steering out the Headmaster's house. She has finally given up maneuvering Maria Petra into a corner for a little divert and flirt. Brad knows Whitley too well. He has one of her morning classes. He calls her the antidote to Jiffy Lube addiction, which is kind of cute. I'm guessing he used peanut butter when he was young to pull his pud, the smooth kind not the crunchy. Although maybe not. You can never tell with Brad. He does severe things to toughen up. Ask him to say about his best Whitley moment. You'll get a needle jump on the laugh meter. One night Brad heaved himself up the gnarly branches of a cedar tree outside Whitley's campus apartment. He wanted to cast a peek because of Wagner opera leaking out her windows. Brad remembered those tunes from a retro Vietnam war movie he was made to watch in English class with attack helicopters riding into battle such as Norse sisters of fate screaming a song of death. He sees Whitley drinking schnapps from the bottle and waving around hands to the sharp voices of warrior bitches. She's wearing a bra of metal hubcaps and a short, tight skirt of black leather, her blubber shaking and her flappy jowls twisting in lip-sync.

Brad gets all sneezy off the rosin of that cedar tree so Whitley comes to the window and calls campus security, which brings Bradley to his first-ever comeuppance with Langly and Socrates, founding members of the Poncy Prep penal colony. These two ancient bald dudes tread on Brad's honor awhile to even the score. Langly behind his desk joggling serious eyes of scorn at Brad and old Soc from behind up on his pillar blind as a fart. All Brad can think while silently laughing through the dress downing from Langly and Socrates is old Whitley flapping to the tunes of napalm helicopters. What a rush!

△

BRAD IS ALMOST AS TROUBLE as Dennis Higgins. But older and more smart, so more slippery, one hand massaging the adult ego, the other making rabbit ears over its head. Take per example Chapel at Poncy every morning but Wednesday. On those Chapel mornings, between prayers and song, faculty take turns at the lectern convincing us unformulated ones that unless we follow their example in some way – such as hike the long trail through punishing bugs and endless rain or finish a PhD one class at a time for ten years while teaching losers like us and living in the dorms and raising a family on cafeteria food – well, unless we have experienced something such as this, our lives will be shit.

What was it the last Chapel before I lynched myself? Oh, yeah, Mr. Gainer's perfunctious vaudeville extravaganza, as advertised on posters of himself in top hat and tails, swinging a cane with one hand, pulling at a bowtie with the other, addressing what he calls the ties that bind. So, in Chapel, he's up there beaming at us, bending us through the correct way to dress for class. We can't slide any more down our benches without being marked absent. He first demonstrates the Windsor knot. Then it's off with the blues & grays, standing there in underwear, crossed legs for laughs. Langly isn't laughing, but Gainer's extravaganza has become tradition, so what can he do? Then on with the tux, and it's all about prom that's soon after spring break. Gainer, the choir director, 250 pounds of tuxified bravado wear, holding a limp bow tie and flashing a Walmart greeter smile. I swear if this man has ever had a nightlife it came in a wet dream.

So he's up there on the dais telling us lesser ones, "Boys," he says, "there will be no clip-on ties in this school! There is no fast way to do it the right way!"

Brad begins to tickle me so I'll sing out and get in trouble. But I give him the fast elbow to stop. Of course, Dennis Higgins from the tenth grade with the nonstop mouth catches a slap back of the head from Mr. Ralph for saying, "Never had a quickie, Mr. Gainer?" Which he ignores, but which we in the pews can't very much. We laugh. Headmaster Langly steps to the dais from his seat with Father Donelli among the chorus and gives us sinners a look that says the floor will open and Hell will grab us by the ankles. So we shut it.

Then Mr. Gainer gives Langly a look of gratitude he's expected to deliver and goes on with his fable of the perfectly tied tie. Goddamn! Gainer is the boringest teachoid on the planet. Higgins earns another slap on the head for saying to Gainer, "Preach it like you teach it!"

After the laughs die, I bag ten minutes naptime dreaming of the metavag that grants wishes when you fuck it. I have to be shaken awake in the pew when Gainer's life lesson is over. Then comes English class with Mr. Ralph. I have to fight for one of the back desks to drop my head to finish my wishes, but instead I dream I have fallen into the digital signal of a robocall and can't climb out.

God's bitches! The beforelife is a really fucked up place. I pity you all. I really do. The only thing I miss is across the street of my home town neighbor Heidi Helsinger's strip tease from her upstairs window and her hand jobs. And, well, I miss Mrs. Vitello.

△

IT STARTED MY SENIOR YEAR of public high school in Lakeville, Connecticut, just before Poncy. Sunny Vitello in a rare social probe drifted into the Mom's yard sale. She was woozy from a brunch of Mimosas which explains why she clipped our neighbor's mailbox with her husband's Mustang. She wanted me to deliver a pine dresser and wanted it taken upstairs to the bedroom. First we hung out in a kitchen with trauma damage and neglect issues – walls scarred from heavy things flung at it, dirty dishes piled in the sink, the ceiling all greasy black with cobweb. But the house felt comfortable, lived in compared to my home, with furniture over-used but practical and comfy, even if what you find side of the road on trash day from the upscale neighbors. It's the original farmhouse to this lake view, dinged and lonesome, proud still even in retirement with acreage sold off to the playing fields of Hotchkiss School.

She mixed fizzy Mimosas that tasted of orange juice gone sour and we talked high school. She had attended an all girls' school in Manhattan with a reveal-nothing dress code where nuns assaulted her with religion. A Catholic tradition, is what she said, and with the name Sunny, miracles expected of her she couldn't deliver. I told her if one of our teachers in public school said a prayer he would be arrested. She laughed and said, "Aren't you the enlightened godless wonder."

She said her husband was out of town on maneuvers. Whatever that means. So I carried the dresser upstairs and we sat together on the bed and we didn't, not really, but we talked it. Then, well, we did. I was so nervous. Didn't know how to move or what to say. Just sat there. She lay me down and went to work. Talked all the way through. I don't remember what about except I balked every time she said Brent, which is her husbands' name. Brent. Better a tool used for metal work, such as "Bring over to me that brent."

She undressed me and the first time she touched me there, I spumed all over. Embarrassing. She laughed, said, "You're a whale,

Herk. An effing whale." I don't know if that means my tool is larger than a brent, or maybe my blowhole produces ponderous gobs of cream. It was my first time doing it, the whole deal. With others until Mrs. V it was BJs and HJs, including neighbor Heidi Helsinger with the body of bay watch and the face of crime. But BJs don't count. Ask any dude. It's not intimate. For me with Sunny Vitello it was the first time and felt the last ever.

Herk is what she calls me and which is my nickname because of the longer version Marvin Herkimer. But so there's Mrs. V on my cell in the early morning of the early days of our together time saying, "Herk, let's redecorate." Which means she has the Mimosas ready and Brent is somewhere off on maneuvers.

So I write another parent excuse for ditching school early, forge the Mom's name and drop it at the Principal's Office. I walk to Mrs. V's place over by the lake, short cut the woods on paths that end at her door. Should of known then what was up because a lot of foot traffic goes that way from a tangle of paths for a reason. I should have earlier read the graffiti brags carved in the birch trees and stayed away. Because she makes me crazy. She really does.

The redecorating happens before other stuff, which must of drove her husband nuts, the forever changes, and maybe also because she's not into cleaning. Dust bunnies the size of tumbleweeds. She doesn't care. The only things dusted are a maze of bookshelves she calls "the mass grave of a dying industry," which I don't really get because there's Kindle. But, anyway, there's also books lying on the floor as toe stubbers. Otherwise, she's deep into environment shaping, terraforming. Only the shelves stay in the same place. What's pinned to the walls moves around, no piece of furniture stays in the same room, no pair of underwear goes in the same drawer. Everything gets moved, expressing its new consideration, just as no partner of redecoration gets much repeat action – except me. She won't say why. But, like, I really don't care. I'm into her. I ask her what's about all the redecorating and she says she's "the queen of smeared lipstick yearning." Which I guess means she's aware how things look but can't help herself.

Her husband, Brent Vitello, he's a sergeant in the military police of Danbury where there's a squad of fighter jets. He's scary as Hellboy. Buzz haircut, a voice authorized to give orders, muscles twisting limbs such as vines growing there, a face red with anger, no patience whatever with change. See his tool shed and it's all gadgets of mysterious purpose hung on the wall where their shapes are penciled on. So how he and Mrs. V ever hooked up, can't say I get it. He throws stuff, a lot. You see holes in the old plaster walls, the lathe showing through, some from those toe stubbers I'm guessing. And in one place in the kitchen where maybe some cast iron was flung, you can read newspaper stuffed in there as insulation. It's an old house. Newspapers are good insulation. Consider the homeless sleeping on the streets of New York City with newspaper under jackets for warmth that I used to see as a sideshow to viewing Macy's windows at Christmas when a kid.

I tell Mrs. V of those windows of Macy's and about later at home us kids Hasbro warping a Christmas nativity scene displayed on the windowsill of our living room with action toy Transformers kicking ass on Decepticons. These are the GI Joes of my generation. And then there's the movie that just came out which is crap. I mean, some teen nitwit buys a shagmobile to woo his girl interest and it's an Autobot? No way! Not even in the toons. And my little brother Matt, he glued together matchsticks then layered on strips of newspaper painted red and brown saying it's Santa, elves, and reindeer, then inserted them all lumpy distortional into our Hasbro

Christmas nativity window combat scene. Way cool he did that. But so I tell all this to Mrs. V and she starts crying, says, "Herk, your childhood memories are so sweet. Shit. Maybe you and I should slow this down."

I say, "It's not just about the sex, is it? I'm into you."

"Right," she says gifting me a come-to eye squint that melts me down and grows my junk. Her hair is white blond, wavy and long, all natural off Icelandic genes, always in her eyes. She pushes away a hank and hands me another Mimosa, my head already spinning from the cheap champagne and from a hardon that won't quit. "You're into me," she says, "and when you're not you want to be." Goddamn! I'm hard all the time. It's not my fault. It's the universal boy teen embarrassment.

"You know what I mean," I say back while she's following behind and tickling the private areas and petting my hair while I'm moving furniture in the living room to make what she calls "intimate conversation groupings" near the fireplace and the window lake overlook. Which groupings will never host more than Mr. V yelling and smashing and Mrs. V crying because Mrs. V is no suburban princess with party friends. And she doesn't have a polite mouth for conversation. She's a poet and says most poets are a bad fit to polite society. She calls herself a "skaldic poet" because living in chains such as some dude that sang words out from a prison cell way before typewriters. I like the strange things she says, but it's her almost transparent white skin that turns me on, her blue, blue eyes, little-girl face expressions, long legs and the gap between her two front teeth. Also, on her cheeks, a constellation of freckles. Those really get me.

Then she says, pulling me down beside her on the sofa, stroking my hair, "I need to remind myself, Herk, you're still making adolescent memories."

"Like I'm some minimal dude?"

"What I mean is I don't want to be a bad memory ten, twenty years from now."

I mouth mash her with my lips to stop the fearsome rambling. She pulls away, says, "Oh, eff it!" And we do it right there on the rug with furniture around in an audience circle and us on the way to stagegasms. Her long pale hair flying loose, freckles lit up in passion, white legs pulling me in, beautiful Icelandic eyes happy and weepy at the same time. Goddammit! Why do Nordic princesses marry trolls? It's always a disaster marriage.

Mrs. Vitello cares too much about her bruises from Mr. V – she's always wearing long sleeve shirts in summer and never shorts even though her legs are beautiful. "They go all the way up" is what the Dad said when he saw her at the yard sale in her tight jeans. He had come by home to hand deliver the overdue child support and had seen Mrs. V sifting a revenge stack of the Dad items going cheap. Anyway, Mrs. V never has a tan. Lives on the lake and hardly ever leaves the house. Except to teach a poetry class at the local community college, which is maybe why all the redecorating. I'd get sick of the inside sights too if I was to over see them. Maybe that's why all the young dude visitations besides my own. But it's so hard to share with others. She won't tell me their names. She's a collector. But as I say, only I get the repeat action. Anyway that's what she says, and that she's grooming me for good to go, and hasn't yet released me because not improved enough to please the ladies. She says, "Call this homework. You'll catch on."

So those paths through the woods that go to her door from all over town, I sometimes follow them and the bark graffiti from her house back through the woods to get a clear idea what neighborhoods she's tapping. There's a few. Including Hotchkiss School other side of the lake. She tells me most that scratch her door she turns away. I doubt that. She's a sucker for feral cats that get handouts from her and spray all over the yard. That's because they still have their balls, she says and winks, which speaks to reasons to avoid domestication. I'm a "keeper," she says, which is now, of course, a relativity term that Einstein pointed out. I've studied Einstein. He said matter and energy are the same. Where I am now, after leaving this life, I have to agree. I'm still me, though without solid form to who I am. I'm all energy and that's a pretty good feeling. The only thing unsolid about Mrs. V is her emotions, which are water on a windy day – all fluttery white caps and changing reflections of sunlight. Sunny Vitello, she's a force of nature. But she's also a very smart woman. It's her husband holding her back.

△

YOU PROBABLY FEEL BAD I checked out so early. Religionists feel that way. Yeah, well, about religion, I'm more an ex-theist now in the afterlife than I was in the beforelife. God didn't make me do it. God's absence neither. I can't find him anywhere here. I've looked. But no one is to blame. My death doesn't need revengineering. Nothing happened to me that anyone needs "laying on" which is from Shakespeare and comes from Macbeth as Macduff is laying on Macbeth with a big sword after the woods have come to his door with bad news. SparkNotes makes a big deal of those woods.

I too know the betraitor nature of those woods. Before sent to Poncy, the paths I took through birch trees to where Mrs. Vitello taught me of love. Those woods so white in the early fall, yellow leaves on the ground and me in Pumas and sweats jogging paths that I told the Mom was to keep in shape for lacrosse. And alongside the lake beginning now to notice the birch marked with rude graffiti of her, Mrs. Vitello, and multiple dude action. Those woods telling me I'm just another one too. Birds mocking and lake water scummy with fertilizer off these perfect lawns, feet slamming the packed dirt. Thomp! Thomp! Thomp! I had pretty big feet that are too flat for running but just right for tangling dudes in a lacrosse face-off or a pick. That doesn't matter now. But she really loved me. I'm sure. And that does matter.

When I saw the graffiti, I did like a really dumb thing. I decided to beat the shit out of every set of initials I found on that white birch. And I did too. Mostly townies like me that backed away quick when I swung and, well, one that didn't work out too good. He's a Hotchkiss lacrosse bro. He was out of my weight class. His fists came at me such as pistons on a hemi. Him and me under the bleachers after a lacrosse game. Townies versus preppies. Big deal occasion, pep rally and all that. When it came time to tangle, him and me, we had audience representation. I had called him out after the game. Because he was chief among the white birch slanderellas. But yeah, even so, he was a bro and I never should have. It's just, Mrs. Vitello made me crazy.

I didn't have the heart to hit the dude. I started it. I swung first and missed by a squeezer his way big nose. Hard to believe I'd miss, except it was intentional. Then he was all over me such as a bad case of Snooki. I kept backpedaling and taking blows. I just couldn't hit back. Because he wasn't any blame. Mostly those woods betrayed me. Mrs. Vitello and me, we had a pure thing. Then I thought otherwise from those initials in the woods. That's what doublethink will get you. Such as Macbeth who thinks nothing bad can happen to him because he was "untimely ripped" from his mother's belly. So he is immune to earthly harm. He was delusional. Me too once.

But so are most beforelifers. This place isn't so perfect either. The afterlife is filled with maladjusted wonder widgets who can't get their heads around this next stage after having slipped past their expiration dates.

△

It was the Mom's idea for me to come to Poncy Prep, this way overmuch testosterone driven correction to the metrosexual, an all boys' boarding school in the middle of nowhere in a field of corn in New Jersey. Because my family, which is from a very posh town in Connecticut, had expected more from me, as I had from myself. More than a C+ student at a mediocre public school. More than a third-tier Connecticut state college accepting me "with proviso" is how they put it. We'll take a chance, college admissions said, but you need to keep the grades up or out you go. Way generous, don't you think? My high school college counselor told the Mom I should do an extra year of high school somewhere with a good academic rep. Dial up the potential levels. Then apply to a real college. But I knew, for me, grades don't matter. It's all about muscle on the proving grounds of lacrosse. I just needed a team with a high ranking in the Eastern Conference.

Post Graduate is what they called me at Poncy. One more year of high school to get it right. But for the school they get PG muscle for football and PG reach for basketball. In my case, PG status but at full pay because my grades sucked so bad and my lacrosse wasn't that great. The whole PG idea is said to go down pretty good at trustee meetings with gin and lime. New uniforms all around! is what they say when the gin moves them to play Corrupt a Wish during which they hand out gut courses to the team with facial hair that beats shit out of those other teams powered on juvenility. But it's the full-paids like me, my father's cash, my mother's bling, that keeps this place afloat.

△

THE DORM PREFECT FOUND ME DEAD, one of Langly's little tadpoles. He snapped my picture to post on Twitter, but because of corporate censors it stayed there less time than the RIP someone else spray painted on the door. My blue and gray body dumped into the back of an ambulance didn't care, my skin blue, veins and eyes bugging out. But why an ambulance? Revive me? As if. But about that RIP on my door. I like the idea and which makes perfect sense because the actor Rip Torn lives in my hometown. You know, the boss dude Zed in Men in Black, the one that when a young actor klonked Norman Mailer on the head with a hammer (lots in line for that job, is what my English teacher Mr. Ralph says). And then arrested for breaking into my hometown bank with a loaded gun. Rehearsing a part is what he said to the judge. Way cool he did it! I shared a tequila fumes conversation with him just a couple hours before. You'll see.

I have posters to Men in Black and Men in Black II taped to my wall in the dorm at Poncy. Well I did. And brother Matt has a Lakeville Gazette article on one of its favorite citizens, aka Zed, hauled away to the hoosegow on a "general misunderstanding" of what defines armed robbery because the bank was closed and he only got so far as a back room office. The judge told him, "Okay, but next time send in the stunt man." Yes and because I am now enlightened to look at the world from a global perspective off planet, because I am no longer "in" the world but "of" it, I can see Rip's point in bringing Hollywood realities to Lakeville. It's a metaphor, really, is what my English teacher Mr. Ralph would say. It's a message of what's going on beneath the surface of things. Which is what metaphors do. Don't put your faith in banks is Rip's meaning. They are, as Zed would say, "betting on the alien occupation." They'll work with anybody. They tanked our economy for a reason. That's what Zed would say. Rip Torn has learned a lot from Zed.

When a kid I used to see Rip Torn driving the streets of Lakeville in his shabby winter jacket bobbing a head all mussed and a face unshaved, steering a rusted Subaru with Chuckie Finster hands gripping the top of the steering wheel. I knew he was out there deflecting identity, a terrestrial anon and sometimes imperial Zed, helmsman of Men in Black. I knew when a kid that extraterrestrials are real and everywhere around us.

I am the generation just old enough to have seen that ponderific event the Twin Towers burn in 2001. I was in 6th grade, eleven years old. All the TV's of middle school rolled on carts into the hallways by teachers with trembly legs and teary voices. The Towers melted and burned right there in the hallways with our teachers lamentably weepy. We were all made to go home with wondersome fear in our hearts.

But I had already been convinced of resident evil by the age of seven when the docuhorror Men in Black exposed to me alien life among us – weird looking dogs suspect, goony looking men in the trades suspect. My neighbor with the hair-lip, Willy Jameson, especially so. Our plumber, Larry Fitzgibbon, might have suspicioned why little Marvin was always over his shoulder. I was spying out his smell, because aliens first kill then inhabit a human host, with the consequent decomposition. And I was looking for vacancy in the eyes, and evidence of seams that would indicate rubberized body wrap, and listening for tinny reverberations of the vocal cords because gills for lungs don't synch well with human speech. Then there was Zed off set and chumming around my hometown but keeping watch of all the aliens on planet Earth and in Lakeville particular.

So when 9/11 happened, me and my fellow wondernuggets were predisposed to think the world had gone out of human control, had fallen into the hands of aliens. Makes sense! Divide and conquer and all that shit. Right? With Muslims and Christians and Jews going at it again, we're back where history started. Aliens can do whatever which with little to no eyes on them. I mean, the Men in Black won't be able to keep up. Even if they wanted to, all their resources have been shuffled to Homeland Security.

Not many know Men in Black II was going to be filmed at the Towers. Then the Towers fell. Seem funny to you? I even have, well had, an advance marquee poster of the movie with the Towers in the background. Talked it off a friend's older brother working at the local theatre that was asked to pull down the poster and toss it. Probably now worth mucho kachink to disaster memory collectors. Little brother, Matt, he has it now. He's fourteen. A good kid but clueless about what the poster means. He only knows it was mine and so has put it on his bedroom wall at home that was once my bedroom– kind of lugubrious, don't you think? I love that word, lugubrious. It's one of my favorite SAT prep words. I did get into a better college, by the way. I mean, like, they had no idea I was dead! Wesleyan of Middletown, Connecticut. Way better than Western Connecticut. So I'm kind of proud of myself for that.

OKAY. THIS IS GETTING WAY SERIOUS. Let's take a trivial break! If you're fidgital, go check that text then come back to hear this. So, as I say, "trivial break." That's what the Dad called it when he used to sit at the dinner table and wanted to cheer up the depressed and withdrawn Mom. He also wanted to show us how clever he is. Or maybe mostly wanted to get the Mom back into mothering vibe which she had lost a couple years before when her own mom died of trichinosis after a family BBQ. That's more irony, when good intentions generate death. The Dad was cooking. The Mom bought the meat and they blame each other. But here's the riddle – what movie star's first name is a verb and last name the past tense of that same verb? Give up? Read back a couple pages and you'll get it – Rip! Torn! Get it? That's a good one, right? Can't say I remember others of the Dad's supper table wit, but that one I always do.

△

THE DAD BEGAN TO HAVE TROUBLE finding motivation to entertain us when the Mom started serving carry out and insisted on reheating and cooking again everything before we ate so it all tasted such as beef jerky or cardboard no matter what its ethnic flavoring. Also when they began discussing me seriously behind closed doors. I was still alive then. That was in my first years of public high school. I'm a PG now, or was. This gets confusing. I'm the second oldest. Was. Still am I guess. I was supposed to carry the name Marvin Herkimer into posterity with fanfare and notable deeds. I was to receive well wishes from dignitaries of state and commerce and sink deep this weedy root of invasive species into the bedrock of founding fathers of this great country.

Our line on my father's side is German. Gustav Herkimer came from Cologne along the Rhine before World War Two and found his place alongside the Mohawk River in a town that shares his name. The Dad grew up there. He says some general named Herkimer took a bullet for the rebel cause in the 1700s and got a whole town named after him. The Dad bragged on that a lot but stopped the day Sherman was killed in Iraq. Little chance Sherman will get a town named after him. Maybe because his cause wasn't so noble. Unless you ask George Dubya or blood-sucking Cheney.

The Dad's dad drove 18 wheelers into Canada and across the provinces for a living. He loved Canada and wanted to live there. The Dad's mom was Canadian English but lived in Quebec. They married in Canada and she determined the move below the 49th parallel. Partly because she spoke no French and didn't care to learn and because she wanted her boy, there was only one, to amount to something besides a farm hand or big rig gypsy. She was glad for Grandpa's road warrior truancy, glad not to hear his voice in the house. Grandpa had minimal education and spoke that way. But she made my father, Randal Herkimer, ambitious for the family name. Another irony, right? I mean, like, imagine my joy hearing "Herkimer jerkimer!" shouted down the dormitory halls of Poncy Prep. Something to make you proud. Teen boys have a way with language. I'm sure you've noticed. But then you need to consider what the name Marvin means, which I did after hearing what my friend of the New Jersey oasis told of his name, which will take awhile to get to. Anyway, the name Marvin means mariner. Not so unexpected really. I mean, I grew up near a lake. Our bodies are 75 percent water. We can live a month without food but only a week without water. And the only time I lived apart from water was Poncy Prep, which didn't feel right. Until I visited the Pine Barrens, which did feel right. You'll see.

△

So, I'm with Mrs. V who says, "He's a pod, that Brent. He's an effing pod. (That's Mrs. V's husband, if you remember.) Don't tell," Mrs. V says, "because my house will be quarantined by the other pods until I'm changed to one of them."

In case you don't know, that's a reference to Invasion of the Body Snatchers. Rad movie. Just as good any day as Men in Black. Revise that: close second. The pod people are violent but have no emotions because vegetable replications of disposed humans. But that's so cool! Notice me and Mrs. Vitello, we have the same kind of mind that accepts aliens.

Mrs. V says, "Don't you see, Marvin? Look at all the upscale homes in Lakeville, the ones around the lake especially, all but mine, all with add-on greenhouses. Do you see? There's a lot! What do you think goes on in those greenhouses?"

She answers her own question. She says, "That's where the pods are grown that do the replication. In those greenhouses." That's what she says. And the pod replicants, Mrs. V says they're right here, easy to see. "Those stay-at-home trophy wives who make the greenhouse scene. House and Garden trenders growing pods in those little glass houses designed to keep dirt off the knees of their effing chinos. Same scene as an equestrianess with a horse in a paddock for one acre of grass." She so right. This is horse country and greenhouse country, northwest Connecticut. A lot of big homes with groomed acreage. Pod country.

When I tell Mrs. Vitello my parents are greasing connections to get me a PG year of high school at Hotchkiss School, the fancy boarding school in our town, she tells me, "Don't be a preppy! They're all effing pods."

She has a point. They dress the same, talk the same, come from all the best families, go to the same colleges, even take spring break at the same ski resorts out West and in Europe. Poncy Prep is not like that. The only thing we at Poncy share is all being fuck ups. Except that while enjoying our natural state of fuckupedness, we bros of lacrosse will forever be tribing up. Even the dude I attacked under the bleachers, though in his case a lesser bro, which I will find out later and so should have connected a fist under those bleachers if I'd known.

Well but maybe some of the black dudes at Poncy have a kind of respect for each other's tats. Maybe they're a different kind of bro. The ones from Philadelphia that throw hate on everyone else, the ones rescued from the gangs who have started their own gangs on campus. They have community, no doubt, from a kind of survival mania. Very Darwin. Others are pretty much lumps of ethnic background that hang together because no one else wants much to do with them. There's lazy Saudis with limitless credit cards and limos that drive all the way in from Philly to schlep them to the movies on weekends. There's Asians who over study every test and whose parents have employed agencies that place them here at Poncy because they are too misinformed to know schools with dress codes don't guarantee a high-class education. There are also many sleep-walking jocks with the ambition of puppies at obedience school. They hang together and bark at everything and bite nothing. Only lax bros have the passion.

The Mom finally caught on to Sunny Vitello when one of the stray cats Sunny had named Crisis followed me home. I don't know why. I hate cats. But this one loved me for some reason. Maybe it was my smell. "Herk," Mrs. V would say nibbling my ear, "your scent, it's a label pasted on a whiskey bottle. Want to know what it says?" I nod sure why not. "It says expect a whiff of back-yard lawn and spice, a little taste of oaky with a base note of shave cream and a touch of mustard seed." That's me polluting the breeze. Just beginning to experiment with the stubble razor and Kiehl's camphor enhancements. That's what Sunny would notice when nibbling. She also gave all them cats creepy names – Abra and Boss and Crisis and Dorable and Earnest and Fatwa. She's up to J in the alphabet. That's a lot of damn cats. Took the Mom awhile to realize this cat Crisis that kept sneaking in the kitchen door meant I had strayed because she was still trying to work out her new life without the Dad, that asshole. Can't believe I once wanted to be like him. She has now tapped her trust fund for spending cash and gone back to work once the Dad shut down the alimony, just after I hung myself. But that's not the reason why I did it, the trouble in our family. The Mom thinks so. She always said I was a good one for inventing an "opt out clause." I guess she thinks my suicide was one.

I have to admit I'm good at excuses. I never do much I don't want to do and that goes way back to my short-leg days. She calls it my "short pants" days, but that's only because my legs were short. The Mom always said she saw my weakness to adapt as "a vein of mineral that was hard to detect but essential to who I am." She said, "Marvin, I fear for your future. I do. There is within you an incapacity to accept conditions as they are." She's like a really smart lady. The Mom is. She never pushed me to do the things I didn't want to do. She was afraid I would make savage damage on the world and leave it raw and bloody. When she learned of me and Mrs.V, she knew to leave me to it or risk Marvin performing sex acts on cigarette machines. The Dad just saw me as slacker-istic. He would say in his best mantra mind control: "You never accept responsibility for where your life is going." Whatever. I guess maybe now he feels I took responsibility. But that's not why I did it, the suicide, to prove him wrong.

△

I convince my lacrosse bro Brad at Poncy Prep to give me a ride back home to sort out the breakup text Sunny Vitello has sent because it's near time I come home for spring break and she's afraid of "getting too deep in." I tell her on my iPhone an abbreviated finger thought:

> how deep u think is cant come
> back cause Im comin back

I tell Brad my plans to AWOL Poncy. He's against it, but he lives in my dorm, it's pretty near spring break anyway and I'm on the team, so what can he do? I'm a bro.

"Hey, Herk, can't it wait for vacation? I mean, dude, I have a fat hangover (too much fast food) and Jesus Fucking Christ what's the rush?"

"The rush, Brad (that's Bradley Turcotte, captain of Poncy Prep lacrosse, early admit to Navy at Annapolis, blonde hair shagged, a C student and proud of it, pink and lime green checked pants, wrinkle-free white shirts, my best friend at Poncy) ... the rush is that my girl is dropping me."

"Herk, bro, girls are like, slide to unlock, that easy. Look, send out a few maintenance texts and see who's interested. You're a good looking dude. A little chunky and maybe too serious for most chicks, but you'll do all right if you just put yourself out there."

"Look, bro, Brad ... I don't have a fuckit list," I say.

"Yeah, well, maybe you should. You think a Swiss army knife is better?"

Brad is not focusing on the problem. He's having a Facebook minute, which is more like an hour and less than engaging on an intellectual level. At least to the extent Brad can be said to engage intellectually.

"Brad, can you get away from your computer and talk to me!"

"Dude," he says, "don't be a parent."

I'm in Brad's dorm room. There's slasher movie posters on the walls and beer adverts of blondes with big titties pouring Bud such as golden showers all over each other. Their cardigan college letter sweaters are unbuttoned at the top and bottom so you see pierced belly buttons and can practically taste the melons. These are female variants of Brad, so when he's pulling his pud, he's getting off on himself, right? Well, better than a lemonparty, such as I imagine Langly and old Soc engaged in old man gay sex. The lights in Brad's room are always off in the daytime and on at night. Because Brad is no dayturnal. He hardly ever makes his morning classes because he's awake all night and sleeps in the day. He knows to make Chapel for head count. Then it's back to bed until lacrosse practice. That's when he's jazzed for Jesus! Hallelujah and pass the Thais stick, the lacrosse stick. Either way that or his pud, some kind of stick is in his hand.

"Okay, sure thing," he says. "I'll put your request for a ride home in my add to cart. Listen, fucktard, I am not Facebooking at present. I am interfacing with the stats on LaxPower. Okay, here it is. Did you know Pontificate Prep has a projected 32nd ranking and our actual score, our current win loss ranking, puts us 48th? Dude! Not acceptable! Those fucking Maryland schools are skewing the stats! Pass me that coozy."

I hand Brad the beverage he wants that's wrapped ceremonially in its foam rubber with the Poncy Prep logo in silver on blue.

"Well, dude, as I give it a think," says Brad doing his version of think, "we're playing the Hill on Saturday. They're going to frag our ass. So, maybe … a road trip could well be diversion worthy. Let me Facebook a couple people and see if they're up for a Bradley Turcotte invasion. You pay for the cab into town. I put in for gas after that. That sound like a deal?"

"Deal."

Brad is, such as me in the beforelife, a PG, although his grades are a little worse and his lacrosse infinitely better, which qualifies him for driving privileges. That's a special deal finessed with Headmaster Langly that no one is supposed to know about where a PG cozies a car off campus at a Poncy Prep day student's home for certain agreed-upon occasions of self-mobilization. Langly thinks he has the only set of keys. But you know how that's going to work out.

△

So now it's a road trip. Rad! Something to do. Something to get my mind off the shit hole I'm falling deeper in. Can't get over thinking there's not much for me to grip ahold of in this before-lifers' life. Not just because Sunny Vitello has dissed me. And not because Mr. Ralph taught me that even words can't be trusted. They change all the time, which makes me wonder why the fuck dictionaries? But because for Gen Y, what should we care about? There's no Hitlerized war to get feverish over, or communist weaponry pointed at our necks, no Vietnam to protest. What we get is pretend victory in Iraq, global warming denial and families cracking up. There's stock markets tanking, Dads losing their cool over losing their retirement, houses shedding investment value and others getting the repo action. The underprivileged dudes joining the army aren't patriots of 9/11. They're broke, bottomed out, and so get IEDs in Iraq, which is what killed my stepbrother.

I mean, with everything on auto correct, and not just the texting app on my iPhone that I have disabled so I can word-warp all I want, but I mean all those imposed life enhancements. Such as finishing high school in middle school and being in college in high school. I mean, Willy Jameson when a high school sophomore in multi-variable calculus, and freshmen in AP Biology, and juniors cutting themselves because of the SAT. So much competition for college we don't get to be kids anymore. And all the lies. Lies about college making a happy future. And then lies about weapons of mass destruction. Lies from Wall Street. Lies from politicians. Lies in your face. Lies, lies, lies, lies! So why even a casual worry over detouring the parental units, or alibi prepping for the thought police? There's just lies everywhere.

If you want us to go batshit crazy right in front of you, take away our tech toys and designer drugs and oral sex. The world has got too serious. We need some fun while waiting to go to pieces via suicide strap-on bombs, or catching the big C drinking water fracked for gas deposits. Sing with me Lana Del Rey. If you want the future to be fun, trust no one. Sing it! And don't look too close in the rearview.

△

BRAD ISN'T HAVING ANY of my dark moods this day. Well, or any other. Brad tosses me one of his sweaters to wear saying, "Dude, brighten your mood!" It's electric yellow. Color therapy he calls it.

Maybe Brad's not so dumb. It's just before lunch on Thursday, 3rd period in which I have English with Mr. Ralph. We call him by his first name because he hates his last one so much. Well, yeah, with a name like Shmatz. We're studying the book Perfume that's very well written but making me paranoid about smells. It seems smell controls your moods and inclinations a lot more than you realize. Which makes me think again of Mrs. V's cat Crisis that took me for its care-mate. Maybe because I sweat the kind of pheromones it mistakes for protection. Bad choice. Look what I did to myself. And there's Theresa Whitley, the art teacher, which you have met, that smells of peanut butter and bacon anytime of her morning classes and bat-fruity schnapps after that. When she leans over to straighten your lines of perspective, it's just as though she's burped morning breakfast or dipped her nose into a fruit pie.

So Brad might worry he's missing another full day of classes, but he's not counting. He's in college already anyway. If Poncy expels him, he says, he'll start summer vacation early where the reefer grows tended by the loving hands of pretty maids all in a row on some tax-shelter island. Bradley knows that island well. He is the son of capitalist Efron Turcotte, the man that turned a ponzi scheme on Ted Turner and got away with it, mostly, except what the feds took away. He kept untouched the Swiss account and the land yacht that ferries him between home and Wall Street and the braghouse on a secret, protected bay of Long Island. Which is a very rich kennel Bradley grew up in and which accounts for his overfriendly, rug-staining, tongue-lapping, untrained puppy habitude.

But Brad's a cool dude never mind that he can overwhelm the uninitiated with casual wealth. It's just how he grew up. His parents are never home. But they have the Velcro touch. He gets perpetual texts from Mom on diet and which bros to friend and from Dad on applying himself and such. Brad's fingers always in motion answering back. They're the ghost in the machine of Brad's iPhone and the soundtrack to his elevator ride. He's always shaking his shag head with the brain buzz from parental node plants.

I've been to his house once for Christmas break. The parental units were somewhere in Italy sharing some Dubya Bush appointee's vacation villa. And there's me and Brad chowing dinner in the kitchen with the live-in help, while Brad texts the parental units all his exam info and his teacher's emails for contact so in case grades don't jibe with Bradley's forecast and so they can plant a thought seed in the ear of Headmaster Langly to make corrections upon his faculty. But mostly Brad smokes the hooch with me while tapping the non-deposit, toss-away cleaning girls from Poland who make his bed at night and then lay in it. Most of the estate population are resident landscaper Mexicans. But a different type from the low crowd of downtown Sapperstown – more gentle, happy to remove snow in winter and pull weeds in summer. Their brown-skin broods live with them on the estate in a far patch of untended ground in the caretakers' cottages where the grass is worn to dirt by small busy feet. At night Señor Rimerez, the patriarch with a fu manchu stash, he occupies the guardhouse at the front entrance to close off the outside world. Which is a good thing because there are antiques in the main house and art on the wall the Met in NYC would be glad to own. Which is funny because no one but Brad during vacations is ever there to see that stuff and but also the cleaning staff I guess.

So Brad and me go to the campus bookstore where I draw out my weekend allowance of $50 and Bradley runs his debit card through the machine and stashes $500. The book store lady, Ms.

Tucker (which we call, Ms. You Wannna, leaving out the Fuck Her part), she leans way over the counter upon which two of the most luscious orbs of honey dew spill out in their loose v-neck sweater. And I swear, my dick sings hail to the chief. I mean, at attention and wallowing in the puckulence of a wet dream. Brad knows I have a thing for Ms. You Wanna, so tosses a ten spot onto the counter and says, "Thanks for the show!" And to me says, "I'd hit that." Then pulls me away to where he can scan his iPhone without Poncy faculty noticing as cell phones are verboten. Which is why so much texting happens in the classrooms under the desks. Brad has a terrible fat finger as a texter. Sometimes you can't make out what he's saying. Or maybe he just can't spell. Or maybe he doesn't care, which if you know, is all about the internet, which is all about breaking the rules.

△

We walk a short way down the big circular drive that leads to Route 22 running alongside barbed-wire fields. The main building of Poncy sits up on a hill, a pondiferous four-story brick that burned down once shortly after it was built. Then rebuilt just as dark and nasty as before. For tradition, you know.

There's a room top of the north tower that provides shark porn initiation for the freshmen and has since the Jaws movies of the 70s. What happens is seniors lock a handful of freshmen in there overnight, take out the light bulbs, and toss vermin in through the old metal grate in the floor up from which the heat used to arrive. Mostly just lab mice, but in the dark, they're scary as shit. This cheery spectacle of brotherly love is usually followed by copious fauxpology and Budweiser binging in the woods up until the little pukers upchuck and stagger back to their dorms to google the NextGen Update.

This was all good and dandy for many years until some little Asian niglet complained of racial hazing. And so the whole thing ended with the expulsion of one pimple-faced broner with steroid lumps and an IQ of 80 that shouldered the blame of thirty years of abuse and so appeased the outraged parents of happy meals. Which is what Poncy calls freshmen.

Brad is really into texting at this particular moment as we sit on a melting snow bank, but is not going to be so impolite as to engage on the phone because I'm here and I'm a bro. But he's texting the same thing over and over, I can tell, and sending it off again and again. Pushing the keys so hard such as he's found the g spot. So I ask what's going down. I pull out the ear buds, Psychobuildings' electric dance beat on my iPod stinging the morning air. Brad says his girl has just broken up with him too. Says he's pissed and sending again and again this message: I'll forget about you if you'll forget about me. I just think that's so beautiful, like, I mean, for a guy to say that. I'll forget about you if you'll forget about me. R.I.P. Deligious! Of course Bradley has never been with this girl in the physical, only skyping. He's seen everything, even if not touched only himself while she does too. So he's not so broke up that a fresh camgirl buddy won't cure him. He mostly likes the ones that speak Russian and Amex.

Brad sits cross-legged on a dirty pile of plowed, melting snow wearing red, wide-whaled corduroy pants and moccasin shoes with little nubs of rubber on the bottom and no socks. His suede jacket opens onto a Poncy sweatshirt and a backpack with lacrosse stick fastened on lies on the ground between his feet. His lips all scrunched duckface and cheeks thick with the shag that blonde dudes get when they haven't shaved a couple days. He unpacks his lips, says, "Dumped me! And she was a diana! A drop dead gorgeous diana. Is that Dr. Dre?"

"No," I say, "it's Psychobuildings."

"Dude! Where's the club?"

"Yeah, like that. But listen, bro," I say, "stream an episode of Degrassi and you'll feel better." Which is, in case you don't know, a show for mostly middle school girls about homosexuality, rape, bullying, school violence, stuff like that my little brother told me of so I watched some of it, but won't tell I did because I might get punched by a laxbro, which is what I was going to tell Brad. If you watch, don't tell. But I mean, like, with no happy endings for anyone, it makes you feel pretty good viewing one of those episodes. But Brad isn't having any. He has just then hooked the cabbie on the phone and is reeling him in to meet us on campus behind the gym where no faculty eyes or security cameras can focus.

△

Two minutes out Poncy drive in the backseat and Bradley lights a spliff sampled to him by the cab driver. He passes it to me. It feels good to have cannabis in the lungs again. The cabbie is an assimulatto but likes to think himself more Mexico gangland than anywhere else. He supplies the bros with street illegals and has a good connection with a drugsmith for cocaine that, in this neighborhood, only preppies and bimmers commuting to Philadelphia can afford. Well, yeah, and he also services the meth addicted that pay with home invasions. The cabbie wears his frayed baseball cap backwards, displays affiliation tats on his arms to impress and uses ganguage to convince. But we know he's a poser.

Brad likes to fuck with him: "Hey, Ese (his name is Ignacio), you're, like, the banger in the barrio that's looking to bone base heads (meaning someone hooked on cocaine). Am I right?"

Ignacio has no idea what Brad might have heard but some idea what he just said. He squirms in his seat, adjusts rap on the radio which Brad calls "crap for the didiot." He reflexes his baseball cap a couple times. Then says, "Yeah, well, homie, I ain't no O.G. (meaning original gangster, meaning having killed someone) but my ruka (meaning gang chick) knocks boots with me anytime I'm in the mood. Don't need no crank (meaning nut case) to get laid. You feel me?"

We don't, no. The shit we're smoking is too rad. The world has fuzzy gloves touching it and sotted eyes seeing it and ears prone to sonar pings. This is not a time for making plans. Our getaway is getting away. Ignacio thinks this is the usual drug buy, so that's why he has gifted a sample then pulls into an alley and parks between two boarded-up businesses in fall-down Sapperstown. Brad and me are too stoned to notice the brick outside our windows just sitting there like us. One wall was once a barbershop. It still has attached the white pole with bloody spirals farther down near the alley exit where sidewalk ice melts in the sun. The other wall was maybe once a deli judging by the pile of tumbled meat delivery boxes outside a back door near the cab. Both walls bravely graffitied.

Brad says, "That's a tooth needs a orthodontist. I tell you what."

He's referring to the profile of a tusked pig stenciled on wooden boxes stacked and rotting in the snow. The meter ticks. Ignacio rolls another joint and passes it to Brad then flashes an exceptionally handsome gold tooth for which Brad is already primed.

Brad says, "Dude, another tooth? Really? Gives me the eye-graine. Put it away!"

But this doesn't faze Ignacio whose smile beams on our horizon with increasing wattage. Maybe he's so generous with that smile because we're idling in his home turf, the meter counting change and a buy of ganja imminent. The graffiti on the walls matches the tats on his arm.

Sapperstown has never been much of a town. It became even less so once the Mexicans moved in. Ignacio tells us this is his alley. We believe it. He says the policía know to leave alone this alley. He tells us crowded spaces make him feel at home. He tells us of the five small ones and his padres that shared a one-room adobe outside the mesa town of Sombrerete. Until his father sold his fields to the marijuana trade and moved his family to Tijuana. Big mistake. Ignacio's two older brothers were killed for cooperating with the policía who were cooperating with the cartels. His sisters became street angels, not because they needed the money. They like the lifestyle. His mother went certifiable. His father rented a coyote to cross the desert to Texas, then bussed himself and his only remaining son to Philadelphia and wandered here to nowherestown in southwest Jersey. Ignacio's father lives with him still in the center of town where the railroad tracks shuttle wealthletes to Philadelphia who park their bimmers at the train station for a quick getaway to their outlying Hummer houses.

Where Ignacio lives with his father is something Dickenese (that's a writer we study in English that's become an adjective). They live in a shambolic hotel that gigantuates above all other buildings in town and tilts unsteady over the sidewalk. So many brown bodies lean out those windows day and night is maybe why. Well but that may seem prejudiced if true but not too much spoken. Which is what prejudice says out loud – the true but not often spoken, is what the Dad says. He's a shit, but even shits get it right sometimes. Then the policía skid into the alley with blue lights and mean smiles on their faces. It's a shake down and maybe a hoosegow for Brad and me unless Ignacio is truly bro to the law.

Guess not. As we watch from inside the cab, snuff the joint and toss it onto alley trash, two dudes in gestapo wear, black with silver beaming from gun belts and badges and dangled restraint wear, they have Ignacio on the ground face down with handcuffs on arms behind his back. Ignacio is singing in his smallest, sweetest voice that he meant to pay up, that business has been slow, that us two are ordering big for a party at Poncy Prep (as if) and that the money will shake out of that (desperate lie). He's smiling despite the shakedown.

The tough cop says, "Hang that tooth out there a little farther. Payback don't come easy."

It doesn't seem to matter to Officer Jake Willis what Ignacio has to say. Officer Willis is the biggest of the two, the alpha dog, a moon face pocked by acne and crooked teeth and very large hairy ears rising over squared shoulders. He spits on Ignacio, kicks a rib or two. Then says to Officer Al Knight, "Toss him in the river or bring him in?"

Officer Knight with short legs and a sideways super lit smile such as dudes on a friending spree, he says to Officer Willis, "Paper work either way when we have to fish out the body."

We all go into the back of the cruiser with more bruises kicked onto Ignacio. This time his thighs and shins as he is last one in and has to be coaxed to squirm in alongside us gringos that are, as Ignacio says, very bad luck. "Mal fortuna," he keeps saying, "Mal fortuna." Such as cut off the chicken's neck and cross yourself three times quick before the legs give out that race around before they know they're dead. Guess Ignacio knows that if the heat is mad enough to arrest rich white boys, his own status is very much up for review and likely to demote even further.

Next thing I remember that tweaks my addled cannabis brain is the stench of urine, mildew, cigarettes and PineSol in our holding cell. Then the sound of knuckle cracking bouncing around those gray cement block walls whose bench Brad and me occupy. Ignacio has been schlepped off to an interrogation room; we can hear him pleading urban survival syndrome. Anyway, it's Headmaster Langly. The knuckles. Yeah, well, I forgot to tell you of the knuckle cracking. It's one of Langly's little rituals, intimidation that sounds of bones breaking. Makes its point. Especially when hosting a trembly happy meal in his big-desk office with Socrates, the old rectal snorkeler, looking down from his perch of a Doric column. And then Langly walking over to old Soc and placing his arm around the statue's shoulders and beaming at you with that embarrassed-for-you rectitude. Then cracking knuckles. Socrates might do the same, but he has no arms. Langly and Socrates. The double-team supreme. Good cop, bad cop. Good philosopher, bad philosopher. You can easy enough figure which is which.

So then back to the cell where somewhere nearby Langly's voice speaks over the knuckles he's cracking. He's declassing the police with a critication of their ineptitude, telling of grievances visited upon him and the school by the hasty and insensitive actions of a police force that has forgotten it works for him. Not, as he says for the tawny-skinned undocumented that fill the town's boarding houses. Not for what remains of the white-collar drunks that pass for its better citizens. Not for the shop keepers who haven't the sense to board up and leave town. Not for the Freemasons whose influence he can assure them has diminished significantly. But for him, Flynt Thrush Langly, Headmaster of Pontificate Preparatory

School and Chairman of the Board of Commerce for the tri-county League of Development.

"And that, boys," Langly says, "is where the power lies! That's where the hiring and the firing, the staffing, and the operations oversight is conducted. You will do well to keep this in mind. And, if you would be so kind to release young Bradly Turcotte. He has an important lacrosse practice this afternoon for tomorrow's pre-season stake against a worthy adversary from a neighboring state."

The smile on Brad's face beams hellacious. Before that he had sunk deep into a pit of self-pity sitting on that splintery bench with me. His iPhone taken away and mine too and my iPod, and but Brad, he had gone deep into disconnect withdrawal. Then jazzed with anger, slamming knees with his hands, likely to pull a mantrum. It's just past Pi Time. The oval clock on the wall with numbers a blind man can see says 3:15. We have spent the whole day in that squared-off detention of zombie apocalypse with the village idiots. The good cop, Officer Knight, he comes over and unlocks the door to let Brad out, says someone is here to see him. I hear in a nearby room a kind of apologetic mewling from Brad I never expected and more of Langly's knuckle cracking. Brad returns briefly to say goodbye, tosses me through the bars a fat envelope and smiles his embarrassment as he wipes away a tear.

"Laxibunga!" Brad says to stir the bro juice and shout away the unequalness of our situation. "Take the car and boldly go. I am wanted to shoot a six-by-six. And I'm the man for that. You know I am!"

He has tossed me my iPhone and the key ring to his mint, sparkling lime green 1970 Chevy Camaro and a handful of dead presidents. Then he's gone. And I have no idea where to find his car.

△

THE VIEW FROM MY CELL is of a laundromat with Mexican signage and an impound parking lot where Ignacio's vintage yellow cab and some other scofflaw autos graze the pavement. The good cop, Al Knight, he shuffles his forever smile over to say Langly has made a phone call to my parents from the precinct desk. Papers are trading hands for signatures to release me.

I ask, "Am I under arrest?"

"No," he says, "detained."

I say, "Well if I'm not under arrest, I want out!"

He says, "Don't push it, kid."

I stuffed the money and iPhone and keys to Brad's Camaro down the front of my pants, thinking safe hiding. But Officer Knight notices the bulge, asks is that a gun in my pocket or am I glad to see him? That makes me laugh. He asks do I know where that line came from. I guess late night Jay Leno.

Al Knight says, "I am sadly disappointed in your education."

I tell him Poncy Prep is good at Shakespeare and Greek mythology but not so big on jailhouse trivia. That places him in an Alex Trebek ponder minute out from which he torques a sad shake of his head. I ask when I'm going to be let out? He says it appears from what he's heard Langly and my dad discuss that I'm not too high up the ladder of lacrosse starters. Unlikely to get out by game time, which is next day. I say story of my insignificant life so far.

He says, "Look, kid, I'll level with you."

I say, "I don't care if you stay vertical."

That makes him laugh. He says, "Look, I'm not supposed to tell you this. But the plan is to sweat you awhile, time to reflect on your wrongdoing. Then let you out to walk back to school. Maybe couple hours more."

I say, "What wrong doing? Why not let me out now?"

He says, "Come on! Consorting with a known drug dealer for one."

I say, "What consorting? We bought nothing. Ignacio took us to an alley and parked. Me and Brad didn't know what was going on."

Al says, "Nice try, kid." But winks, holds up a polite finger and goes off to consult add-on bad cop Jake Willis. They argubate the degree of my criminality, after which Al returns somewhat beat down but lets me out, hands over my wallet and says, "Okay, just go. Out the back door. Quietly."

So I go. Out where Ignacio's yellow cab sits on splayed wheels such as a big old beached whale with jaundice, which our school nurse says is a condition you get from disliking vegetables. We had a diet lecture from her one morning before classes in Chapel. That was an intense sleepathon. Don't know why I remember the jaundice part. A brain is a funny thing. All kinds of earworms get in there. So but the keys are in Ignacio's cab, permanently stuck in the steering column. I'm thinking, why get a bro in more trouble? I don't know where to find Brad's car anyway. So I thieve the cab which is mostly a gift anyway and get curiosity looks from the Mexican laundromat I pass by because of a white boy behind the wheel of a known Latino enterprise.

One little Mexican looks out the window. He thinks he knows me. But then his expression changes when he sees more clearly, and as his mom folds clothes, he morphs into his best gangsta meme pointing a Mr. 9mm finger at me such as I'm ridin' dirty (carrying drugs) on spinners (hub cabs that spin). Then I see the little dude's whole life flash by – his ten-year-old self with Cheetos dust on chin and a round taco tummy and baggy capri shorts and Phillies base-ball cap, which become low riders with underwear showing, and a wise ass in high school so dudes will respect him and the girlies will want him and the teachers will hate him. And then after school pil-laging shops along the sidewalks of fall-down Sapperstown which earns him a rep. And so then Uncle Ignacio priming him for a narco (drug dealer) and gifting him a deuce-deuce (.22 pistol) so hot he thinks it makes the devil sweat, and him getting much too much paper (money) too young and swag (style) off that. And then five shots, face down on pavement, blood pouring out from a drive by. His mom standing over him, doe eyes disbelieving and too pained and sad to cry. I swear, life is just too much headed nowhere but dead sometimes.

I stop at the PO on my way out of town to mail the Camaro keys to Brad back at Poncy. It seems an efficient outfit, the Sapperstown PO. All aliens is what I used to think because judging by the distor-tion features and awkward gestures and disregard for the ugly wear issued to render them customer friendly. A sort of declassed version of the Poncy dress code. These aliens have become quite virtuoso in government protocol. Good infiltration practice, starting at the bottom so as to work their way up. I take a moment to remember mail delivery at my house, the dude with the foul breath at our door with packages, a noticeable limp he said he got from the first Iraq war that I thought probably most likely comes from an improper fit of his alien limbs to human form. I carry this thought with me to a pit stop at a Shell station to invest coin in gasoline and a chili dog. It spills most onto my chinos and Brad's yellow sweater when one-arming down the grimy streets of Sapperstown away from the Delaware River toward the coastal highway north and more sex-ucation with Sunny Vitello. No one will think to look for me in

Ignacio's cab. But some determination must be made because, well, Ignacio's cab is a virtual resource drain.

It registers 57,000 odometer miles but as a 1970s Caprice retired from the Big Apple, the medallion pinned to its fender expired by a sum of years near my own, must have run a hundred-thousand miles twice around. It chugs gasoline and misbehaves off that with fumes and chattering such as grandpa Herkimer that tipped Canadian Club by the bottle the few days he was home and farted rainbows in his favorite easy chair by the TV. Even in his sleep. Another reason grandma wanted him gone.

Ignacio's car lumbers corners, no longer absorbs shocks, the engine knocking, spewing black smoke from its muffler. I'm driving through descending night on back roads of farm houses and sleeping small towns, the orange sun in my rearview mirror saying Eastbound. Cash half gone. Tank half full after emptying itself once already. I pull over to nap. Then, the night is gone. I must of slept. I crank down the window in the cool early morning of the early spring of growers season and start again rolling down farmland roads. Dirt furrows rise through a crust of snow, crows peck corn stalks, the thawing ground smells of rust. Trees have open sores from budding. They stand there black and white and black and white again. Birch with yellow leaves just a little at the tops and the odometer turning, the engine giddy on combustion. Shivering in the chill, I crank the smelly heater and sing from Michael Franti about it being early morning and that I need to wash my face and how lonely it is to be a hundred thousand miles away from everyplace.

△

THEN ANOTHER HUNDRED MILES on back roads following the sunrise. I have to find a place to eat. It's getting harder staying off main roads – the population expands; my stomach shrinks. School busses throttle down and flash their loading lights every couple miles piling in book bags with little humans attached. Highway signs appear. The circuit board of suburb planning routes me to Walmarts and McDonalds and Dunkin' Donuts. Distinctly every-where America. Success of the corporate ad-man for plastics and polyunsaturates. Parents buying throw-away stuff from China and diabeating the kids. The drive-through windows of life. One of which I steer towards for a sugar doughnut. After that, at an inter-section of desperation and what-the-hell, I turn down a slant street into the weeds and away from industrial landscaping. I follow an old pick-up truck with scruffy fat farmer dudes trolling that road, arms out windows even in the chill dawn, the slowest common denominators I have got behind yet.

The road soon becomes dirt, ruts and washboard, which I try to maneuver. The truck goes straight through clattering steel, hicks bobbing up and down on the fat of buttermilk hips. Then I see, popping up from the lap of one of those hefty dudes, a blond ponytailed hotty with frothy lips from having gone downtown on one of them. They're laughing and she pulling on their equip-ment, as I judge by her arm motion. Then the driver pushes down her head in his lap and I'm thinking – is this the dutiful daughter of the NRA?

When passenger dude spots me close behind he motions the driver to have a looksee. Yeah, well, there I am, a little stark – vintage yellow cab on a dirt road to nowhere looking for a paying customer? Then I grab an idea. They hit their brakes. I do the same. They hit the gas spewing mud and rock. Me too. They stop and the driver steps out pulling at suspenders that snap his man boobs in a torn and dirty white T. He's a very big dude, kegger proportions, stroking a waist-long, wizard-thin ZZ Top beard, his bald head gleaming, carpenter jeans bulging from tree-trunk thighs. As he ambles over, his passenger steps out, also large and shaggy bearded, also gray with white but lots of hair on his head, most gathered into a ponytail and the bluest eyes. He reaches behind his seat for a shotgun which he cradles in his arm. Riding shotgun must be. What's to protect? He stands there waiting for orders.

I roll down the window and say to the driver leaning in, "You looking for a ride?"

He says, "What you say?" I repeat myself, after which he says, "You ain't barely old enough to drive, son. You think I be looking for my brownstone condo? Little man, you must of made a wrong turn off the Brooklyn Bridge." He laughs.

But I stare at him in my best serious. I say, "I am the pay-what-you-can taxicab. I take customers wherever they want and they pay what they can. So long as the gas gets paid and there's roadside meals, and as I sleep here in my vehicle (he scans my long, wide back seat, nods approvingly), I go where the fares take me. I'm here because I took a customer to the bus station off Exit 36 of the Garden State. I'm sick of highways so looking for my next fare here on these beautiful back roads. This is nice country, mister."

He says, "Ain't it though. Jest a minute" and shifts fluidly back over to his friends at the truck. I can hear him telling me and chuckling. The cute blonde ogles me through the back window. He drifts back and says, "We do have travel on our minds and was thinking Greyhound but could avail ourselves of your services should you not mind following us to our farmstead from which we can offer stomach comfort and a bunk to sleep as payment (he takes a breath) if you're of a mind (he takes another breath) and a ride thereafter in the morning. If that suits you."

"Suits me fine," I say in rhythm with his country patter that's so infection to the tongue organ.

So I follow close behind, spattered in slung mud, the old Ford truck whining from its transmission such as all Fords do. My family plumber, Larry Fitzgibbon, that I told you of as suspect of alien possession, he drives a Ford panel truck that whines the same. Ignacio's Chevy Caprice isn't the only mechanical songster on the road these days. But this Ford truck lays down a serious opera track, clatters percussion with attendant diva wail rising out from its transmission. Yeah, I know, a woozy metaphor. Can't help that. During my growing up moments, the Mom throbbed around the house all day with Madonna on CD and vacuum in tow. Madonna's apocalypse sex triangles and breaking apart woes shouting out from the black box of digital drama. Strange isn't it. The Mom and Ms. Whitley sharing a fondness for diversion ear trauma and both very much educated. But then maybe that's the place outside the boundaries of a dull life where they can safely travel.

But anyway, soon we arrive at fields of thistle and weed and snow crust enclosed in rusted barbed wire on rotted fall-down posts. And a set of weathered barns leaning badly with windows broken and black wood rot creeping up from the ground. Then a farm house of white clapboard gone to weathered gray with a roof of slate that gleams with patches of tin such as aphids shining. When we brake beside the house, I look around for animal life, cows or chickens or pigs or any other kind. There are none. Not even a house cat. Strange kind of farm that has no animals is what I'm thinking.

△

As I step out from the cab, blue eyes introduces himself as Little-G and the driver as Big-D. When I ask about animals, I'm told the family has fallen on hard times of late and has eaten most anything available with fur or feathers. "Barn cats taste good beer roasted" is what Little-G says, the one riding shotgun, the one not so little except when compared to Big-D. Little-G says, "A George Forman cooker works best." He makes a pause for that to sink in, winks and says further, "No shortage of wandering kitties to be had." He smiles at me, blue eyes disappearing behind a lappet of weathered skin and I'm thinking, Oh, shit! It's Leatherface, Texas Chainsaw Massacre! It's 1974 again. The scariest movie ever made and I'm in it! Ignacio's 1970s Caprice ... it's a time machine. I really do begin to think my days over, even sooner than they are now already.

I mean, dude, backwoods insanity, more than personal. Think beautiful young things tied up in a dirt basement with severed limbs hung from ceiling beams and what I can see for sure – mobiles of cat bone and various jawbones chattering on the porch. I swear I hear screaming down in the basement, but I'm hoping that's only a sonar tweak from my expectation brain. Bradley Turcotte will envy I'm living the movie, his favorite. Brad has the '74 movie poster on his wall and thumbnail poster art of all the others, maybe altogether six spinoffs, stored on his MacBook desktop. And all there in kodachrome digital the '74 poster again as his homescreen. He has the soundtrack of sawed-apart Sally screaming as his iPhone ringtone when he takes it off vibrate when Poncy faculty are scarce.

When the driver, Big-D, shoves a pile of material away from

the front door on the porch to pull at the screen door and one of those items is a chainsaw, I just know. Shit I *am* living the movie! But I'm not scared. I'm like so pissed not to be scared. These ZZ Top chainsaw amputaters should have placed me in a reset freeze crash. That's what a good scare does for you. That's why it's so cool to have a scare that goes so deep inside your gut the sphincter tightens and the nads pull deep into scrotum. And you just know you would push anybody out the way to be first out the door, to change the scenery, to change the underwear, to smell something other than your own fear. But this as a theory will not go down well with Bradley Turcotte. He wants "scared shitless" a permanent condition. He needs that much stimulation high.

So about the ZZ Top lookalikes – I find out they're cousins. All of them. Even the girl that never speaks, and so her reaction to a question is eyes to the ground, shoulders raised then lowered such as lifting barbells. They invite me inside the house, which is cave dark with the shades drawn. Little-G that rides shotgun, he skips outside the back door from which I hear cussing and mechanical sputtering. Then the growl of a gasoline generator after which TV springs to life beaming Judge Judy, and a radio tuned to country twangs tinny from the kitchen. A couple overhead bulbs spotlight the dust and tossed-around mess of this cousin-shared insanity pad.

I don't see really how no-name girl cousin fits here besides the BJ's, not until Big-D orders breakfast of whatever is hanging above the kitchen sink gutted and wanting flaying and singeing in a hot-buttered pan. I don't know what I'm about to eat. Maybe a neighbor's dog, a barn cat, someone from the basement. But god damn it tastes better than good! Of course it helps they pass around canning jars of 90 proof distilled "sweet mash." I'm cockeyed and spinning off the planet pretty soon, which they know and place me prone on a dusty sofa cushion where I pass out and dream twenty years back into the lives of these ZZ Top cousins.

I nod off to the throbbing pulse of the generator as Judge Judy has been turned off and the radio is indistinct. The vibration is soothing. Then I'm in the dream and it's me buzzing. I'm looking down from above a field of corn. I'm flying! I'm fiercely attracted to a scent. No. It's more than that. It's spoor, and I'm a mosquito with mosaic vision because of a hundred small-screen lenses for eyes and fuzzy antennae that smell. And there below comes what I hunt. It's Little Darnell and Gaylord. It's the sweat and hot-pumping blood I smell. They're running through the high corn, lost from the world in a maze of high growth, screaming with delight such as little boys will. Until Darnell trips over human remains.

Gaylord chokes on air to get his breath because inhaling the grisly sight as Darnell goes quiet and curious. Darnell looks more closely at the blown-away back shoulder of the face-down corpse, the buckshot having taken muscle down to splintered bone. He knows at once the plaid flannel shirt of the young hired hand that lives in the trailer beside the cow barn.

The young man in the cornfield comes from one of the welfare families the Baptist Church sponsors. The young man is said to be at risk because keeps no job, drinks a lot, steals sometimes. But Pap wanted to impress the congregation with his generosity. He wanted to sponsor some ne'er-do-well for his evangelical work. Timothy Quantry, the boy with his face in the dirt, is about as needy both spiritually and materially as they come. So Pap brought the boy onto the farm and prepared him for the river baptism that would change his life. Well but even though he never did get Timothy river wet, he did purge him of his habit of drink (sifting through his trailer routinely when the boy was off fixing fences or plowing in the John Deere), and he did put back in its place whatever he could find Timothy had relocated from the farm to his trailer with quick, treacherous fingers.

But when Timothy got found in a late-night wrestle of naked, tangled limbs with no-name blond cousin only twelve-years-old but blossoming and willing to learn (some of those early lessons having come from Big-D and Shotgun-G), Pap has had enough. He tells that boy he is through and get off the farm. But Timothy sets him back on his heels saying, "Sure. And next you know maybe your house burns down. And maybe with you in it." So Pap throttles back the threat, says, "Fine. One more chance." Then sends Timothy into the corn to shoot crows while he follows behind. Timothy got one crow before Pap got him. Seemed routine to Pap.

But to Big-D this is a wonder of farm life he hasn't yet ciphered. Killing happens indiscriminately and then also by design all around the farm of many breathing things for meals and money. But to take a life for other reasons? Well, Big-D can't sort it. Yet he is awed by the spectacle. He swears Gaylord to silence and revisits the corpse with a skinning knife which he uses to remove the carcass from Timothy's bloated remains, easier to skin than most animal life because buttery and hairless. He brings that carpet of hide to the dirt basement of their home where he sprays it pliable with leather cure, then shapes it best he can stuffed in rag ticking until Timothy has the aspect of a ghoulish Pillsbury Doughboy that Big-D sets upon a busted ladder-back chair. Then places on the floor candles lit and begins to wail such as a banshee middle of the night waiting for Pap who, big joke, descends the stairs perplexed, sees the apparition and goes directly into cardiac dead.

The farm wife goes fast into decline after that, having seen her son's skinning display and the effects on Pap and not knowing who killed Timothy. Thinking maybe Pap because of the bad blood between them, but then thinking maybe Darnell and having to remain silent to keep her brood out of trouble. Then too the government paying them not to grow crops and them with many acres of government subsidy, so the boys, the cousins, they quit high school in the 10th grade. The silent and comely cousin that Timothy had got nakedly ugly with, she claims a disability and gets paid for that. Although I can't see much disability but am afraid to ask and she wouldn't answer anyway, which is maybe her disability. And the cousins living off the government very comfortably since teenagers. Then the farm wife dying from a full measure of liquid Drano upon the first anniversary of Pap's death. Big-D saying at the funeral she opened up her pipes something fierce. They all laugh.

And there's me again. I land on Big-D's arm and probe the fat of this sweaty, heavy breather with a needle snout. But he's quick with a swat, and so I'm a squashed bug. Why am I still vibrating? Oh, shit! It's my cell phone. But I wake as me, because waking as a bug only happens in books, which this is not, if you remember.

△

I HAVE LOOKED FOR BIG-D'S PAP where I am in the afterlife, but don't think to have found him yet. There are farmers here, but mostly poppy growers blown up from the war in Afghanistan and they are hella lost. Who can blame them? Poking around for Allah, finding none. Otherwise, I don't see much here representative of murderous farmer dudes. Mostly urban jetsters that crashed from the skies and highway accident casualties still in shock, HIV and cancer victims, the "untimely ripped" ones that should have lived more years but didn't. But for Big-D to lose his father and to be the cause and to know his father had murdered Timothy, he must have a whole other perspective on life: such as expect the worst from anybody anywhere, including your own self. Which is a really depressing philosophy. One I might share. But that's not why I killed myself.

So that vibration from my iPhone that woke me from my nap on the couch ... another text from Brad. One among a vastness I have not bothered to answer, mostly from the parental units. I am in text recovery at the moment, disinclined to answer, and Shotgun-G leans down over watching me from the railing of the stairs overhead. I know I'm a good looking dude, but this is a disturbing development. I'm large for my age but not too awkward moving it around, solid muscle from my father's German genes, which is why the Vikings kicked ass, and dark hair wavy and eyes brown and direct, white skin the Mom calls Geisha slick. I don't yet shave more than just my chin, though for appearances at Poncy I do sometimes run an electric razor all over in the A.M. to impose a masculine habitude.

So here I am reading from guilt the latest post from Brad:

> jw (just wondering) r u ok? wat up?
> ttyl (talk to you later) gtg (got to go)
> back 2 homework

Yeah right, I think while collecting a leer from Shotgun-G then texting back this:

> have fallen in 2 leatherface dream. cant wake up :(

Now, as I've said, all this history of backwoods cousins I was gifted from breathing deep the intoxicant sofa dust. Which is maybe something you will not like to believe. I say believe. The dream is real. It came from somewhere real. If you find this detour one-toke-over-the-line, call me unreliable, but believe in the journey. That's real enough. Everything in the universe ties together. It's a complex of motion and action reaction with recorded images that ground us. But when one part of the machine falls out of sync, after a while all moving parts will grind down from friction. Think of the celluloid motion picture of olden times, frame by frame, fed into the machine of light projected through patterns. Then a gear off center, jamming cogs and intense light melting the film, then fire, then the black of nothing. I have seen our world grinding slow to its final rest and I have trembled to see. But this is not a worry you need to share. The generators are still humming. The images are still projecting.

△

So there will be no more stops made by the pay-what-you-can cab among the spooky blooms of corn country New Jersey. Now it's Atlantic City. I drive the three cousins there to gamble, a once-a-year migration is their story, and highway all the way. Which makes for impersonal miles and me burning silver off the rear-view mirror with nervous eyes thinking sometime soon a sharp knife is going to cut across my throat from Big-D, and Little-G will laugh, and the silent hot chick is going to lap the blood. This is not a pleasant way to travel, but I get America's fascination with the road. I mean, it's no different from a video-game effect of fast images and fast info and potential violence: metallic birds playing gotcha tag with your bumper, scroll-shock scenery whizzing by so fast it makes you skate horny, random billboards shouting for their cranium moment. I see a billboard with the surveillance video profile of a recent bank robber: Have you seen this man? it says. Phone 1-800 bag the bastard. As if! Bonnie and Clyde would not of had a chance at phenom in this day's time.

So I drive into Atlantic City as the sun falls off the opposite side of America.

For the desperate of luck there is billboard signage suggesting buckets of coin presented by adorable cocktail babes leaning their glowing bangers. This I see from the backs of boardwalk hotels, ocean views obscured, as I drive past one empty parking lot after another. Either the city has been tapped out as potential bonanza or its riches have shifted to Mohegan casinos up in Connecticut. The Mohegans are those ones that once grew strips of hair down the center and shaved all else to skull, such as what punk rockers copied. But in my home state even the Indians have gone corporate. On the Rez means a whole other thing. No teepees or wampum or deer hide stretched out to cure, and no massacres of late, unless maybe at the gaming tables.

The Connecticut Indians have come crashing back after the next-to-last Mohegan went dead-fall off a cliff in a Daniel Day Lewis flick. Daniel Day Lewis – now there's a versatility dude. He's English but plays American Indians and also a gang leader in Tammany NYC, which is where gangs started. Never mind what's going down in the cartels. They've got nothing on Bill the Butcher. Daniel Day Lewis is a pod buster if ever there was. Him and Rip Torn. They take the movies into their personal lives. Rip robs banks. Daniel beats shit out of fellow actors with bowling balls. They both stay in character after the set's torn down and the camera's switched off. Pod busters. Those dudes make the rest of us inertiatic. Really. They are the anti-pods to which we aspire.

So I pull into one of those anonymous blacktop passenger exchanges that all look alike, such as a Jetsonian overhang roof you get at any tri-state mall and the bright blue phosphorescent lights within of soul snatching club glitter. A doorman smiles a fake welcome, such as tending the gates to eject posers and wannabes. Well, standards have fallen off some. The Leatherface cousins walk right in. They have been drinking firewater in preserve jars and snuggling the silent one between them who giggled the whole ride out and performed acts of sexual gratification I tried to ignore. I watch them stumble out the cab and shimmy into disco lighting, hardly a prestalgia moment. Then gather the nerve to glance something wrapped in tinfoil Little-G pulled out from a pocket and left beside me on the seat as what they're paying that they can. Something maybe best left wrapped, about which Little-G says,

"Juicy and tendersome. Ignore the hairy parts." His blue eyes twinkle inside a smile that folds the skin around them.

The scent of severed parts cooked to tender fill the cab. I distract myself with a far-gone memory – I've been here before. Atlantic City. Ten years ago for News Years. I was nine. Younger brother Matt was five and the reason for this family outing was my stepbrother Sherman turning eighteen and enlisting for Iraq. The Father freaked. He thought a family intervention would keep his son from a marriage gone bad away from a life gone bad, or at least one free of IEDs and jihad suicides. It didn't work. Sherman burned alive inside his Humvee. That which was left of him after the explosion.

What I remember of Atlantic City is my little brother Matt just old enough to keep the Mom busy the whole weekend chasing salt-water taffy, kicking frozen beach sand for frozen clamshells, riding the fair-go-round, and the Mom dragging him along to shop the boardwalk outlet stores. A Madonna concert had top billing for New Year's Eve entertainment. The Mom had to loner it because the Dad wanted one more night with Sherman to psychosuade him off his path of self-destruction. So I pulled Matt duty in front of the numbing tube while the Mom brought her mid-life insecurities to a Madonna concert to retool her potential, channeling Madonna's multiples lives. One of which was then promoting her new album Ray of Light, which is all about eastern meditation and Hinduism and Buddhism and the Kabbalah and yoga and blah, blah, blah. Which explains the Mom's one-time obsession with sweat pants and sandals and dim lighting and rubber mats doing yoga to identical skinny people stretched out on the tube. Spiders doing pushups on a mirror.

My best memories are of the Dad and me and Sherman at the red-button bandits on New Years' Day spinning fruit with pockets of quarters. The Dad was so depressed he handed out money such as Willy Wanka's Golden Tickets. The Dad had wanted to bond with his eldest son before it was too late, but only just had argued Sherman into defying him. I was too young to know what was happening but wanted to hang with the family dudes and wide-eye worshiped my older brother that I really, really wanted to get to know. Well, it wasn't going to happen. And so I wonder if everything in life is a gamble, or if it's already decided.

I have since found Sherman here in the afterlife. His voice led me to him, the same voice except blunted by war, downgrading the tone and quality of his words, harnessed to the worry instincts of a hunted and destroyed animal. This was no wonderment of a reunion. He told me there are friends of his here in the afterlife that have shared his IED blitheration. He called it that: "blitheration." He said it matter-of-fact in a dark whisper, such as falling off the bed from a bad dream and fearful of telling details from the mouth of madness. But, like, what jacked me into dizzy was him saying how cool that he and his bros had died together. He said it's fathoming the afterlife that has him spooked. He didn't remember me too much, though he knew he had won money in Atlantic City before his memories had mostly shattered from the explosion. He didn't remember the Dad much at all either and that's maybe a good thing. I'd like to forget him too. I think the Dad is why Sherman killed himself. Going to Iraq is the most sure way to kill who you once were, even if you come back alive, which Sherman had not managed. He is for sure one of the untimely RIPped ones.

Sherman Bartel Herkimer. That's his full name, my stepbrother that I saw here in the afterlife. I knew about him in the beforelife mostly from spilled over conversation from phone calls the Dad made to his first wife that were supposed to be private. And, of course, there was Atlantic City and me obsessing over him. I couldn't help myself. I had an older brother. I wondered what he thought about me. I thought he must think of me most all the time such as I did him. Such as what did he talk about with the Dad? What can his mom be like? Has he got laid? Then I learned he got married and wondered what she was like. Would she like me? If she likes me, would then he? I don't think he knew he's the one had the Dad's attention, the one he worried over, the one he mourned over when dead from Iraq. How could I compete with that? I was supposed to carry the Herkimer name to new heights after the Dad, but how do you beat a hero's death? But that's not why I killed myself.

Sherman was there when the statue of Saddam Hussein was toppled in Firdos Square. Very big score on the hypo-meter. American servicemen watching the video thinking to have won a great victory. Liberated citizens smiling their gratitude, an enemy military machine shamed and routed, a time to rebuild, douse the fires of drilling rigs and bring back the black crude. But Sherman had from that day an uneasy feeling. The event was staged. Only but a handful was there. The small box of the camera lens made it seem all of Badhdad had turned out. That square was empty. Some handpicked Iraquis, a Humvee off-camera with a cable pulling at the statue that was supposed to be citizens, a cordon of American tanks. Spoof to the world. No better than the ghost of weapons of mass destruction Saddam had amassed. No great turn out of happy citizens. No justified uprising.

Then months later, nervous bivouacs and unease among the officers, extreme heat and sandy winds and broken buildings, suspect citizens, resistance rising up, and IEDs everywhere. Sherman's Humvee on patrol, the directive of some nitwit fobbit (a "forward base operative" lounging mindless in the air conditioning), a tight alleyway leading to a broader avenue which Sherman never got to. His thinly armored vehicle torn apart by the explosion. And the thing he most remembers of that moment, as he told me in the afterlife, the smell, because tinnitus ends all sound but its own frantic ringing – that is a lasting condition of explosion the lucky ones get. But for the unlucky, the smell of cordite and flesh burning, the smell of blood and heat, the smell of absence. Yeah, that's what he said, "absence."

He said he knew to put the Humvee in reverse, but he could hardly see from the blood in his eyes. It wasn't his blood. But he didn't know that and then, once he blinked away the blood, there was no gear shift and then, no hand, no arm, no shoulder. And when he looked to the passenger seat from where the explosion had ripped, he saw there was no passenger. Sergeant Dewey was gone, just gone. Only a splash of red everywhere and nothing solid. And then he passed out and passed over to the afterlife as fire consumed him. He said he found particularly moving the change that came over him. Nothing hurt anymore and nothing mattered anymore, not the army, not the girl he had left behind in the trailer he had rented to make a home for a surprise pregnancy that had miscarried while he was in Iraq. He said these things to me in the afterlife and then he stopped. He thought he heard Sergeant Dewey's voice off on a wind. He had to follow that voice.

But these are memories from the afterlife. Back when I was alive and thinking about my brother Sherman at New Years, leaving behind Big-D and Little-G, I was driving the Garden State at night with Atlantic City well behind and Connecticut ahead. I was driving through a refinery hell of smoke stacks spewing fire and slag dumped in the marshes and rude drivers anytime of day and so I texted Brad:

> karmaquesting down the highway to
> hell ... u?

Which I think is pretty cool because back then I knew I had driven into a hell contrived by Henry Ford, god of combustion, to which we sacrifice our time and income and our planet's resources and weather. So there I am riding the fumes of dinosaur waste that Ford has refined and mechanized, and so as if on cue, an 18-wheeler wails its horn, and me thinking Celebrate the road! But I get that wrong, because while drifting between lanes texting I see a beefy arm such as a post extending a rude finger out the window of that semi. The yellow cab chatters along unfazed and drifts some more between lanes with me as tight on the reins as Bamm-Bamm's grip on Snorkasaurus Dino. Then my phone which by habit goes into my deep pocket vibrates the testicles which is Brad saying:

> u & nik cage ... bcnul8r maybe,
> oops! mr ralfph tapped me

Which tells me Brad is in English class lapping his phone beneath his desk with Mr. Ralph gone keen on Brad's junk safe and hovering sputnik.

But then the skyline of NYC glitters over across the wetlands. Condos replace industrial dumps, and refineries fall away, and the gagging smell has blown out across the bay. Then the Hudson River. The suck of money chased by a swarm pulls me across the George Washington Bridge lit up and smoldering hot such as a skyscraper has fallen across between the two worlds (not an original thought to Marvin Herkimer, as you will soon learn). On those girded sides I slide along in the clattering cab then loop-d-loop at the butt-end tie strings of its tourniquet off-ramp collecting centrifugal speed. Then off toward north where Connecticut turns on its side to switch off the lights. And there blinking in wakeful expectation glam the destination eyes of Sunny Vitello.

△

I'M WIRED IN AND DRIVING straight into the black night of conduit road through small towns that spread out from Westport such as firewalls on the net of protected secrets. Such as quiet divorces with Zoloft children, unbalanced dinner parties, Mexican nannies ganking jewelry, swimming pools glinting headaches to hangovers, gardenias with the spotted blight, PTA meetings to shout down unfavored teachers, smugbots of the country clubs. The white fences of white clapboard colonial homes with brick sidewalks and black shuttered windows quietly dissing developments outside those Paul Revere streets. That's where me and Matt and the Mom lived in an unhistoric cul-de-sac development of road signs named after sanctuary memes such as species of trees or birds or historic persons.

But it's home and thinking of home gives me a big, fat nostalgia boner. Because there's no place like home. My once-upon-a-time English teacher, Mr. Ralph, he said a cliché is a truth you're sick of hearing about. Now there's a truth burger to chew on. So go ahead and click your heels and nostagibate! Like, give me one reason Dorothy wants home so much while tearing up the yellow brick with those loveable furry and clanking tagalongs to dry her tears and turbo boost her courage. Dude! Get a clue! It's just another road back home. What's the fame without the family? So there I am leaning out the open window of Ignacio's run-down yellow cab leaking bravado, sleepy Connecticut blowing across my face inspiring the watery tearstosterone. I'm going home. I'm a kid again.

There's four-year-old Marvin laughing hard, proud to be the item of the Dad's eye glow, him watching and me bouncing the yard in my new, candy-red, battery-spun plastic Jeep that the Dad has guilt-gifted me. It's the slow month of June with a cloud of mosquitoes following behind. My step-brother Sherman has recently entered the calendar year of teenager dumb and advertises as much to the law of Bridgeport by inhaling whippets from a supermarket then staggering the isles. The Dad gets the call night before my red Jeep purchase. He must of by then been on the law's insta-dial menu. Next day he opens his wallet and out pours to me the love Sherman wanted.

So there's the Mom, her day-bright eyes beaming from dishes at the kitchen window, framed there such as a museum portrait and waving courage at me from our perfect house of the perfect neighborhood of the perfect marriage in the perfect state of Connecticut. Dude! Take notes! This will be the offset to the brodak moment that captured me dead hanging from a Poncy Prep tie. So I ask you: Where does truth lay its troubled head at night? I'm sorry to have to give you the truth ache, but aside from Sunny Vitello's bed, there be nowhere anywhere in Connecticut to find that truth.

Per example. Here's a retina-freeze slide show of Connecticut poser truth –

Slide One » Me and little brother Matt in our winter jammies sipping hot cocoa while the Mom hovers her Cheshire Smile shuffling happily in pink fur Christmas slippers. And the Dad there too laughing together with us tittering rubes and nuzzling the Mom as we make plans to family slide the hills that rise above the frozen duck pond, and make angels in the snow when we fall off our sleds. Never happened.

Slide Two » Me at junior lax making cut backs on little bro defensemen and flattening the hacks, laying lumber on the mary gaits then going low-high at the goal with mustard and score! Little dude Marvin does it again! The Dad stands proud in the bleachers and glad hands the other parentards while crooning my name. Never happened again.

Slide Three» The Mom and the Dad laughing and chasing the other around the bedroom naked and dripping shower water, loving it up on the shag throw rug, the Dad cooing love words from a Merle Haggard song until little me and baby Matt knock the door to join the fun. And so their joy expands to secret giggles and fast clothes and comfort hugs for us little security-starved twaddles. Never happened times three.

Connecticut is a fairyland of should have been and might have could, and that's what makes me cry. I breathe again the heavy night air of what's to come. The back roads through farmland gone to development housing and the towns of colonial houses with mailboxes built to look such as the houses they service. Doesn't Connecticut just overdo cute? Well, there's nothing cute about my prefab neighborhood built in the 70s as add-on luxury outside the old money of downtown Lakeville. So I drive into our development where big-screen oscillations of pre-canceled network serial TV light the cul-de-sac of my childhood. Picture windows beam at me blue and white and green, such as airline pilots must see coming in to land. But this is a landing to a very sad house that will disabilitate me badly. So I circle again and again such as drilling down to find the fond memories.

Then I brake a moment beside my brick home of ranch design with a screaming rooster weathervane over a heated garage because cars get the most care in my house. I can see inside the white-on-white décor the Mom prefers, lamps and sofas and rugs and walls all white. Which is what the Dad calls a break-up color because of the Beatles white album, its empty cover meant to hide the conflicts that disbanded them and that did too the Mom and the Dad. Anyway, there's the back of the Mom's shag hair over the sofa facing the full-wall screen TV, she the generation of the big screen and me of the small screen. I know she must be freaked because by now she's heard I have escaped Poncy. Even still multiple text and voice mail neglect will be tops on her complaint list. But I can't educate her the reasons for all this just now, so I drive another circle round and there sits Willy Jameson's house across the street. He that used to wing rocks at my pug dog Rufus. Willy was two years ahead of me in school and likely to remind me in the rudest way, and him an only child with an ogle-worthy hair lip I couldn't ever ignore – physical imperfections being, if you remember, signs of alien occupation – and Willy not given enough attention for that oddity so taken to acing his classes in high school and hating his parents. So there I see Willy bringing out the trash and dressed in something shiny and wearing sunglasses at night. With Olympic tonsil extension I say to him while pressing on the brake, "Dude, those bags? Your parents cut to pieces? You finally make good the righteous threat?"

He says back with that lispy swirl of word sounds from his damaged lip, "Dude!" he says, "Isss that you, Herk? God damn! You bussssting my nutsss again! I have sssome Rufus rocksss here in my pocket could be for you."

"Catch me if you can!" I say then step the gas but brake to query: "Willy, why you still living at home?"

"Parentssss can't find the eject button. If they don't sssoon I'm due to lay a Virginia Tech masssacre on thisss town."

So I'm not so far off in my assessment of good'ol Willy the delay bomb. I lean on the accelerator, punch the horn and announce to the neighborhood a case of parental malpractice. "Free Willy! Free Willy!" I shout thinking maybe he can go to some other town to shoot people. The Jameson's porch light beams on in my rearview mirror. Willy's dad peeks out the door. He tosses a mouthful of disgrace words at Willy who performs the sequel to rude with a dismissive hand gesture aimed at his Dad who points to me while reviewing in his labyrinth mind reasons for an ancient yellow cab circling the neighborhood in the dark with a voice pouring out.

Then I remember. Shit! Zed calculates 90% of all cab drivers from NYC are aliens, which brings a more profound reality tweak: a yellow cab just about vibrates otherness in this town of same. How will I stay a secret in Lakeville in Ignacio's ride? But can't say I'd be any more remarkable than Willy on his porch in chain mail and pointy metal shoes and sweats, cleft lip sneering. Then I remember, oh yeah, the SCAdians have reeled him in and maybe saved his life. Which is obsessive historic reenactment that want jousting back and chivalry, which if you don't know is code whereby the dude must love a married lady he can't have. Something I understand very well. I need to drive off and find Mrs. V, but can't just yet stop the loopathon. Not just yet.

Because there next door to my house is Heidi Helsinger's upstairs window that has lit a night time blaze of lust into my own upstairs bedroom window for many years. Her little girl puberty mellons squished against the glass, laughing with a bright red throat that would soon swallow me down semen and all, a brain-spin of simulated sex. We never did have sex. Only just oral. Which was enough to almost impeach Bill Clinton. What ridiculousness. I mean ... invite the teeth, become impeached, and Heidi another Monica whose face would launch ships the opposite direction.

As I slide the big yellow car past her house and my own, there's Heidi's mother, Priscilla Helsinger, seated in the dark on porch steps dressed in jammies and a winter coat. Smoking a cigarette and engaged in dreamathon. She looks only a little bit curious noticing the cab wheeling around the circle. When I brake and roll the window and shout hello, she mostly absorbs the oddity, hardly a movement except lifting the ciggie to her lips. Maybe because my Willy conversation a couple houses away alerted her of my return.

She says, "Marvin, how are you?" As if this is my usual way to reclaim the old life. Then says, "Your mom, Marvin, she's in not so good a mood lately. Pretty abrupt with Heidi. I know her music is loud sometimes, but that Madonna shit your mom plays all day is no bird song either. You come to see Heidi? She's been asking about you."

I say, "No, Mrs. Helsinger, only just come home to see a friend ... Mrs. Vitello. But thought I'd cruise the neighborhood before. Please say hi to Heidi."

"Yeah, sure, Marvin. Whatever. If you want to see Heidi, she's at the Mobil snack deli in town behind the counter. Any shift no one else wants she's there. She'd love to see you."

"Okay. Will do. Thanks. Later!"

With that I cast a parting look at the Mom's bobbing head in the picture window. She's absorbing another episode of Survivor which is a bunker habitude she developed because the Dad's x-wife, Sherman's mother, up until the Dad scrapped his second marriage, she phoned all the time to bitch out the Mom for taking money out of her pocket. She made threats, which had the Mom thinking she was being followed, likely to be kidnapped, looking over her shoulder for anyone talking into a wrist, behaving toward the Dad such as he is Zeus that seduced her as a swan so now she has to forever watch out for his angry x-wife.

Then I see Matt from my old upstairs bedroom sitting at a desk facing Heidi's window. The blue glow of his computer screen ghosts his serious face plucking at the code-buster algorithms he uses to change the drive-thru window orders at the McDonalds in Millertown or hacking into the Hotchkiss School server to schedule a fire drill. He's a way better keyboard warrior than I ever was. But really why he's here in my room, Matt must of wanted the view to Heidi's sexucation. Can't blame the little dude. I toot and Matt waves an unsure hand while the Mom sits there lost in her wall of cascading pixels. She's in the matrix, I think, and shudder, and wonder if maybe the Mom has become a pod? But I shake that off and gun the cab out from its spiral into the old life then back onto the main road and away such as out from a sling to Mrs. V's.

△

I KNOW YOU'RE THINKING why tell Heidi's mom I'm intimate with Mrs. V, right? Not much of what we do in the beforelife rates explaining. Really. I mean, if the moon bullies the ocean tides, why not us. Why not me? I'm 75% water, right? But no, there's a reason. Have you never told a stranger the complete truth sometimes? I mean, isn't it nice to tell the truth sometimes? And believe me, Mrs. Helsinger qualifies as strange. And maybe I wanted to be found out. Maybe that. I'm no different from anyone else glitching their way through this life. But mostly there's no way she's tickling the ear of the Mom with this confession nugget. All they share is a hand wave backing out the driveway. Maybe on account of Heidi and me in seventh grade studying gender anatomy in the upstairs closet one day in Heidi's house. After Heidi pushed her bare chest against her bedroom window at night and signaled come over with a finger wiggle. Mrs. H found us and laughed. The Mom cried and grounded me a week. Heidi and me spent the weeks following exposing gender parts across the window span of our bedrooms, yanking and rubbing to get off, a week of mojo preparation almost as radical as Mrs. V's tutoring. Heidi and me became tight sex friends after that.

I'm so turned on thinking of Heidi as I drive off to see Mrs. V that I almost stop for a back-room release with Heidi at the Mobil to calm the idiot energy assailing my nervous system. But I don't. Instead I drive off the hill Lakeville High School occupies, turn right onto Main Street already gone to sleep. Except for those few restaurants still serving the chic its faux ethnic fix. There's an upscale Chinese, a French brasserie, and near the lake in an old millhouse of Revolutionary times, a black-tie swankery serving authentic old-world American meat pies. I think of Big-D and Little-G's cat stews while driving past. Do we ever really know what we eat? Anyway, otherwise, this town is three streetlights long with colonial houses each side of the street. There's an obsolete book store for the gray hairs, a couple galleries for artards and shallow lawns one side of the street, but deep as an acre from the street to lakeside where every house but Mrs. V's ponies up more taxes than my tuition at Poncy.

I park the cab behind the bank that Zed will soon rob and open the trunk to throw in Bradley's yellow sweater which a Chinese gas attendant on the NJ Turnpike reminded me is no kind of anonymous wear.

"Dude," he said, "welcome to the oasis. You will be the distraction from my distraction."

I had walked in on him in the late-hour of his cell-phone porn streaming at the cash register. All around him isles of candy and rows of sugar-water drinks in coolers explode in color density. "Dude," he said, pointing at me, pointing to the yellow cab, "a canary in a canary coach! And I thought the yellow race is me. Where's the migration going?"

I said, "No migration necessary. I live here. Well, I mean, not on the turnpike. I mean here in the States."

He said, "Yeah, me too, but canaries have wings you know. Migration can be a good thing."

"Okay, maybe a small migration. A couple hours north. But which minority are you?" I was referring to his Afro that has a retro feel about it and confused me all to hell because his face and eyes say Chinese.

"Oh," he said, patting his hair. "It's a jewfro. Anyway, my dad wants to think so. He's a Brooklyn Jew. Mom's from Bejing but grew up here in China Town. She likes to think there's black Caesar in the mix. Seen that movie?"

"No, never."

"Yeah, well, Mom had a thing for Jim Brown that took his football legs to the movies but says she scored costar Fred Williamson that was making a gangster of Harlem flick that she gave a massage to … don't ask. My guess is she only just orgasmed to his nudies in Playgirl. Now if you want to see an Afro, my mom rocks it! It's a complete salon tease and spray freeze, but I swear she kills it! Whatever. I'm a Chinese black Jew. My dad calls me Baskin Robbins. "

"Sweet," I said with all kinds of identity envy.

"My family never owned a laundry. Never. Check it! Dad's a lawyer in Brooklyn. Mom sells vintage clothes here in sweet-smelling Jersey. I migrate between the two. It's the migratory hustle! I was born to it. Mom lives in Hackensack, this side the Washington Bridge. Hey … about that bridge … did you know it started out a skyscraper that fell across the river. So they hung lights and drive on it. Did you know?"

"Never heard that."

"Where's your American history? Dude. Seriously. Yellow man to yellow man. Learn your American history. Whatever."

"All right, I will. But why aren't you in college skewing the curves on math tests? What are you doing behind the counter of a freeway oasis?"

"No geek genes, bro. I'm into politics. This is a political appointment. Not so easy to score."

"No shit! You need connections to get this kind of work?"

"State job. It's a long slide into Jersey politics from here but I'm greasing it. No dead end if you're paying attention. I meet all the dark suits motorboasting from the Trenton State House to Wallstreet. All kinds of secrets shared in this late night oasis. What's your secret?"

"Do I have one?"

"Can't bless the migration without you have one. But, whatever."

When he made the cash register deposit, I remembered the

Chinese pretty much own America and I didn't want to madden the overlord. So I said and only really by reflex, "Okay. I'm going to kill myself at the end of this trip."

"No shit! Cool. Haven't heard that one before. 54.40 for the gas but have a Snickers bar on me and best of luck in the afterlife."

"The afterlife?"

"Whatever."

That's the first time I heard the term "afterlife " applied to me. And that's when I realized the true nature of my personal migration. Didn't know why. But I knew it was what was going to happen. I was going to kill myself. Could be fate. The kind I remember from Macbeth. I mean, if not for the witches, if not for his wife, would he have killed Duncan? The fates say no. Well there are those woods that betrayed him, such as the woods that did me too that surround Mrs. V's lake-side house. But, I mean, the big thing, the really big thing was his wife. Choosing your woman is a major reset. I mean, the fates say you're doing this but you choose a woman leads you the direction of that, and there it is. Fate's big reset. I chose Mrs. V, and so I'm dead. Is that what happened? Something like, yeah. But let me ask, how many shoes does it take to get somewhere? Mrs. V was one of those shoes, but not all of them.

△

SO I PARK AT THE EDGE of a street lamp beam of light back of Zed's bank, the one he'll soon contrive to rob. I'm out in the damp, muddy air springing open the trunk of Ignacio's cab intending to stash Bradley Turcotte's yellow sweater. But then, what the hey! He's a drug dealer. Sapperstown cops aren't so bright. Give the spare tire well a looksee. When I lift the swatch of carpet, there underneath all scrunched into a round space lay nothing like a tire, but rather instead a duffel of black nylon containing Ignacio's personal whatnot. I know I can't gank a drug dealer's stash without reciprocation worries. But again, what the hey! He's in jail. I'm not. So I pull on the bag. It's heavy. I close the trunk, lay it on top, unzip and ... this will be proof I'm genius. There's drugs, a small caliber hand gun, and best of all, cash. Also, a black hoodie. Preferware to any teenage son that doesn't attend Poncy Prep or Hotchkiss School. Most decidedly the big diff between preppies and townies of Lakeville High. Well, that and destinies warped by families with big money.

I put on the hoodie and even with khakis riding the hips, I'm transported to who I was pre-preppy. Then I stuff the roll of cash into the hoodie's deep pocket. I toss two shrink-wrapped bricks of marijuana over a wet snow bank because suggestive of a transfer to reform school. I hide the gun in the glove box. I walk into the night, down a path beside the lake toward the woods that lets out where Mrs. V lives.

When I get there, Brent Vitello's Ford Mustang is ticking still from a cooling engine. It's suppertime. Things are boiling over in the kitchen, probably because it's late for supper – Mrs. V not the kind that keeps to schedule – and, well, there's afternoon Mimosas. I sneak up the porch stairs, kick a path through a pride of cats scratching the kitchen door and just laying around. I peek in the window, bend to tickle the ears of Crisis for which I am gifted a purr and face-rub requital. That's another SAT word, requital. I would definitely have impressed the word wonks of college.

So, anyway, Sunny and her husband, Brent, are by now faced-off shouting hystericals. I'm standing there outside the kitchen window two yards away and they don't know. They are so about conflict. I hear Brent cuss a barracks degrade of late dinners and untidy housekeeping. That soars to overdrawn checking account and then onto all the little boys that skip away when Brent answers the door. Then he's telling of the grocer's help whose giggles betoken scandal when he walks in for his six of beers. Then cussing those damn cats overtaking the yard so he can't get in and out of the Stang without fur attached to his boots. I kind of see his point there.

Mrs. V says, "Yes, that's right. I've seen how fur gets the effing boot for friendliness."

Then the spaghetti sauce boils over and as Brent complains about that and reaches back to kill the gas jet, he notices me outside and goes off: "Here we go! Another juvie dick for redecorating. Isn't that what you call it, Sunneva? (which is her real name from Iceland that only Mr. V uses). Well, shit. Maybe after I deal with this I'll unwind on commissary beers and drive the long way home. Or better yet stop at The Dancing Mouse and feel up the first white thigh that sits beside me at the bar. Give you time to clean him up after I'm done whooping his ass!" He starts towards the door as I jump off the porch and Sunny comes between.

I climb the trellis attached to the garage that's attached to the house. I break a slat or two going up as not properly engineered for Marvin weight. I throw the sash from the garage roof and step into the bedroom. Instant boner! Can't help myself. Just the scent of her room spins me into jizbomb. I push the boner down and prepare to do a UFC beat down on that fucker below. I hear things smashed, Mrs. V crying, Mr. V shouting. I run down the stairs and there's Mrs. V with a kitchen chair raised over her head, beaten, crying still, collapsed in a corner, waiting for the blow. I swear to all that's holy or forever mistaken as such, for the first time, I know what it is to be in the afterlife. Because in Mrs. V's kitchen at this moment, I feel everything at once. I am so positively sure of what I am and where I've been that brought me here and where I'm going and embracing the exposed selves of unsure and scared shitless but determined and channeling those DC comics from my youth that show so much heroic darkness and noble self-sacrifice and this while aswim in every molecule and particle atom of that place. I mean there in Mrs. V's kitchen, I understand for the first time it's her intimate battle ground with the man that knows places of her I haven't yet explored and never will. And the smell of burnt food is really the scent of naked anger and gears un-synched that grind and smoke. And the funky green wallpaper and dirty yellow cabinets and the greasy exhaust fan huffing still over the stove where sauce burns in a pan and, dude! I'm not ready for this! It's information overload.

So I stop the cognition treadmill and run up to and give a wimpy shove from behind. Brent Vitello thumps the wall with his head. He turns slowly and unfazed smiles the most evil grin I've ever seen outside Benicio Del Toro pimping it out in Sin City. Mr. V must feel the pimp vibe when he looks at me because his hands become hammers.

What comes next is so unexpected. Mrs. V off the floor fast and taking hold of a cast iron fry pan from the kitchen counter, shouts, "Eff you!" Then nails Mr. V side of the head but which only reminds him there's a second front to this war, so shifts his face toward Mrs. V where he takes a second blow. Mr. V wobbles and collapses, but again shakes it off, rises unsteady, grabs the chair, slams it against the floor where it shatters, picks up one of the legs and smiles, gathers strength for a rush at me. But Mrs. V crashes down again and again from behind with the fry pan until Mr. V begins to leak blood from a crack at the back of his skull and already from his mangled face.

When Mrs. V factors what she's done, she curses me, throws arms around Mr. V who is on the floor silent and bleeding. She begins throwing pieces of chair at me, cursing and shouting, "Get out! Get out, you little effer, you! Get out! Go find a virgin. Leave me alone!"

But I can't leave. If you remember, I'm fascinated with deformity. I can't take eyes off the expanding rosette of blood that stains the beige throw rug with Brent Vitello's brain juice leaking and his face all shanked out of recognition. I wonder if he'll go hairlipped such as Willy Jameson that I could never stop creep peeping when a kid. But I shake off the fascination horrors and take Mrs. V by the arm and tell her, "Get up. Get out! You've got to get out!"

She looks at me a long time, blue eyes empty but for tears. Then she gets it. Pushes aside Mr. V and wipes her bloody hands on his uniform and stands up shaky. I reach for her, but she pushes me away, smoothes a hank of blonde hair behind her ears, pulls down her blouse inside the pink-flower patterned cardigan sweater, tells me in a voice so calm it's scary, "Meet me at the Hotchkiss boathouse. Not the new one. The old, fall-down one." I hesitate. "Get!" she says. So I get.

△

I'm running down paths in the woods, branches welting the face, tripping on roots in the dark because distracted by the sometimes ghost graffiti of Mrs. V and a posse of intimates other than me dancing on the blue trees lit by my cell phone. Then a turf monster grips my shoe. I'm making furrows with knees in the muck of early spring. When I stand, everything hurts. I rub the mud away, wash hands in a patch of snow, and become like really pissed. I pull out a sharp rock in the shallow underground that struck my knee and scratch away a selection of hook-up brags from off the blue birch, those ones maximum queasy because I know the dude. But there are so many. I have to remind myself I'm looking for a mostly forgotten path of weedy overgrowth. It leads to an abandoned Hotchkiss boathouse become disused from lake shrinkage off a water table siphoned by expanded population. Mrs. V often complains of thirsty houses gone up around the lake.

The woods are speaking to me. A spooky combination of owls, frogs, and a panther scream the Mom corrected as only red fox but that raises the short hairs anyway. And wind-bent branches slap together such as brooms sweeping the air. Cleaning away bad dreams is what the Mom used to say. Woods have a job to do. They don't sleep at night. I begin to wonder when will I? It's been since that alcohol-induced psycho drama on the sofa of dream-filled Little-G and Big-D accommodation that I last slept. The adrenalin rush that propelled me to here has drained off leaving mostly woozy. I begin to feel the emotions brother Sherman must of in Iraq: the ups of combat overload and the downs of inactivity underload. I'm ready to give it up, whatever this is with Mrs. V and me, curl beside a scrub of windbreak on a carpet of moss and sleep.

Then a memory of me in the woods near my house when a kid. In summer, wandering off to nap in the deep quiet. The Mom carrying me home from where she knew to look on a patch of sun-lit moss. Maybe the Mom will find me in the morning and wake me again from the dream that carries me here. Every night the same dream from the same bedtime story: That very night in Max's room a forest grew .... There can't be more than a hundred words in the entire book. I remember them all. Every one. I can say them backwards: hot still was it ... and ... him for waiting ... supper... Yeah, well, sleep and food. Pretty basic. What you come to expect until it's no longer given. And these woods, they're not a Max habitat. They belong to Hotchkiss School preppies, less easy to tame than wild things.

I stumble my vitality-sapped feet onto a faded dirt path down which stands in a gray mist the abandoned boathouse all weathered and tilted, mossy, boarded up and creepy at the edge of the mud suck of what will in summer become malarial swamp. Boathouse paradise reduced to a shallows of cattails and red winged blackbirds and black mud. A place to rest.

The door is firm and padlocked shut. I tear off nailed boards and break glass to pull in through a window. So of course I rip pants at the crotch and cut my hand, which is not so bad compared to the remodeled face of Mr. V. Although he might be too dead to notice. Feet land on a spongy floor of mushroom spores and wet-wood sheen upon which I slip and quick snag a rail to prevent tipping into a cutaway floor over pond water. It's here where once bobbed the famous Hotchkiss prowl boat with nose painted in furry likeness of the school's muskrat mascot. The boat's stored another place now but still spins the lake to stir a crowd before crew race regattas, and seated in the stern a megaphoned dude braggadouching the fame to come.

I dig out the iPhone again to light a stairs to drier digs above. I score a mattress on the floor of single proportion. A futurelicious hope of bod-on-bod stirs the juices. There's a wine bottle with candle stuffed in waxy useful and a BIC disposable too. Condoms peek out from the room's corners. As if I wouldn't know the implication scenario of this little accommodation scene. But for now, that mattress pulls me into deadfall. Complete sleep best expressed here. No thoughts. No worries. Because the sensory neurons have shut down even with Mrs. V out there somewhere in a fog of homicide panic and accomplice guilt of the carnal arts. The mattress smells putrid, but even this won't detour a crash into senseless.

I dream this time of a future woods. I see the boathouse of better days painted white with deck off the upstairs where I'm sleeping that leans over water shining silvery on wind ripples. Turtles on logs, trees across the lake in bright fall colors, the sugary scent of wood burned for heat. Foxes play where the brook lets into the lake. And Mrs. V and me in the afternoon sun on that deck drinking Mimosas, holding hands, laying claim to this little corner of paradise.

I wake with the pounding head of hunger. My hand has bled all over the mattress. I haven't eaten more than a Snickers gifted to me by Baskin Robbins, the politico of Jersey highways. That was a day ago. But the pounding, it comes with a voice. I realize, finally, the voice of Sunny Vitello. A desperate whisper. "Marvin," it says. "Marvin, where are you? Are you there? Shit! Herk, are you there?"

Takes me awhile to realize she can't get in the door, probably doesn't see the broken window, doesn't know I'm here.

I flip open the iPhone to light my way down the stairs, speak softly as I descend and at the other side of the door tell her, "I'm here. Be cool. I'll get you in."

I slam my shoulder into the door. Mrs. V screams. She didn't hear me speak, must be, and so I say again, louder, "It's me! I'm here! Be cool!" and lean again so the door cracks in the middle. I push out a thin, square panel of wood above the padlock and see Mrs. V shivering in the mist with a wash of moonlight pouring down. She's wearing the same bloody clothes and nothing more, vastly underdressed for New England woods of early spring. Her cardigan sweater open, white blouse pink with blood she tried to clean away that clings to skin so you can see there's no bra. Which is a habit she finds hard to break from early days when it took forever to grow breasts. That's an explain mote I never will forget. Tight jeans make her seem that young still. And pink fuzzy slippers all mud she has forgot to change. And the tone of undecided in her voice maxes the cougar attraction for young ones such as me that take flying lessons from the Lemmings. That's what Mrs. V often says to me that she references again taking softly my hand because notices the bloody cut. "So," she says, "another hard landing?" I make a raspberry response but she knows I'm jazzed to waltz with her together at the edge of any steep overhang.

So there we are separated by a half inch of weathered door deep in the watershed of preppy abandonment with her shivering there and me shivering the other side. We have to get our two bodies together for warmth and sympathy. I tell her, "Hold on Mrs. V. I'm going to open this door!" and shine my iPhone into the corners looking for the persuasion tool from which to do exactly that.

I take stock. There's sail rigging wrapped, stuffed high in the rafters, a shine-back reflection of another set of windows other side of the hole where water slops below, some rusted lockers and a life vest hanging on a hook. There is too, I notice, a door open onto a bathroom remodel never finished with only just a hole in the floor that vents to the pond below (evacuation the old way). There's metal pipe on the floor and a porcelain toilet on its side that never did assert its design function. But then I realize that pipe could make a tool and remove a section, lean into the hole of the door and tell Mrs. V to stand back, as this is a masculine gesture I can't resist. I reach outside with just my hands and that pipe and torque the padlock hasp out from the wood splintering less than just pulling out from the rot. Could have sprung that loose with a twig. But no need to inform Mrs. V and buzz-kill the moment.

We hug. She smells different this time. Maybe sweat. Mostly I think it's worry stink and fear. She's clingy. More than ever before and it's usually me not her. So this is way different. I lead her upstairs with my iPhone beam. She collapses on the mattress, curls knees to her chin and cries. She's desperate, cold, scared, unlikely to want my hard-on up against her on the mattress. So I take another explore downstairs to those lockers, poke around inside, carry away a ripped Hotchkiss sweatshirt, a water bottle, a pair of flip-flops with one broken toe strap, good tread for slippers. I rip out the other toe strap.

Then I leap at a stack of sailcloth, pull down a load, bring all upstairs where Mrs. V, all squishy white, glistening wet, has become a ball of mollusk looking for its shell. I lay on top of her covers of moldy sail that bring her up from herself and out from herself. Her watery blues blink a connection with what's me and what's her. Me: a hoodified bundle of red-blooded uncertainty runaway. Her: a housefrau exploded of sexy uncertainty runaway. We have become the same.

△

I sit beside Mrs. V on the mattress and ask softly is she okay? No answer. I ask about Mr. V. Is he dead? She forgets to breathe, coughs into her hands, takes a bite of the air, dislikes the taste of mildew, stale sex and fugitive worries, pulls a face and says she doesn't know. I ask was he moving? She says no. I ask did she feel his breath? Hear his breathing. She says no. I say, he's dead. More silence, then, "I need to go back, Marvin."

"No way! We stay here awhile. Then run."

"Run where?" She is now sitting up, wiping tears with the back of a hand. "I have a class to teach."

I tell her, "I think you need to take a personal day."

She laughs in a batshit way. Eyes narrow, arms belted at the chest, a sinful grin that mutates into a laugh track that sounds too on cue to be real, her face a mask of prepared emotion. The engine of her lungs sucking away our oxygen, deep breaths whirlpooling everything not tied down, such as what pulled under the Odysseus boat and me thinking where's the fig tree to hang onto? I know she needs this. But I'm not going to let her pull me in. It's me that has to be the reality consultant. I laugh with her as convincing as I can then say let's make a life of the pay-what-you-can taxi cab. I'm thinking her and me on the road to nowhere permanent, maybe back to Big-G and Little-D's for mouthwatering feral cat that I'll say is possum and divert her mothering habitude to those sweet young things tied up down in the basement. Sneaking away the grateful darlings in a daring rescue that will go down as an app for cell phone distraction such as digital Nosferatu running from the sun.

But not just yet. She gives me a look of come together vibe and dude! We become animal. It must be 40 degrees in this unheated loft as we tear off clothes and attach. Me totally gone into thoughtlessness which she knows and slows down a fraction with her two hands framing my face and those sharp blues telling me this time it counts. You might think that would send the nads and their attendant bad boy running for cover. But not so, my droogs! I get so hard I could batter the doors of Troy, or fulcrum shift the rotation spiral of the moon. Her and me become so welded and tight of lips and legs that we share together one skin, become one single heart beneath one single skin. It's a beautiful thing. I mean, have you ever felt infinite?

△

THEN ABRUPT SUNLIGHT. It's morning and we can see how temporary is our hideaway crib: sun through cracks between pine board and from knots pushed out with only just 2x4 studs as interior wall, wetness within from a roof gone spongy on top that soaks water then releases in drips, two grimy windows either end of the gables filtering light such as we have settled under water. The place filthy with fast-food litter, beer cans, cigarette butts, a syringe near the mattress. Condoms, of course. Initials carved into walls, some I recognize from the birch trees outside. Insult language sprayed on in bright colors from townie invaders such as Blow Me Hotchkiss Fags. These are my once ago high school bros avenging fears of worthlessness and of homos coming out from closets. I must plead guilty to some of these thoughts. There's also empty liquor bottles from Dad's home stock gone missing during Hotchkiss vacations. Then others here with us more domestic that have a better claim to this rickety outpost. Beaky noise makers, little carnival barkers announcing a nest above in the rafters from which mamma red wing shuttles out and back again through broken window glass with food and rude announcements. All while shitting on us, feathers coming loose spiraling down.

Mrs. V says, pointing above, reaching for a pinwheeling feather, "Look what she's lost in parenting, Marvin. (She misses, feels around on the floor beside her.) Did your mother dash around the house that way, Marvin, did she go frantic making a home for you? My mother never did."

I want to give her a serenity hug but instead keep arms straight along my sides, the better to absorb my own body heat. Under this sailcloth is no kind of warm and Mrs. V won't let me near. I tried sneaking an arm over her shoulder but she rolled away. The smells are oily and musty and make a faucet of my nose. You'd never know we had warmed it up under here last night with our passion.

I tell her, "The most the Mom did with us kids was keep us under control when the Dad came home. Unless singing country, we could tell he was in a bad mood when going over the month's sales at the kitchen table, comparing projections to units sold. That's what he calls a car, a unit. Sometimes, when in a good mood, he'd call me and Matt units. He'd say, Maddie, that's the Mom's name from Madison, dress up the units to sell. Let's take them to lunch and see what offers we get. One time Matt thought the Dad really meant to sell us. He ran into the restaurant bathroom and wouldn't come out. But mostly the Dad was saying for us to shut it, especially when his dealership ads played on the radio."

"I've heard those ads. More obnoxious than a robocall. Hope that's not your dad speed talking. If so, his mantra needs refreshing."

"Well said, Mrs. V! Very spiritual technological of you. Very L. Ron Hubbard. And no, about the Dad, not his voice. Some silver-tongued nabob become the industry standard for fast speak, right out of the Simpsons if you ask me. Mrs. V, why don't you have kids?"

And then, right away, I know – wrong thing to say. She looks at me with the recoil shock of a physical attack equal to a Brent Vitello bloodletting. She looks away. I say, "I didn't mean ...."

"No, it's a good question." She pushes the sailcloth down to her chest, brings her hands to her face, wipes off tears, pats the cheeks lightly, maybe to bring warmth to her white skin become all blue veins and goose bumps. Or maybe to awake the poet in her that knows words matter and says, "Bad womb. Bad odds. One miscarriage was enough."

"I didn't mean ..."

"I know," she says, "nobody does. Nobody means anything anymore. Brent didn't mean to become the punishing misogynist. And I didn't mean to become a hermit poet, a drunk-by-noon lech, a spoiler of youth. Oh, eff me. Sorry."

"No, but I ..."

"What I want to know is how it came to this?"

Then I get a little heated. I try not to show it, but I mean, a spoiler of youth? Really? And what exactly is this? I mean, what? Diversion reality? I'm a diversion? Or is this the end of her life as she knows it? Well, yeah, maybe. But that could be a good thing. She goes silent. Rolls over facing the wall. Then me going assertive saying, "This time, Mrs. V, you and me ... you better believe it's the beginning of something."

I tell her I'm going to take her here and there. Introduce her to him and them and she saying with the force of a bell rung with a cotton ball clanger, saying with no energy, no excitement, no trust, "That's so nice."

Then me saying, because I just think of it, "Why not Mexico? Run a cab service. Cheap digs and namelessness," and she saying, "Maybe."

Then me saying, "Forever sunshine. No more school" – which works for me, but not so much for her. She smiles and says, "Maybe."

Then she licks my ear. Can you believe? I mean, she rolls back over and licks my ear! Cat woman. Hella sexy. But then says, "Shit!" and pulling the musty sailcloth up over her head says, "I shouldn't get you involved in this ... whatever it is. Go back to school, Marvin. I'll be all right. I'll tell the police what happened, take my punishment in the cell blocks with my sister assassins. Another rat in the maze."

"Yeah," I say, "I get it. But that's me every day. Remember me, the Lemming? Leaping with the Lemmings, remember? You said you like that about me. Why not like that about you?"

"Shit, Herk," she says with only just her eyes out from the sail cloth, "you're maybe too smart for school. But those Lemmings ... what I haven't told you ... when they leap they don't come back."

"Okay, sure, if you say. But me and Mr. Ralph, when I asked if he knew about the Lemmings, we googled them back at Poncy. We found them on youtube. What we saw was a documurder of a little gang of Lemmings trucked off a cliff and filmed such as a migration gone wrong. It's a lie, a big lie. That's about your Lemmings, if you want to know."

"Who did that?"

"Disney. They're all about myth making. Maybe time to reframe the childhood memories."

"Not my memories. More like my parents'."

"Okay, sure, but I never trusted the Disney plan. I mean, never grow up? Never grow old? I mean, it just has no relevance. Sesame Street too. Adults talking to puppets? But, I was a mature pre-schooler, so, I mean, friendly monsters just don't feel right."

"Yes, better the aliens."

"Better the Pods."

"Right," she says, tongue inside her mouth pushing at the gap between front teeth, eyes to the ceiling. "I wonder have the pods already replaced me now that I've left home? Will they feed the cats? Will they teach my effing class?"

As you can imagine, that places me right there with her in a ponder moment as to how much I should tell because pods have no emotions, so the cats won't get fed. And about poetry, I've known teachers who do the poetry scan thing, same as diagramming sentences, with as much feeling as a pod replicant, naming parts, taking the soul out of what the words say. So yeah, I guess, poetry can be taught by pods and pretty effectively too if you like autopsies.

She sees me going deep into the silence of my factoring so unbuttons her frown and adjusts her face to lighten the mood, says, "This discussion can wait." Mrs. V jams fuzzy feet inside busted flip-flops and bounces down the stairs to gather swamp flowers and arrange them in the Hotchkiss water bottle. As she goes she's singing, "Cuckoo, jug-jug, pu-we, to-witta-woo! Quoth the songbird. Oh, and," she says at the bottom of the stairs, "there are fiddlehead ferns to be had that are good to eat when boiled. Best fried with butter, but, oh eff it, boiled works." I'm thinking that would take a fire, a dead giveaway to our hideout. I can't tell her this without the shade returning, so I balk. But so nice for her to do, the flowers, the fern, the bird song. Mrs. V and red-winged blackbird making a busy life of swamp gathering and feeding their young. But then I think no, that's messed up. She's a songbird not a mother and has not flown even as much distance from the nest as me.

So I'm here alone inside the loft but for momma bird up in the rafters freaking out. Flapping crazy, bumping against walls. How can it have forgot how to get out? I don't get this. It's shitting everywhere and screaming its fear, which has erased its memory. At night I heard the fox and owl again. Now it's peepers and this crazy bird that still can't get out, but then another comes in with food, and I'm brooding as regards this tag-team feeding of black birds mated. I'm wondering would the Dad benefit from a pair of wings. And, also, when do Mrs.

V and me talk about the dead husband? Then Mrs. V comes back with a pluck of spring flowers, some yellows, some whites, shoes off, feet and hands black with mud, pockets filled with circles of tight curled fern. She places them on the floor in a tin can she found and filled with pond water saying, "Heat this, drain, and eat."

My face shows the vast unlikeliness of this green shit going down my throat whether heated or raw. She gives me a pout so severe I get a boner alert shaping below and above hesitation eye contact. She knows. I have to divert attention so as to avoid embarrassment. I tell her, "Okay, green breakfast then the fast road out of town." So what if smoke tells our location. Nothing is permanent. She looks amused. I run off to gather wood scraps to burn. There's a small woodstove upstairs tucked in a corner that I light with pages ripped out from a moldy Hotchkiss yearbook lying around and dead wood I collect outside. I place the tin can with fern on top of the stove to heat. But the smoke backs up so bad I think we must be on fire. She laughs. Then runs outside then back and hands me a rock. Says get up on the roof and drop it down the pipe. So I climb a tree to the roof and do a slip-slide on mossy growth over cedar shakes then drop the rock. I hear Mrs. V scream with the clatter and go back down and inside to find her kneeling and teary holding a bird's nest with broken eggs inside. So we relight the stove and warm the place and boil the water with fern and eat. Too bad we can't eat those eggs is what I think but don't say it.

$$\triangle$$

Mrs. V says, "Herk, look at that sky. It's all sun."

I look up through the gable window. Even with the grime my eyes dilate from the brightness.

"That's a sun to warm us," she says. "Let's go outside by the water."

So we do and can't resist rolling pants legs to wade in such as a day at the beach. We trip over waterlogged tree branches complicating a small patch of sandy ripple beside the bank. Black muck to our knees of rotting leaves. Some ice still at the edges of the pond in the shade. The water brown in which we poke our hands, our skin yellow and bloated looking. Perch and shiners swim around. I splash her and laugh. She gives a sad smile, walks out to the shoreline beside the boathouse of compact dirt from many feet putting in and pulling out crew shells, some granite boulders large enough to make seats. Around the pond otherwise, at our hidden end, the shoreline dark with woods down to the edge where cattails and weeds grow. Away from us and after a bend, manicured lawns down to the water's edge of homes with rooflines the size of airplane hangers. Then at the far end, the red brick of Hotchkiss School spread out in military bulk and imposing formality but with little red berries jogging the sidewalks and lawns: students in red and white uniforms between classes. Boys in red jackets with the gold Hotchkiss crest, white pants. And girls in white blouses with red skirts. Townies call them burberries.

Mrs. V sits on a granite boulder with knees drawn to chest, hugging herself for warmth, but more ... making a statement of there's not much I can do to comfort her. She looks at her feet, fuzzy slippers stuffed into broken flip-flops, wipes legs dry with the Hotchkiss sweatshirt. Another dark smile. A sadness too deep for me to tease away. She says, "Marvin, I have killed a husband."

I say, "We don't know that (thinking maybe, yeah). He could be mostly fine. Only just rubbing away a head-thump the better to make him think. I bet he's brewing coffee right now and wishing he wasn't such a fucktard."

She goes quiet, wipes tears, then a brave smile and "Where do you get those freaky words?"

"Which ones? You mean fucktard? (She smiles yes.) I'm terraforming."

"Oh, sure," she says with her irony voice then kicks sand on me.

"Okay, it's like this sand (I kick back). Same with words. Terraform. Which, if you don't know, is a major component of some of the best games out there such as Wurm Online. Many woozy hours tweaking platforms to that mind bender."

"I think we live by a different set of dictionaries, Marvin."

"I'm just saying. When I terraform ... still the same beach if different. You see? You do the same with stuff in your house. Move it all around. But still the same house. Words don't stay the same anymore even if the same language. Haven't you noticed? Dictionaries mostly now fuckall worthless. They just don't keep up."

"Fuck is in the dictionary, Marvin. Even the OED."

"Yeah, well, maybe on your permanence beach that's not been kicked around much you'll find the word fuck. But where I come from, that word will have a twenty-page documentation."

"I don't think so."

"Then where's the truth? Fuck has become an ingredient word. Even I need add-ons to complete me. Do you see I am so separation anxious I run to you? What's about that? I still worry over stepping barefoot on legos, but I can make hella bad words you can't catalogue fast enough."

Mrs. V reaches out a hand for me to join her on the rock seat. I give her the cut hand then change that out for the unhurt one, which she notices. She takes in her hands my damaged wing, wipes away with the sleeve of the Hotchkiss sweatshirt the dirt and dried blood smeared now from pond water. I begin to wonder how much of Mrs. V I have been sharing with husband Brent. Maybe because of a song the Mom lip-synced on Valentines for the Dad to reference a piece of chalk in his Hallmark card. Matt & me laughed. The Dad walked out from the room. The song told of a dude loving up a fat chick, making chalk marks where he'd been, then finding other chalk marks not from him, then another dude with chalk in his hand. At least Brent Vitello has not left chalk marks that I can see, unless you count the bruises.

"I know, Marvin, you feel nothing is solid. Nothing is sure. Marriages too. Yours truly by example," she says walking to the lake, dipping the sleeve of her sweatshirt and back again. I make brave as she cleans the cut. "Well, shit," she says, holding up the arm of her bloody sweatshirt, "listen to me ... Lorena Bobbitt playing the victim."

"Who?"

"Sorry. Time capsule item. Going to happen a lot now that we're talking more and fucking less."

"Crude. I like it when you're crude."

She pinches my thigh, pushes her tongue into the space between her teeth. Bonerfic crude!

"Are you feeling sexy right now," I say, "because ...."

Mrs. V shakes her head no, but her smile nearly sends me to soulgasm. She holds my damaged hand. We sit awhile. Scan the pond. Ducks and geese on the water with their brood. Foot paths at the pond's edge as ancient as the first native tribes. The water just starting to pull away farther from shore from its not long ago highest level off melting snow. Alder and willow sending bone-white roots down exposed at the water's edge, holding together the steep bank-side dirt. A thicket of cranberry making some of the water's edge unapproachable and these bushes already flowering. Peepers sounding beside the shore in the wreckage of the fall foliage that litters the ground.

She sees me following the abuse trail of black and blue printed on her white legs, covers them with her arms and says, "These aren't the places that hurt most. There are deeper injuries."

I say, "Yeah, I get it."

Then she says, "Look, Marvin, I'm not a possessive person. I know my husband played around. I didn't much care. And I'm not making claims on you. This lasts only as long as it lasts."

"Yeah, okay, I get that too, but all those stray cats and those multiple dudes coming by regular as the dandruff itch. That's a possession I think."

"No," she says, "Marvin, those are visitations. I've been under house arrest."

"Not anymore. Why not come with me to Mexico?"

"Maybe." She pushes strands of hair behind ears, a swoonable gesture I don't see done nearly enough, not even in the movies.

We smile nervously and a little embarrassed because making plans and look away from each other back across the pond. Dense, skinny trees rise such as a palisades to keep our eyes and feet away.

Mrs. V says, "Thoreau says a lake is the Earth's eye and that looking into a lake exposes the depths of our own natures."

That's so beautiful, but I don't get it. I take another look at what makes those words come out. The surface of the pond, where the sun lets you see, it dimples and boils. Maybe the ripples say there's a life beneath of a sunk Atlantis where commerce and wars are constant and secret. Such as an alien off-world might see from high as the Moon above Earth where we busy humans appear as a sometimes blast with smoke or satellites blinking across the surface of our high atmosphere, such as bugs that skate across a lake's surface, and below that surface all the shit happening you can't see. But it's there. So now I get it.

Mrs. V tells me Thoreau's pond has a metal chest at the bottom from Revolution War days that sometimes floats to the top that no one can catch and open, though many have tried, and which is a metaphor for riches you can't get but want badly. She says Thoreau's riches are time, such as floating down a river in a dream, which she says is me in the yellow cab. I don't get it. Seems to me time is the same for everyone. And right now, what I see mostly is trash from pond visits of fishermen and hikers and mostly Hotchkiss preppies that toss in beer bottles and used condoms and cigarette packs. No one here in Lakeville is going all philoso-rapper over time.

I look again at the pond view offered this boathouse and those outsized houses and Hotchkiss School. The sun is going away. Cloud and mist are moving in. But still I can see this is no working pond. There are no ruins of mills, no rock walls that lead cows here to drink within a pasture claim and no dams with pipes to regulate water flow out from a reservoir project. This is pure pond and its own universe. Somehow, it seems more real in the mist. As I sit on the rock boulder with Mrs. V and ponder, we see on the other side of the bank an old timer fisherman packing up to move on with the weather change. He has come by to pull out a string of bullhead catfish. Which if you don't know is a fish with an identity conflict, what any teen would know about. Anyway, he's an LL Bean catalogue of adventure wear so must probably inhabit one of the glory houses that own those expansive lawns cared for by teams of mower jockeys. He waves as do we and it's all so perfect. Until we remember we've been found. There's still smoke climbing out the woodstove pipe and now we're getting neighbor waves. Time to move on.

△

So we trek the woodsy paths, Mrs. V blushing past the personals etched on trees. I say nothing. It's mid-morning, but the sky is darkening with rain cloud then comes rain. I mean, we weren't exactly singing our greatest hits of the Hotchkiss boathouse retreat. Even if we wanted to, the damp and cold pretty much put an Elvis-has-left-the-building coda on that idea. I tell her of the Caprice taxicab heater fan. I say it's noisy but effective, and that quickens our step. Then the black tar of the bank's Saturday parking lot empty and pooling from the more heavy rain that's damned up by a ring of dirt encrusted, plowed snow. And there's the cab floating on its fat tires, open and waiting, yellow and shining. Thoreau's treasure chest could be what it is, if you consider the cash Ignacio left behind. I reach inside the kangaroo pocket of the hoodie to be sure. It's still there, but I haven't yet told Mrs. V of the money and she doesn't seem to be making the Thoreau connection anymore. Maybe because I left the windows open. It'll need bailing out. But it fires up quick. The heater throws a cloud of vapor on the inside windshield. Mrs. V says mist seems to be our element. I thought an element was something solid, but okay, yeah, in this case. We rub hands together and for fun blow vapor cloud out our mouths on each other until the warm of the heater makes a difference.

Then a premeditated romance gesture. I take out from the hoodie pocket a candle and that BIC lighter from the boathouse, melt the wax just enough to attach it to the dashboard, light the candle. What is it about candlelight that's so sexy? We make out. Until the refresh Jesus I forgot about hanging from the rearview begins to smoke, blessed saint of the drive-by would be Ignacio's intention, and Mrs. V slapping Jesus with fire-suppression intentions but knocking off the candle that gutters out in my lap making me jump and squeal. We laugh. That's really what we needed.

We stop at the Mobil for gas and something to eat besides soggy fiddleheads. Barfage! But I would never tell Mrs. V this. Anyway, behind the counter of the deli appears Heidi Helsinger, a possible detour of future plans because, as Priscilla Helsinger said, she'll be all torqued with the expectation of renewed vows, my neighbor and fellow exploitainment junky in the land of gropes and hopes and ... shit! She sees me filling the cab with gas, sees Mrs. V sitting there soiled and woodsy same as me. And as I go inside, lay down a bag of chips, pull a twenty off a roll of same, her eyes narrow to something of a secret understanding.

She says, leaning over the counter with those gorgeous anatomy anchors, "So, Marvin, there have been adventures in your life lately?"

"Yeah," I say, "more than you know."

She says, "So, Marvin, that's Sunny Vitello? Her husband would be glad to know she's still in town. He's been asking about her. She know that? She know anything about his face bandages and his really bad mood? "

I give her that hide-a-fact look we have practiced so often to neutralize the parents' tribunal, then say, "She might. We're together. Heidi, I think I'm in love," which I say ironic to make her think the opposite.

"Well, shit, bro," Heidi says with a fist bump, "I'm glad for you."

"Did you say Mr. V has been here? How recent?" (This I say understated with adrenalin levels rising.)

"About an hour before."

Shit, I'm thinking. Still alive. Do I tell Mrs. V or let her think wife beater is out of her life forever?

"Hey, Marvin," Heidi says, her voice a pinball rattling my thoughts and then an offer that ends that game but starts another: "Before you go, want to meet in the little girl's room for a lipwrap? A little forget-me-not from the neighborhood."

What a suggestion. How can I resist. I mean, what would you do? May I say, resistance is futile.

Now I'm back in the cab with two secrets on my mind added to a list of don't tells and that's a load to bear. I remember the Mom saying about the Dad behaving badly is because damaged his psychotic nerve from carrying the weight of the world, meaning having kids, meaning me and Matt and Sherman way earlier. Then, an epic nightmare. The Mom pulls up in her Ford Explorer throwing gamma rays around with an angry, confused, hysterical look on her face. She notices me in the yellow cab. Her eyes go hard the way they do when she has applied her lawyer's brain to the words she's about to say. She's out of the Explorer before I can warn Mrs. V. Then I get it. Heidi has tapped out a text to the Mom before our bathroom goodbyes. These girls. They're a sisterhood of witchery. Macbeth never had a chance. No bro would ever on purpose put the hurt on another bro like this, which is a cloogy thought I will change soon down the road. But I have to deal. I get out of the cab quick so maybe Mrs. V will blend with the seat covers.

The Mom trots over to me with perfect hair bouncing and the latest flash-your-body wear, as wrapped and clinged to as cheese melt and who wants to see the Mom like this? But there she is and gives me a breath-pausing hug, then pushes me away, smacks my chest with both hands.

"What the hell, Marvin! Why are you here and not in school? You had me so worried! I haven't slept in a week. Your dad's in New Jersey talking to the police. The Headmaster called. And your lacrosse buddy. He called too. Brad ... somebody. Your dad's hired a private investigator. Are there still such things? What the hell is going on, Marvin?"

I can't tell her much that's true about Mrs. V and me, but there's Poncy Prep I can summarize to squeeze glue back in the mother-son relationship. So I tell her about how I can't stand prep school, how I developed a need rash for early vacation.

"And that explains getting arrested for drugs? Breaking out of jail? No communication with your parents so we might know you're still alive. At least!"

"Yeah, I know. Sorry. I had to act quick to get away from school. And I didn't break jail. I was let out. That what they told you?"

"Yes. You were given a bathroom visit but never came back. There's a bulletin out for your arrest in Jersey. Did you know? You're going to have a criminal record! Shit, Marvin." Now the tears.

"So that's why the bros are mass texting. I'm famous. They all wanna know what's up. I'm not telling them. So don't worry. No one knows where I am. Except you."

She hugs me again, kisses my cheek, calls me her "little fugitive," which makes me beam, then an observation truly diminishing.

"Did you take a cab all the way from New Jersey? I think your allowance is over-generous." She looks inside, not yet connecting that I stepped out from the driver's seat. She sees Mrs. V, says, "Who's that? Is it that married woman? Shit, Marvin!'

"No, well, yeah, maybe. Mom, she's a friend. She's helping me out. I can trust her."

"It's that cat woman! Vitello? I thought that was over."

"I don't think I want to go there."

That's when the Mom loses it. It's, like, all that time alone and the Madonna stimulation Heidi's mom complains of. As if to confirm, there's Heidi viewing the scene from her deli window, pretending shock horror, but mostly amusement on her face. So nice to be the entertainment. The Mom goes spastic in a brainspin of opera voice and nonsense words gobsmackingly incoherent but so the universe will know of my blundering. Nice to be so cared over. Even the Dad has given more of himself to my truancy than I had thought would happen. The problem now is to unhook myself with dignity from the over-caring parental inhibiter. Oh, fuck it!

"Mom," I say giving a hug, "I've got to go. I'll text you soon. Let you know where I am. Promise."

"No! You come right home! Now!"

"Mom, I'm nineteen."

It's the first time I have optioned the Free Willy signifier for myself. It's a sad day. I'm asking for release. But she isn't having any.

"Not while I'm paying the bills you're not. Far as I'm concerned, you're still in short pants, even in a hoodie. Where did you get that thing anyway? Is it prep-school issue these days?"

"Mom," I say, pulling back to give the eyeball caress, but holding her still by the arms, "this is my cab. I'm making a living off these wheels. I've got paid all the way here from Jersey (okay, a small lie), and I'm going to start saving for college soon (yeah, okay, a bigger lie this time). I promise (mega lie)."

She wraps herself in her own arms and squeezes eyes shut to stop the tears as I step into the cab and drive away. Heidi not even a pixel in the rearview mirror.

Mrs. V puts an arm around my shoulder, hands me the opened bag of chips, says,

"Family sucks, doesn't it?" I nod yes, eyes tearing up. Shit! I'm a five-year-old again. Only the Mom can do that to me. Then silence awhile as I drive directionless down the road. Then Mrs. V punches me on the shoulder, a funk buster is what she thinks and says, "Listen, we need to say a formal goodbye to Lakeville. Don't you think, Herk? Something ritual. More than just a calendar day. What do you say?"

Well, I don't really know what to think, but I say, "Such as visit the police to confess our tag-team skills. So I go back to jail? And maybe you? Better a graveyard visit to find a plot for Mr. V don't you think? But no, too lugubrious," which is double dipping again my SAT prep and thanks to Mr. Ralph for me cogitating a word that's invaded my DNA. And pretty dope of me to apply the dictionary in the real world as if some truce has ceased my word warping. But no. Right now, I'm not at peace with anything.

Mrs. V throws a tight grin of surprise at my word choice and tenses with disappointment because I'm not inclined to throw a milestone in our path and there's no small concern I can be so mean. In my defense, self-involved is what teens are supposed to be. But then I'm reminded this is a small request from a lady I love, and I feel guilt pleasure from the Heidi interruption, and some upset still over the Mom's hysterics, and I haven't yet told her Mr. V is still breathing which has made some relief for me but not yet her. So I say, "Okay. Whatever. What's the plan?" I get only silence.

△

IT'S ALMOST NOON on the road that leads out from Connecticut to the New York State Thruway and the long road south to Mexico's weightless sunshine. This will take us past the Dad's Jeep dealership.

I tell Mrs. V maybe I should text him to say I'm okay. Meet for lunch or something. Maybe he could be part of the goodbye plan.

"What?" she says in her grown-up voice, "Not a good idea. You'll disclose too much, Marvin, or too little. Either way, bad idea."

I'm not taking this well, her veto of the Dad visit, but she's probably right. It will take a week of chin-tuck texting to say all I need to say to the man that's supposed to protect me from all this. But I still want to signal my seed benefactor. I'm probably more looking for a father than he is a son. You'd think Mrs. V might understand. Just as I'm about to engage an aggrievesome moment with Mrs. V to show it's me that's in the driver's seat, there in the lot of the Dancing Mouse, a dive bar at the edge of town, the only place anywhere near that's open early for alcohol breakfast, there sits Rip Torn's battered Subaru wagon with the dented, rusted side panel. I lock brakes, apologize for the whiplash, and tell Mrs. V there's someone here I definitely want to say goodbye to. It's not the Dad, but maybe this will qualify as ritual farewell. She says maybe so in her unconvinced voice.

It's dark in the Mouse day and night. Louie the bartender that's also the owner keeps his patrons anonymous as in, "What can I get for you, Mickey?" Which is his name for customers. There's no road noise inside, maybe because padded walls with maroon faux leather dimpled by tacks adhering it to the foam behind. Even the door. So this place is just as often called the "padded walls" and the regulars "nutsos." Since 11 a.m. the regulars are here – those designated imbibement devotees who bear the load of the world for the rest of us and so can't start the day anyway but drunk. Among those Rip Torn abides just another Mickey. Which is what he wants. So there's Rip. He's shaggy and brooding. He's licking the salt and throwing back tequila, maybe to quiet the paranoia inside his head that alien awareness brings. He's seated at the bar, his goatee dense and wiry gray, spreading up his cheeks, forehead planted on the bar soaking the juice of a pile of lime slices. He's muttering to himself. There's a hammer on the bar beside his drink.

When me and Mrs. V step into the dark, lonesome place, I don't at first recognize him, but I know the voice. I want to tell him how important Men In Black is to my worldview. How I'm still awed by physical imperfection in the human form, how what's wrenched out of spec is more real ever than Connecticut cute. Thanks to him I still feel the deepest suspicion that the perfect among us could be aliens hiding grotesqueries behind a painted front. This is me in psych-charge stimulation, powering up for a first ever confession to the great Zed.

When stepping inside the Mouse, Mrs. V turns for the lady's room, so I make a home beside Rip's left ear with a chunk missing that looks animal bit. And inside a ponderous growth of ear hair that I could dive into such as Florida with my bros for spring lacrosse practice where I snorkeled the bay in an underworld of waving tentacle sea anemones. Can ear hair be another sign of alien occupation? Can Rip be alien occupied? But then, no, I remember the Dad trimming ear hair in the bathroom of his shaving ritual. And he's way human. I relax, take a breath, begin to tell Rip of our shared alien fetish. I don't get too far before he says, "Who are you? Speak up!"

The bartender leans over, whispers, "This Mickey, he's half deaf."

So I raise the decibels and Rip says, "Jesus, kid, why you shouting?"

Rip lifts his head off the bar, cops an adjustment look at me, blinks, reaches out, touches my face, says, "Good profile." He grips my chin, pushes my face left then right, shakes his head maybe not. He's looking at me such as I do others that wear the face before rehab. Which queases me to the core. Mrs. V appears behind us and says quietly, "What's he doing?" Upon which Rip twinkles his Hollywood star shine intending to impress and maybe bed the Icelandic, luscious Mrs. V. But he can't find his words such as more used to rubber dolls with response limitations. Or he's just too drunk. His mouth forms unsaid words as he reaches for her. She yelps and moves away. He becomes all smile with a little drool, eyes disappearing in a wrinkle grin. He says, "You with him?" Meaning me. Mrs. V. looks at me unsure, then shakes her head yes. Upon which he says, "Okay... fine ... that's fine" (mumble, mumble) then, "Is it the hammer scares you? You know Dennis Hopper? He's a a-hole. But I took a lottta money from him ... and that's all right. So he gives Jack Nicholson the part. I mean, what the fuck?" Rip shakes his head violently. Something in his speech box clicks back into place. He sits upright a moment, says with authority, "Says I pulled a knife on him. I never!"

I whisper Rip's hard of hearing, which registers no surprise and so she says to Rip with an abrupt torque in volume, "You pulled a knife on Dennis Hopper?"

Rip shakes his head, tries to focus, says to Mrs. V, "Who told you that?" He grips the hammer.

I can't believe he's talking to Mrs. V like this. I love the guy. I try to tell him but don't get too far before he says, "You keep out of this!"

Mrs. V jumps in says, "He's a good kid." Which is what a teacher might say about me, or a friend of the family. It nearly erases all the intimate we have stroked and talked recently and hurts my feelings. I think she notices. Mrs. V puts her arm around my shoulder. But that only makes me the misfit toy to my significant adult. I shake off the arm. She barely notices because so into Rip's performance.

"He's good for what?" says Rip. "Speak up! Shit. Okay, you here to apologize for Terry Southern? Don't bother! I know what's what."

"So tell us what's what!" Mrs. V shouts back.

"Damn, woman. You want I say it out loud? Even in the Mouse we're taking a risk."

"You can tell me," she says placing a hand on his shoulder.

"Okay, fine," he says scanning the tiny scatter of fellow imbibers, one under a hoodie that looks a lot like a dude I shared physics lab with in high school, his dad the town cop. And there's a couple others ready for the grave. "I'll tell you," he says, then something mumbled, then, "I could be a science experiment. Marvel comics would know. I'm more than one person. I mean, way more. There's many people inside here. (He taps his head, then his heart.) I know their terrors ... their failures. It's too much," which could make you think he's wandered the afterlife. But no. Rip is very definitely a beforelifer only with empathy overload.

"What people do you feel?" says Mrs. V.

"Oh, shit, Mrs. V. Let it go. He's lost in the movies. He's had too much liquid suppression. Let it go."

"I heard... I heard that! Mind your manners, boy." Anger seems to be a sobering emotion for Rip. His words come at us clear and with velocity. But he's making me sad, putting me down, such as he's a peer-reviewed j-stor to my stub-length wiki. He says more: "I haven't yet had enough. The juices that numb (he says to me), I've not had nearly enough" (he says to Mrs. V, then turns to the bar and stares at his multiple selves in the reflecting mirror).

He starts down an inspiration rant, a religion manifesto, his voice dipping into that familiar Zed baritone of wisdom. Mrs. V pulls up a bar stool and takes a seat to listen such as it matters.

"I mean, I'm not the one lives in movies. You're the one does. Every step you take, you think you're in a movie. But if you look in here (knocks his head with a fist), you'd see. The movies, they live in me."

"Oh, yes, the Lee Strasberg method," says Mrs. V.

"What? Don't put me off my stride. What I'm saying is ... directors ... what they want ... they want actors to be their silly putty. Same with you. It's the bankers, politicians, lawyers, billionaires. They all want you to be their silly putty. But these Hollywood directors. They're the worst. Maybe they're alien occupied. That's what Zed would say. Maybe they're lizard people. Sometimes you see the faces change. Zed sees this. Some of their children ... born with reptile tails. Did you know? Fact! Documented fact. Movie director kids. See them naked, you'll know."

Mrs. V says, "I don't understand. This is a movie script you're practicing on us, method acting. You're living the part?"

"Oh, I'm living the part. We all are. Aren't you listening? (He reaches inside his winter down jacket, looks confused, sees the hammer on the bar top, grips and flourishes it.) This for the reptiles. There's a nice little branch of the Litchfield far too successful in the financial downturn. Must have lizard ties. I'm starting there."

That's just too much. Imagine a drunk Rip Torn that should be taking his first of twelve steps while reciting the AA mantra, but instead he's looking for someone to hammer, and while I have a little of the alien paranoia still, it's an itch I don't want to scratch with a knife. Mrs. V and me give a look to each other that says it's time to vamoose down to Mexico. That's when the Mouse becomes a mousetrap.

△

As we push open the door to the parking lot to begin our trek south, I see a roadblock advancing on us, a scrum of Hotchkiss preppies dressed in schoolyard togs, red blazers with the Hotchkiss crest, school ties. It's just after Saturday classes. They will be expected for sports practice soon. They're in a hurry. The rain has stopped but could come back. They squeeze out from a muddy path in the woods beside the lake coming toward the Mouse. They become large fast with the smooth grace of athletes, kicking stones, shoving one then the other playfully out from the circle, bending and dancing with the conversation, seething forward in one solid wave of testosterone threat. They are in the sum of their parts formidable. Even before facial recognition, somehow I know, they are enemy bros, lacrosse players from games I have played in opposition when in my senior year of Lakeville High School. They haven't yet seen me, but I know they will once I'm outside the door. Mrs. V feels my hesitation, asks what's wrong. My eyes say it and then she feels it too: in that scrum of enemy bros one or two has shared her bed. Her eyes go wide in worry metrics. We slip back into the Mouse to prepare our defense, mostly emotional but also maybe in the physical, if it comes to that. Rip notices, sees we're in retreat, says something referential only Mrs. V gets: "Oh, I see. It's Katy bar the door is it? Who's after you?"

Louie looks up from his newspaper, hears the commotion before he sees it, says, "Shit, them again."

In comes the scrum noisy, raunchy, threatening in motion.

Louie says, "Hey, Mickey, I can't serve you. Don't even try."

"No worries, Louie, old dude, we're only here for a top off," says him with the muscles and attackman prowess, a real baller this one, hair buzzed to prickles and a hook nose proudly assertive.

"That's right, Louie, dude. Relax. We've brought our own container. Reusable. Like save the planet and all that shit," says the smaller, overcompensating bro with perfect diction and a mouth of corrected teeth. He's probably the team's black hole. When he gets the ball, there will be no intention to share, ever. But in this case, he does: passing along a silver flask that's been since before entering the Mouse passed around making faces red and voices loud.

There must be five or six of them. I don't know for sure because Mrs. V and me have taken a table in a dark corner. I'm under my hood with eyes sheltered away and Mrs. V has her back to the enemy bros.

Louie says, "I don't think so. Bring it outside. I want you out of my bar."

That makes a brief sobering moment. But no longer than a gnat's love life in Alaska. Hook nose is the one I tried to beat down under the bleachers after a Hotchkiss versus Lakeville High lax game, the one I also know from birch trees insults of time with Mrs. V. He makes a grin with a message and, like, goes over to the dark side. He says, "Louie, you know that's not going to happen. Don't be laying on the bros a cross check. Play nice or this will end ugly. And," he says looking around the bar at the few shadowy imbibement junkies, then Rip, then me and Mrs. V, "no one here is going to help you out. But for me," he gathers in the bros, throws arms around the nearest two, "these here are the eyes back of my head and the spikes in my turf shoes and my food finders when I'm hungry and, Louie, I'm starving thirsty right now."

Louie blanches white. He doesn't know what button to push. Then Rip goes off script, something he's prone to, and makes a machismo mistake.

"Boys," he says, "the proprietor says we don't serve burberries here. Go fuck yourselves!"

Those drunks other than Rip chug drinks, lower their heads and shoulders as if ducking flack while going out the door, because as expected, this does not go down well with hook nose. He thinks his words have so filled the place there's no room for others to sound out. He's wrong. Yes, unfortunately. Mrs. V turns in her chair and says in a surprise moment of verbal contention, "Dieter Vollander! You need to calm down and go back to school."

The one Mickey I had thought once a classmate, he stops before pushing out the padded door, gives a look, eyes red inside the hood, and a smile of broken teeth, makes the face of travel agent Grim Reaper from the game Grim Fandango that assesses a player's transportation merits through the Underworld. He's sending a message. I get a late model vintage cab. Makes me shiver, until I remember the game comes only on Windows, so how seriously can it be taken? Dieter's face is more threatening: shocked, repulsed, then twisted with hate. Rip snickers, which brings bro Dieter additional heart burn, because he so hates his name the other bros know to only call him Gunner. Which calls attention to his enviable shooting arm, while teachers at Hotchkiss call him Deet per the parental request.

Dieter has not yet recognized Mrs. V or me, and we can see he's a little off balance, shifting to find the right response to a room that is moving out of his scoring zone. Dieter points to the shortest support dude for the flask, takes a long drink, drains and tosses it at Louie who bobble catches it against his chest, then lifts it off the bar, gives a sniff, says, "I can't do that … Dieter dear."

More laughs from Rip, which Dieter wants to ignore then says to Louie with the mouth of malice, "Fill it up, old dude. Make it top shelf. And we'll be gone."

"Top shelf seltzer it is, Dieter dear," says Louie in the security of patron approval, meaning Rip, which just about pours gasoline on Dieter's smoldering ego. But that's not the worst. He fills the flask with the seltzer hose and tosses it back to Dieter which hits him on the chest and sprays him in wet then clatters to the floor. Well and then, God screws with me and I laugh. It just launches out. Dieter takes a serious look our way and knows Mrs. V and me for who we are same time his short back-up bro says, "Hey, Gunner, that the enemy bro wanted you beat down under the bleachers? You recognize him? I'm sure that's him."

"Yeah," says Dieter, "I know him."

Which is bad enough but then even worse when one of the other scrum bros who has until now remained mute says, "And look who he's with. It's the bruised MILF we don't write home about. Am I right? Dude, that's her!"

Shit. I'm seeing no way out of this but the wrong way. I stand up with two fists knotted and ready. Mrs. V puts her hand on my leg but that only makes Dieter more filled with hate. He begins a hack sway toward our table, which is a lacrosse move that's intent on punishment, eyes lasered on me. That's when Rip makes his move. He's off the bar stool tapping Dieter on the shoulder who makes the instinctive cut back and gets a glance blow off the cheek of Rip's roundhouse that only maddens him more and hardly sets him off pace. Dieter shoves Rip over into a collapse of free-fall curses and old bones clattering the floor which brings me out from under my hoodie and up into Dieter's face with defiance of his scrum superiority despite having already once been the victim of a beatdown under the bleachers.

This will be the moment where I hesitate. I should launch on this laxer dude and take his head off for what he's done to me and mine. But I can't. I get cold down my spine and freeze entirely. That's what cowards do. I must so accuse myself. But who could so easy step again into those fists that had a time ago pulped my face and closed my left eye so bad the parents wanted to bring in the 5-0 and assign blame to the damage. And my lacrosse bros hanging heads in disgrace over losing the game and then the fight under the bleachers too.

In my frozen moment, Mrs. V is now on the floor at Rip's side as he has hit his head on the corner of a table going down and makes pathetic choking sounds confirming his farther down fall-from-grace. Dieter says, "This is going to be fun. Laxabunga, bro!" He takes a handful of hoodie under my chin with his left hand and brings me near for a Chuck Norris beatdown when he screams, collapses and grabs his knee. There beside Rip on the floor is Mrs. V with Rip's hammer in her hand and a very surprised look on her beautiful face.

The bros are smirking, anticipating major carnage, but now make confused denial gestures, such as fist bumps missing target, shoulder pats off-aimed and smacking the ears of fellow bros, all while sounding together on "Laxabunga" meant to encourage their leader but that morph into girly squeals embarrassing the scrum. This is a neutered machismo machine. Reminds me of those young boys of Shakespeare time that misfortunately lived in Italy and had poor families and sweet high voices that lost their nads to opera. Talk about your sacrifice for art. Holy fuck! I mean, if that's what it takes to carry a tune, I want no part of the singalong.

As a bro of the finest game on the planet, I should not, you might think, take satisfaction from the downgrading of another bro. But to be sure, such laxifaction arising from the correction of a wrong can't be all wrong itself. I mean, even a major laxoholic will admit to the need for degrees of correctitude applied to bring a bro into compliance with the code. This is a given, as my Poncy coach will say. "He to whom lax is given, much will be expected," is what he says at practice and which applies a kind of denomination friendly religion thankfulness.

We take with us the stuttering Rip and make out the door with Louie behind tending the unhinged Hotchkiss preppy that's loudly pouring out threats of our ultimate destruction by his hands and me shouting back, "Yeah, if only," and his fellow bros confused of action with their leader fallen and Mrs. V ... well, she's a changed woman. This makes two bravado dudes lowered to the ground by her sweet little hands in just forty-eight hours time.

She has Rip by one arm, me by the other, and she's glowing with the grace of accomplishment, her pace smooth and quick, nothing slowed by the door she kicks open. So I think again of why clichés are so smart. I mean, one door opens and another door closes. The Dancing Mouse has sent us away on the road in the best possible way.

"Mrs. V," I say, "I think I love you."

"It's spring fever," is what she says back.

"What's the cure?"

"Summer."

"I don't know if I have that long."

"Maybe not," is what she says with that third eye of sight poets have and I could be sad but I'm not. We are no longer victims! We have become destinous!

△

LET'S TAKE A MICRO BREAK. You're now half way to the end of my rope. You might by now feel overexposed to an endless selfie. Or worse, trapped in a loop waiting for the interrupt. Maybe you should stop listening. Go ahead and text or google or Facebook. I mean, not to put you in a shoegaze moment, but the beforelife is of the moment, about the moment, momentary and to be enjoyed by the nanosecond, or whatever quick-second count you live by. If a nanosecond, you have 11.8 inches before the moment is over. That's the exact length of wire electricity passes in a nanosecond. One billionth of one second. It's a short step but it can be forever. It's a Buddhist thing. But for us westies that have never rode the orient express, time can seem to be adversary, out there, expanding beyond reach, because broken promises have canceled our futures. You with me there Ese, farmers in the dell, PHD wannabe's, potential botox beauties of the housewives collective? All you scene kids that have detoured here upon these words, dudes and dudettes, since there's no future to prepare for, there will be joy taken from the impermanent moment. It is so decreed – video games that never end starring action hero you, posts of Facebook that forever morph to attract approving thumbs, reality TV serials, 500 Instagram photos a day to document your every move. These are the things that matter to us that embrace no future. But even so, impermanence is a sexy moment, don't you think?

△

SO WE'RE PUSHING RIP into the back seat of the cab. He's all crunked and nonsense as the beatdown from enemy bros has placed him back to muttering zombie. Mrs. V has Rip's hammer in her hand. She's double-thinking her part in all this. She's blinking denial syndrome, eyes sucking in the sights but seeing only shadow of recent events. Reliving that. And Rip, he is become entirely Zed. He mumbles his disgust of reptiles making babies off humans and sending them to posh boarding schools for training in world domination through politics, film, and banks. I begin to ponder whether Zed thinks me a reptile. But then I guess not because he knows nothing of me and Poncy Prep, and I'm all swagged out in townie gear. Must be he's thinking enemy bros. Rip's bent over rubbing the back of his head, feeling sorry for himself, then entirely vertical with lopsided smile, says, "That's the fuckin'… that's it, the bank I told you of (points across the street with a shaky finger). The fucking Litchfield. Get me … (leaning way over the seat for emphasis) get me there, junior!"

Mrs. V begins to shake because shivery dressed in minimal wardrobe. But, no, that's not it. These aren't shivers but waves that start in the gut and snap her shoulders. She's verging on a big cry. I want to dive in with a life vest but this is Rip's moment to feel the transformation powers of Ignacio's conversion cab. And I am the designated driver. Mrs. V will have to tread water by herself awhile. I feel sorry for her though. This can't be the world she's been hoping to find once she's left her poet's hideaway. Has she found the world outside as limited as her cat-infested, young dude visitation retreat where her sometimes husband beats her for sport? Or has the violence potential of her core self been realized and needs a personality tweak to accommodate?

"Here! Right fuckin' here!" says Rip. I turn again into the parking lot of the Litchfield Bank. He's suddenly so much more drunk seeming. Should be leaning a forehead onto the bar top at the Dancing Mouse. But that's okay. I don't want him to see me repossessing Ignacio's drugs. They must come with because, well, just because. I don't know why. But I'm nervous of exposing to Rip a street dogg profile. I admire the guy. I don't want him to think bad of me. Respect is the one currency that spends anywhere, which is a cliché the Dad says often that is himself bankrupt in ways other than money.

So I'm quick out the cab and down over the snow bank spidering back with bricks of weed that Rip somehow notices even in his inebrious state. Then in my seat behind the wheel with a thousand excuse stories running through my head. I'm popping open the glove box to insert the weed as Rip leans over the seats to assess my sly moves and I have finally landed a phat story to burn away the guilt (something about finding a drop-zone and making this dispose snatch to protect the children). He sobers from what he's seen, says, "Shit, son, that a firearm? Trade a hammer for a gun? What you say?" So I'm forced to detour my thinking and move on to fuck the weed as this conversation is about Ignacio's gun that has no doubt committed crime and needs a home away from me. And so I say, "Why not!" I take the hammer from Mrs. V's hand, which she lets go unwillingly. I place that in the glove box along with the weed. Rip takes the gun, makes busy hands balancing it, yanks at the door and leaping out grips the frame for support of his mostly useless legs. Mrs. V peeks out from her overthinking and makes the face of disbelief as Rip shakes that gun at the bank, says with volume and intention worthy of Jihad: "Muther-fuckin' snakes!"

Mrs. V says, "Marvin, the way things are going, we'd maybe better not be here right now."

That's agreeable. But I must first make a respectful gesture of goodbye. Because I love this man. He will forever resist the grown-up hang-ups. So I roll down the window and say to Rip, "Mr. Torn, I just want to say ..." but he's already tipping around toward the back of the bank. We hear more cussing, then glass breaking, and as I press the pedal and we spin on ice onto the main road, I see him in the rearview climbing into the bank through a broken window.

Not the smoothest rollout for Zed's threat extravaganza. But I can't think of any revolution that's been much understood and loved at the very first. Ask Steve Jobs, the computer theologian. His garage-tinkered Windows-evaders were dumped and forgotten before their conversion karma conquered it all. Didn't America start out dumping tea? I don't think that translated too early on as Old Glory flag waving and don't tread on me. Which now I remember is a snake rattling its intention to strike. Can you believe? The reptiles! Even then. Has Zed got it right? It's so awesome to hang with the great Zed. This could be the most historic of chapters. Bring it to school. Teach it!

△

So I'm motoring with pace following the yellow line from Connecticut to the Dad's Jeep dealership in New York State where he's Sales Manager. Mrs. V sits beside me diminished. She's tipped inside herself, arms crossed, small cuticle-bit hands holding herself together, leaning toward the windshield. Wrinkles under eyes and on her forehead become worry tracks, such as drop a stylus and play a sad song. Ignacio's cab takes a bump in the road with graceless recovery springs and the flap of skin under her chin jiggles. I'm reminded cougars have a use-by spoilage date. I'm rudely considering what's her date? Can't help thinking. I sometimes forget she's of my father's generation that raised their kids as ad campaigns. They are so expectation-driven they become brand consultants instead of parents. But Mrs. V, she's a mold breaker, a consumer of the shit that happens. And I'm happy to be the shit that happens. Despite the worries collecting at her brow, I'd like to think she's done with marriage, committed to the road, accepting of the transformative powers of the Caprice yellow cab.

As the dirty snow banks of retreating winter fly past our windows I say, "Mrs. V, this could be a road trip of epic proportion. Don't you think? With a start such as ours, we're the update to Bonnie and Clyde."

She blinks away tension, smiles out from an empty place, looks away, says, "Who? Oh yeah. I'm more a Thelma and Louise criminal, Marvin. Since I've killed a husband... and, well, where else does the road lead?" She says this with a voice ashamed in the confessional. And I'm thinking, many confessions must of been said to drivers of this yellow cab? Once again, so easy to tell a stranger the truth. Or, someone you love.

"Mexico is what I thought," I say. "I don't know those ones, Thelma and ...?"

"Louise. Thelma and Louise. It's a beautiful story," she says having found a place to come out from herself, that indefinite look of her eyes still there but now unloading some weight and worry from ugly memories and unsure expectations. "They kill a rapist, Marvin. Thelma and Louise do. It's self-defense. I think I know that one. And as they're chased by police, they hold hands and drive over a cliff. End of the road." Whatever she's looking at in the distance has made her weightless. Her arms have come unclasped and float in the air by her sides.

"Over a cliff? Again? Look, Mrs. V, we have to get over this Lemmings thing. I have no desire to jump the shark in Ignacio's ride. I don't need a reset in my eternity clock," is what I say without just then considering I will soon down the road change my mind about this.

"Okay, then, maybe instead we're more Jack Kerouac and Neal Cassady."

"You're saying that book? Kerouac's book?"

"You know that book? On the Road."

"Mr. Ralph made me read it."

"Did you like it?"

" Yeah, mostly."

"Outdated?"

"Yeah that but some of it not so much. Mr. Ralph says the whole thing is a jazz song. I don't know. Maybe. I say Neal Cassady is a rap seducer. Mr. Ralph had us memorize a passage to please himself. He said make it part of your DNA, which is pretty rad of him to say. So I grafted on these words. Care to listen?"

"Love to."

"Okay, goes like this: 'dancing down the street such as dinglebodies'.... What the fuck's a 'dinglebodies'? Makes you wonder. But anyway, the rest goes '... these are the only ones for me, the ones mad to live' and then there's a whole lot more madness that I like. He says, 'mad to talk, mad to be saved, desirous of everything at the same time, the ones that never say common stuff, but burn in fiendish all-day all-night talk proportions.' Dude! From a 50s book? Correction: this is now! This is what I call rap seduction."

Mrs. V says, "You know, Marvin, you surprise me sometimes. That your favorite book?"

"I don't read much."

"You don't have a favorite book?"

"Mrs. V, catch up! Books have gone away with albums and Blockbuster and the Cosby sweater and dial-up connections and VCR's and home ownership ... and pretty soon honeybees."

"But, Marvin, On the Road is a book."

"Yeah, score that, but not a normal book. I mean better than most. (Mrs. V gives an adult look of concern.) I'm just sayin'. And okay Mr. Ralph made a good case for retro immersion. I mean, words can be music all by themselves sometimes. Right?"

"You're talking to a poet."

"Yeah, I guess ... I don't get it."

"That's okay. You don't have to."

"Sometimes I worry, Mrs. V, that I'll never make a friend so tight as Jack and Neal, and but maybe that's because I haven't found a dude so much inspirational reckless such as Neal Cassady, except maybe Rip Torn. But Rip's a loner. I can tell. Also, there's what Mr. Ralph said of the whole bio thing of Kerouac and travel buddies in that book that have a sex thing going making them tight and committed to each other. It's not like a banned book or anything. I mean, Mr. Ralph says the perverty stuff of On the Road is all between the lines. I don't really get it but Mr. Ralph is like a really smart dude, so I guess he knows. I'm talkin' homo shit, which I'll never understand, but I worry I'll never make a friend of a dude that will turn the pyramid upside down and share the road with him because I'm not a fag. I tried to bring my best bro Bradley Turcotte on the road but then the police and then Brad's parents and the Headmaster and lacrosse. Anything but time alone with Herk! What's about that?"

Mrs. V gives a sympathy look she might give Crisis the cat. I'm now, at least temporarily, a diminished dude.

"Hey, Mrs. V, don't color me wrong. I'm not about flying the rainbow spectrum. But it's just sometimes in the shower with the bros, when the energy is high, the laughter loud, towels snapping asses, I get a hard-on from the love I feel for those guys. What's about that?"

Mrs. V says, "Marvin, that's narcissism not homosexuality, if that's what you're worried over. (She pats my leg then and with the back of her hand slides up and around my groin and thighs where the monkey jumps to life.) You see? Your hetero motor is running just fine."

Mrs. V has such a soft and sexy way of talking dirty that I'm about to pull over and nuzzle her ear except this road is just too familiar to be comfortable. How many times have I motored these miles to visit the Dad in the Mom's car when I was just a little wonder nugget and she preparing a public embarrassment from the Dad's dalliances or, before that, when things were good, to do a little scrap-book moment. But that's not where I am now even if on the same road. And yet it's still there with me, squatting on my shoulder such as a three-eyed toad from the museum of hoaxes. Such as Mrs. V's third eye. It's real? It's not real? Which?

When lawyers got involved my parents' marriage became shaky as a Jeep's warranty promise. If you don't know, Jeep is one of those car companies that promote performance over reliability to sell cars. The Dad's reliability warranty comes from Jeep. Grievous moments of the Mom are most remembered because most frequent and most recent and most dramatic. They started when I began seventh grade. The parents would break up, sue for divorce, get back together then break up and rehire the lawyers. Some particulars: the froth of the Mom's spittle in those sharp, put-down words at the Jeep dealership followed by a sit-down feast of hand-churned ice cream at a boutique sweet shop on the way back home; the Mom keying the sides of display autos inside the showroom which the Dad sees as unjustified revenge but ignores anyway; the Dad's hands inside his pants pockets holding his balls, squeezing himself calm, then the Mom's teasing, a public goodbye kiss with her hand on the Dad's Johnson pulling the lever, watching to see if the fruit lines up in his eyes. These are the most worthy memories separate from the good times which produced unreliable GIF moments. Rare and not to be trusted because likely to have received the digital buff and sheen of Photoshop.

Mrs. V's shivers become real when the cab's heater fan has busted from its overwork at warm, making chattering sounds and refusing to throw off heat. I turn off the heater fan and suggest a wardrobe change, extract my roll of Andrew Jacksons which gets her attention. We talk where the money came from. Mrs. V begins to feel more criminal. She starts to hyper-breathe. Says she thinks she's having a panic attack. I wonder what that is. She says it's about things being out of synch and unlikely to ever be normal again. I don't understand panic attack. Seems to me the thing least trustworthy and most likely to unbalance someone is what the suits and their attendant baby incubators call normal. What's normal? A setting on the wash machine? That's what the Mom calls it. Maybe that's more irony. I'll have to ask Mr. Ralph.

△

WE COME TO THE DAD'S JEEP DEALERSHIP. Red, white and blue triangle flags hanging limp off antennas in the lot. Patriotism sells. All Jeeps have the same toothy front-end grill, snappy piranhas hungry at the world, which is why it's so intimidating to have a

Jeep lock onto your rear bumper, driver leaning into the steering wheel, hands squeezed to white, eyes another pair of headlights boring into the back of your skull. This is SOP for drivers of Jeep. Type A personality is what the Dad says. Aggression compensating for competence is what I say. The exceptional ones drive Jeep or Yugo is what the Dad says. The blandsome ones seeking to avoid trendenitis drive Chevy and Toyota. I've never seen a Yugo, but imagine it a sweet ride. The Dad is no mindless non-factor. He's pretty smart for an old dude though still a shit. He always says about Lakeville it's a good place to raise a car. That's what mostly thrives there, what's most cared for. Kids go on the deferred maintenance plan. About people, he says making plans is a good way to hear God laugh.

Me and Mrs. V spin the cab through the Dad's shoal of omnivore machinery quivering restraint as the slow yellow cab swims among them. Mrs. V cranks down the window, leans and squints a look into the fluorescent dealership showroom. I tell her, "He's the one in the back office you won't see until it's time to close a deal. He's very good at nudging reluctant buyers into debt. Ask the Mom."

"What's he look like?" she says picking herself most off the seat to look deep into corners.

I'm not sure what to say. I don't remember being asked before to describe someone I have tried so hard not to see in so many ways. Books describe people all the time. But that's a one-dimensional media and from an emotional distance. This is the real world. Best to expose the Dad in song, such as emptiness wrapped in skin. That's from an AFI tune. Ice in the nucleus of the cell. Like that. Or maybe go with the man that wastes time chasing cars around his head. That's Snow Patrol. But what's most easy to say is the ears, door knob ears which we have both got beneath a wave of hair grown partly over, unless out from the shower then it's Hello, Dumbo! But there is too Grandpa Herkimer's thick neck, which brother Sherman and the Dad have got but not me. And the Dad's perfect teeth which I have definitely not got because have not sat long enough in the dentist chair to receive correction. And there's Grandma Herkimer's catbird grin that Grandpa called it, the most smile the Dad ever gives. Stuff this all in a dark suit pinned by a red tie and that's him. But of course what I say is, "He's the smooth one."

"Oh, yes, I see him. He's standing beside a cubicle office."

"Yeah," I say, tapping the brake, "he's there. How did you guess?" I get a what's-the-diff lift of the shoulders. I'm thinking that's a sales rep's desk he's leaning over talking hockey, replaying Stanley Cup stats from the perspective of a twenty-year Canuck shutout. It's the only time he shows emotion other than pissed. He hires only reps with the hockey gene. Or maybe the Dad's listening to a nice bit of fluff. He hires women sometimes, if they're easy, moony around the eyes, and chatty. Then it's just her talking and the Dad listening with self-interest. He gives a lady room for words. He's known for that. Very much liked by the girls for that.

"You interested?" I say. "The Mom says he's long on short-term portfolio management. Whatever."

"Bad investment."

"Yeah, I guess."

She's interested. I can tell. She's stretching neck cartilage to cop a parting look as I gas past a line of cars facing the street clipping with the cab's bumper a Cherokee tail light that leaks a wail from it's invasion detection alarm. And I'm thinking, that's right you bastard … you've been invaded! The Dad makes like a prairie dog in a cube farm to scan the evidence I've gone way beyond his influence, and then we're off down the street into town center Millertown, NY.

It's a place that attracts artsy browsers and locavore grazers from Lakeville that spread cash out among those paying less property tax because no lake and no posh boarding school but talk the same and vote the same and so pass the snob test. I hate this place and its wannabe inhabitations. I kick the cab's transmission into whine, scattering daytrippers trusting the crosswalks, swerve past cars stopped for red that leave room enough for me to skim by very near the sidewalk steppers that scatter to the muddy lawns of the town green. And I'm thinking, you too have been invaded! Mrs. V scoots lower in her seat giving me room to grow. A pair of red squirrels skitter down a butternut tree. One lands beneath the wheels of the yellow Caprice. I see in the rearview the struck rodent flip once in the air then lay dead. Mrs. V follows my eyes out the back window. The second squirrel sniffs its dead friend. She calls me a "shit." I guess I agree. I tell her I'm sorry but what does she expect? The way I feel, it's, like, contents under pressure. Don't even try to shake me out of this. I tell her, "I'm saying goodbye to my childhood. Never done that?"

"No! Not like this."

I didn't want to say, but on our way here, the ice cream shop where I used to stop with the Mom coming and going from Millertown, it's boarded shut. There's a driveway of crushed marble stone I used to sift through collecting the best to bring home. I like the ones with green veins. Might still be some in the bottom drawer of my dresser if little brother Matt hasn't already removed them. Matt can't keep his hands off my stuff. But, like, this is a drive-by goodbye to all that and I'm pissed about it. I don't know why.

"Well," says Mrs. V, "when you get this out of your system, tell me how you imagine yourself at your dad's age."

So I pull the cab off the road outside of town, a place soaked in sunlight, the tires squishing mud, turn off the motor, lean back, close my eyes, tell her, "I see myself in Mexico. Small town. I'm the only gringo. I lean on a wall in the shade chewing a blade of grass, an empty bottle of Dos Equis in my hand, the other resting on a very large stomach."

"Nothing like your dad."

"Right." Then I say, "What do you see when you look up into the sun with closed eyes?"

She tries it, says, "I see spots."

"Not spots," I say. "Look again close."

So she does and says, "Still spots."

I say, "I used to think spots too, but wondered why they jog all over. Then one time I see wings poke out. It's birds. Black silhouettes of way-out-there birds flying near the sun, secret, out of range, safe, and that's so cool. It calms me."

"What do you do when the sun's not out?"

"I just stay pissed, like this..." and I pull up the dark hoodie, sink back into the shade such as Darth Vader in his storm trooper togs. I know I'm rocking it. Mrs. V laughs, calls me dark matter, which brings me up out from the hood with a questmessage clogging my response. She knows. She tells me dark matter is known by its effects on things but can never be seen and understood as itself. I say I like that. I say, call me the dark matter. We smooch awhile in our sunlit hideaway. I notice her skin way cold to the touch so pull the yellow sweater Brad gifted me out from the trunk and explain to Mrs. V its color therapy value that she will appreciate and she does.

△

WE'RE ON ONE OF THOSE SMALL ROADS known only by a number that empties out onto the New York State Thruway. It's a road

I know from family visits to New York City and from a five-months-ago delivery to Poncy Prep. There's a house I have imagined living in with a family I've wanted for my own. Red brick pitted with age and faded paint on trim forty feet off the road in a stand of tall pine. Kids' toys in the yard year long, even in winter covered in snow from which some peek out and some become igloo mounds. The grass not often cut in summer and snow never plowed in winter, tire tracks leading to a garage. Evidence of human life but no human life evident. I've never seen anyone in the yard or looking out windows, but lights always on and in winter a thin trail of smoke out the chimney. Today is sunny but cold with patches of snow still under the pines, toys scattered and muddy on the lawn. The usual smoke from the chimney. Maybe it's because I've never seen the family I think their lives together are so perfect.

I tell this to Mrs. V then say, "I mean, Mrs. V, the freedom to leave toys around, to let the grass alone to grow and snow to pile up. That's a kind of love, isn't it?"

Mrs. V says, "No, it's neglect."

"But no pestering. No pressure."

"There's black mold in the sink and teeth with cavities and stained underwear. The kids lack manners, don't eat well, don't read and don't listen to adults. If that's what you like, sure, why not call it love."

"What aren't you telling me?"

"I had a stepdad that got too familiar and a mother that didn't know ... or didn't care."

"Oh, shit. What did he do to you?"

"Not as much as he wanted."

"How did you stop him?"

"He had a tomcat he liked. I did something with scissors to that cat that awoke him to the possibilities."

"Oh, shit, Mrs. V, you love cats."

"Not the males. I only keep them if they've been doctored. I don't do it myself anymore. I know a vet gives group discounts. I don't have a male cat anywhere near my home that hasn't been doctored. You haven't noticed?"

"I don't tip cats for inspection. Maybe I should inspect myself."

"You a cat?"

"Don't think so."

"Don't bother."

"What's this got to do with me wanting to live in that house?"

"Oh, right. I can't remember."

"Me neither."

We waste miles together argubating the nature of freedom applied to cats and kids. But we don't revisit house specifics until home furnishings cause a jam of parked cars on the thruway. It happens like this. We're way north of any major city. There shouldn't be traffic. But we're stuck. No way through. Except an emergency vehicle flashing past in the breakdown lane and also the road rage warriors that gauge every blip in their drive-by lives a personal insult. One of these, a German warship pulling with all four wheels, high off the turf on outsized rims, black lacquer and plate glass gleaming, it clips the side mirror of the yellow cab because I have drifted into its lane a notch to peek around the stalled lines of pulsing metal. It's no more than plastic on plastic, our sideviews, but that black SUV slams brakes then redlines reverse to confront our insignificant selves. Mrs. V is noticeably shaken. No so me.

I pull up the hoodie channeling my best gangster meme as the bimmer screams tire rubber braking beside the cab. I pull Rip's hammer from out the glove box and point the handle at the window over Mrs. V's hunkered insecurity as noise barks at us from that pissed-off interceptor parked at the passenger door, window down with kaiser mustache emoting. He's going off about what he's going to do to me, and Mrs. V too, amping up the threat trauma. Until the metal claw head of the hammer that I have gripped such as the trigger of a deuce deuce pointed at him glints through his red rage. And then he's all about diarrhea mouth: "Shit! Shit Shit," he says, "Shit!" and steps the gas for a quick release from insult collateral.

"Well," I say to quiet the vibe, "that went well."

"Even better than scissors," Mrs. V says and laughs which presents more affirmation proof for why I'm so right to love this woman.

△

WE'RE MOVING AGAIN, SLOW. I turn off and on the Caprice engine because it's overheating and sending blue fumes behind that tailgaters say with their horn tapping was banned by the Geneva Convention or something. Whatever. Us being noxious and them obnoxious. Which is worse? I don't restart the cab until the car ahead has gone two lengths or more. Which makes sense to me but not them behind. Hell of a wail from horn tapping. Then a dead stop for what seems hours because highway speed has infected the pulse making nerves twitch, such as the effects of a buffering media stream. We move a few yards. Then stop again. Our lives on and off freeze pause. God's spastic hands on the remote. Then a wonky sound makes me think the yellow cab won't be our transport to paradise, the clank of metal breaking apart beneath the right front wheel. I'm thinking this can't be a simple fix, as if I know, but I'm the guy here and so must seem to know despite ignorance of all things mechanical. I tell Mrs. V, "A brake shoe has broken off. That's okay though. We have three more."

I'm inspired by my assertive diagnostic to prepare a detailed explain of a simple road-side fix. But Mrs. V is unconvinced. She begins to cuss, freckles igniting, racing around slamming into each other, a crash-car universe of angry stars. I feel instant deflation from knowing I can't compete with wife-beater, military trained, Gen X greasers with sprocket wrench fingers and transmission schematics as bedtime stories. Mr. V's bashed in face sits beside me smiling venom.

But it's not my automotive idiocy that has her riled. I realize she's going off on litter offenders. There's cast-off debris covering the road. All manner of stuff. We have hit a clothes iron, which explains the clattering metal. There's also pillows exploded of white feathers that makes me think angel road kill, and broken lamps and furniture, and then we sideswipe an already dented metal file cabinet with drawers out and confetti streams of paper that places me back in the office of our family shrink. Those filing cabinets of Doctor Westover's office, they creep me out. They think they know me. They have dissected and prescribed me. They say I'm ADHD because zoned out at school, but really it was from all-night video games, where I was very much in-the-zone. I've gone off the meds since the Mom quit paying the Westover bill because the Dad had too. Then the car to my left splinters an upturned dining table with three of its eight legs upright, dying a centipede death. Weird shit like that is what we're seeing. Then we really see it. Just ahead a moving van on its side with exploded cargo.

"God has stomped a tissue box," is what Mrs. V says. I don't get it but I like it. And then I see why she said it. From out the seams of that jackknifed semi a billowing of white sheets. That's what you see first. There's also brown cardboard scattered, some still squared and glistening in packaging tape but much of it flattened with contents leaking out. Then we see where it's going. There's a broken guardrail over which the back of the trailer hangs and out from which stuff pours and tumbles down into a river below. Most of the emergency responders stand there looking down at the mess. One takes pictures with his cell phone. Someone in a turned over car calls for help. Everyone is stunned. Can't get their shit together. A neighbor car says, Looks like terrorists! Another says, More like Katrina! Everyone has his own version of catastrophe. If Zed was here, he'd be looking for evidence of alien invasion. No one gets out to help. No one seems to want to leave the security of their escape pod. I like best Mrs. V's pissed off God stomping us.

We slow the cab to a crawl, look down to where the river has taken a family's collectibles somewhere unscheduled. Everyone else does too which is why the jam. We see a steep ravine, trees and bushes clinging somehow to rock ledge with bras and skivvies attached. The boxes that delivered this display have all crashed through to the river below, some carried downstream, some lodged in tight channels between river rocks. I wonder if this undie exposé will rate a superfund clean up. Probably not. Too small a catastrophe. But huge for the family that lost everything. Mrs. V doesn't agree. She says, "Insurance will cover it."

I guess she's right. But it won't cover attachment items such as group photos of family that hung on walls now busted off frames and wearing tire tracks more ugly than DNA patterns. There's also kid toys. A pink broken apart girl's bike with pink basket still attached to a handlebar separated from the rest. Plastic dinosaurs crushed under tires. A box of video games tumbled from the back end of the van that has become lodged in ripped guardrail. An emergency responder picks through to recycle the best entertainment. So nice to see someone worry this stuff will go to waste.

I think again about that brick house with scattered toys I like so much because neglect is freedom. I don't see attachment issues at that house, and I don't see freedom in this van filled with stuff. I see stuff mistaken for life. And having seen the future of all "stuff," which is landfill, I say, put it in the cloud, and which is a rad idea that could save the planet. Don't lug it around with you, is what I say. If you must own it, put it in the cloud. Travel light. If the family in the brick house was to move, the yard will still be a deposit of toys and the house will be less than clean and furniture will be left for the new owners to use. I could live in that house. I could live in this cab. I could live in the cloud. Maybe I will. Maybe I am.

△

So we're moving again at the posted speed, wind outside pushing debris around but only in the rearview. A noise such as diesel trains from behind invades our separate thoughts that have drifted into and closed the doors to separate rooms. Mrs. V peeks out from behind her door, says, "A phalanx is thrusting at us" and winks at me. I look at my crotch but that bad boy is sleepy and zipped. I don't know what she's talking about. Then a hogly bike rider beneath a skull cap helmet, weighing three hundred pounds, shaking blubber inside a leather cocoon, and seated on a Harley, he zags between cars behind us, then bedside us, then to the front of us. And another and another and many more. Shaggy beards flat in the wind and swept behind such as a bad case of gorilla neck hair. Even in the cold many with jean jackets short sleeved exposing inked skin. Then women in pink helmets with Mohawk stands of pink hair attached. Some grandmotherly, jowly, pissed off looking because maybe blood in the urine and cysts and bad teeth. Billboard sized backs promote the Angry Bear Adirondack Chapter biker club with a patch pasted on of a snarling grizzly standing on two legs holding a skull. All of them together in a V cracking apart the space in front of us with noise and formation acrobatics. Long wind-knotted manes both male and female whip out from helmets.

"See," Mrs. V says again, "a phalanx."

She says that's a Greek word for a military formation. I say, I thought so. But then above, what Mr. Ralph calls counterpoint, another V parts the air which I point out to Mrs. V. She leans into the dashboard, looks up through the windshield glass where in and out again a smudge of cloud flies a wedge of Canadian geese. We hear their honking even with the Harley noise.

I say, "What's that mean? One phalanx goes south, another north. Maybe it's nothing. I'm beginning to feel stupid looking for signs."

Mrs. V says, "The Greeks looked to birds for signs all the time. The Greeks aren't stupid."

"I guess. If you say. But what's it mean? Which phalanx do we follow? Back north to Lakeville or south to Mexico? I'd like to know."

Mrs. V says, "Sometimes you have to made a choice and find out later what the signs are telling you."

"Oh," I say, "that from the Greeks too? Real helpful."

"Look," she says, "my stepfather was a son of a bitch, but I always paid attention. Call it self-preservation. When my mother died after too many years married to the creep, he says to me he was just starting to get used to her. He said the day of her death he knew he had been right to marry her."

"So," I say back, "you're telling me wait till you die and by then I'll know if following the Harleys south or the geese north is the best idea?"

"Something like that," she says pointing south. She being the most significant V in my life, I press the gas and move into the Harley phalanx jet stream.

She says, "Good choice!" and closes again the door onto her thoughts.

△

WE DRIVE A LONG WAY together in our separate silences down the high-speed blacktop. This is where the lonesome truck driver plays country twang on the radio, such as Grandpa Herkimer that exposed the Dad to Merle Haggard, but the Caprice radio has gone to mostly static so no company there. Although I'm tempted to filter for alien communications. You never know. It has become night hours ago, and dark inside the cab except for Mrs. V's face that shines thoughtful and worried in the radiation glow of the cab's instrument dash. Probably brooding on a dead husband and the retribution karma she'll pay. She'll be surprised to know there's nothing to pay but a reset time out. I'm thinking she's going to leave me when she knows Brent Vitello is only just mad he's the one bruised and left behind. I'm not ready to spill the truth. Then we're near Albany and even in the late hour, traffic is getting thick with urgent drivers maxing the miles. Semis mostly. No more motorcycles. They're already somewhere in a trailer park refuge bumping nose candy and slamming Budweisers.

Now our wheels roll over Jersey and the tolls want a bite of our getaway budget. Which is no big thing given the size of the roll of bills Ignacio has gifted us, except I have spent the top layer of the roll down to its core of hundreds and don't want to peel off a hundred at the off ramp. Too much drug reference. I have this ticket that needs a cash exchange and not sure yet what I'll do. But that's a later problem. Now it's exhaustion. The day's events have left me woozy and beset with sleep nods. Mrs. V is already dozing. Her eyes flutter shut and her chin taps her chest. She shakes it off, looks at me. Same thing multiple times. I really need sleep. Then I remember friend Baskin Robbins at the highway oasis down by the refineries and grip the wheel with the assurance of a destination tag.

I drive an hour or more longer in the draft end of a rumbling semi as this cab burns through gas and I need a moving pick to get me down the field. He knows I'm here. Must have a nostalgia node humming in his brain with fondness for vintage yellow cabs. I pull into his rearview sometimes and wave a thank you after which he switches his lights on/off hello. I'm a sucker fish to a whale. He knows and he's okay with that. The cab rocks gently in the airstream behind his rig. Mrs. V has gone deep into dreams as the burn-off stacks of refinery chimneys make a torchlight appearance. I'm thinking Marvin Herkimer drawn to the flame. Another singeing coming soon somewhere down the road.

When we pull under the yellow lights of the oasis, the Caprice is overheating. I have stayed awake spinning the radio dial for the occasional slide-by moments of talk-show hosts stinging their audiences with reasons to embrace their particular hatreds. These reasons have periodically startled me awake. Goes to show shock jocks are good for something. A white cloud drifts out from the hood. I shut the Caprice down alongside public bathrooms. It backfires, shudders and clatters itself still. No other cars but us parked in the lot. Only just one semi at the edge near the highway ramp snoozing. No one gassing up. Mrs. V sleeping.

I pull the hood of my hoodie up around my face to mock a gang initiation for Baskin Robbins' entertainment, close the cab door quietly so as not to waken Mrs. V. She's so cute, helpless and unsure without home decorations to fuss over. Mrs. V has become the stray she likes to give a home to. She's bent sideways into her seat. Her neck is going to hurt like hell when she wakes up. Put that on the list of sometime later reckonings. So I creep around to the entrance and there's oasis friend inside. He's sleeping too. Forehead settled deadman on the counter, fro bushing out. That's a surprise. I thought vigilance a job requirement. But then I remember the Dad has tweaked his job description a vast number of turns to better fit his personality. Maybe Baskin has negotiated a catnap requisite to offset his daylight activities.

I push open the door, my other hand inside the hoodie's kangaroo pocket pointing the handle of Rip's hammer at oasis friend, my face deep inside the hood, just a shadow, an electronic ping saying wakie-wakie which pulls Baskin Robbins' head up such as a string attached and his eyes go as wide as sloe eyes can go at my Darth Vader slither in from the dark night mysteries. Dark matter is what I want once again to think of myself, which is a Mrs. V original if you remember. He's reaching for something under the counter. Fumbling with eyes on me, he drops it. Heavy thump on the floor. Then knees bent so I only see the top of his fro. He stands, slams down on the counter a tire iron, hesitates, then raises his hands. I laugh. His mouth goes off center in an unsure response twitch. Then I pull off the hood, smile and say, "Hey, dude! Yellow friend to yellow friend! Remember me?" He takes a minute to sift the memory compost then pulls out a good vibe tangled in food scraps and dead leaves and blotchy sunlight from all the shit memories he's tossed there from this stream-of-faces job banquet. He smiles, then not so much and says, "Dude ... yellow friend? We still kicking that down the road? Damn. Whatever. You scared me shitless."

So in walks Mrs. V yawning, massaging her neck, then spreading arms in a windmill motion, fingers snatching pockets of air, releasing, snatching again, all encased in a yellow sweater. She stops with both arms raised because feeling disturbance in the air from recent events. She drops her arms, says, "Marvin, what's going on?" and Baskin says, "Dude! The migration brings its mother along?"

That's a wake-up to caffeinate a Mrs. V response. I'm the only one in the room not experiencing wake shock. Mrs. V plants her feet as if bracing for a breaker wave. Hands on hips. She makes defiant elbows, says, "Hey, kid, Herk and I, we're fuck buddies. Isn't that what you call it (she says to me)?"

"Yeah, I guess... but..."

Baskin's laugh rips away my response which would include the hope Mrs. V and me are much more, then slips into camofraudulent to hide his inadequacy fears because he senses Mrs. V's takedown readiness. He processes all this info-overload with some difficulty, embarrassment fumbling again the tire iron which he places back under the counter. He stands, hugs his chest with arms behind which flashes a fluorescent orange T-shirt with traffic safety engineer in black silhouette and the motto: flaggers do it in the road.

I make introductions and tell with abbreviations our getaway strategy from points north to points south, leaving out the tangled relationship woes, but tell of the signs that say what and where and ask can the oasis provide a temporary rest from our road weariness? At least a reset moment to refresh, fill up on artificial flavoring, nap in the car awhile until his shift ends? By now it's more close to morning than night but still dark outside. Baskin nods okay sure and signals for us to walk with him the isles of snack delights whose bold packaging vie for most worthy. Mrs. V follows. I sit up on the counter watching the fun. They are sizing each other, noting the uncertainty levels expressed in those things separate from the words they choose.

Mrs. V's machisma surprises me. There's nothing shy about her anymore. She gives Baskin the direct eye while he takes the side-glance evasion tactic. They could be talking waste-words on the weather. It doesn't matter. It's all about giveaway responses in tone of voice and his dancing eyes and Mrs. V's solid stare. Him pointing to the best options, telling his reasoning. Mrs. V ignoring his words, saying only "uh, huh" and stepping in as he steps back. All this to expose which of the three of us is a match. They both take each other for a friend of Marvin Herkimer with significant history as yet unexplained which accounts for the definition probes. I've never felt so much wanted before. I'm the bone these little doggies pull from both ends. I count for something more than dark matter it seems. Maybe I am the pink marrow.

Baskin has the disadvantage of work-reference exposure. Mrs. V judges him totally by his bondage selection. So he is what, she wonders? As Mrs. V sizes the operation here at the turnpike oasis, he seems a high school dropout with vampire tendencies and no kind of future plan. She doesn't yet know of the politician hands he shakes and the skin tax he plans to collect off that contact from Trenton's finest. And then, too, he has little to use for judging Mrs.

V. He probably thinks her a cougar tagalong Elmo, in that fuzzy yellow sweater, with a special needs fixation from an antisocial personality disorder. That last bit is a label given my stepbrother that's now blown to pieces in the beforelife, but that when once all of one piece was said by our family shrink, to the Dad that asked, to be suffering from antisocial personality disorder. Which explains his trouble with the police but not with the Dad that couldn't caretake a vegetable garden.

△

OASIS FRIEND FILLS A PLASTIC BAG with preferred snacks which he hands to Mrs. V, says, "No charge for the migration, which has, I'm sorry to see, gone through the mud." I hop off the counter, shrug affirmation and leak a small laugh while giving him the gangsta hand slap followed by a hand grab, then a shoulder bang which we fuck up and that hurts some. But it sets us laughing. He takes Mrs. V to the employees' restroom to clean up and me behind the glass case refrigeration to where an improv hang out exploits an unused storage space inside a pile of wooden skids. Purposeful emptiness. When Mrs. V comes back, we sit on boxes filled with Snickers nougat bars I imagine melting from the heat of our bottoms. There's a banged up lamp table where Baskin has placed a brown and droopy potted plant and a vintage Rolodex and a stained and empty coffee cup. Baskin takes the card rotary in his hand to explain to Mrs. V his political motivation for taking this job. It's all about the needs of "the collective" is what he says, and as proof runs a finger across those cards to expose the ink stains of networking. He says he wants to lean a shoulder in to get the right pivot off our social policies. I'm thinking fantasy land,

Baskin wanting to make a control spin of our planet's wobbly tilt trajectory.

Mrs. V says, "You might have over-estimated the power of your shoulder. Unless your name is Atlas?"

Oasis friend says leaning farther away from Mrs. V, "You don't understand. Okay, reference this."

He tells about Tuong Lu Kim of South Park that was asked of city residents to build a wall to protect the kids from abduction. He says, "Big surprise. A Chinese man asked to build a wall."

I say, "Dude, I remember that episode. The Kim character is a multiple personality. He makes a Japanese rival commit shame suicide because his other identity is a shrink."

Baskin says, "You're so right. Don't I just love the toons. What I say is, the walls come down. Many hands built it. Many hands will be needed to tear it down. It's the many hands theory."

I've never met someone my own age so smart already. Mrs. V is not so convinced. He tosses me a Slim Jim and I'm chowing on that slimy meat concoction as Mrs. V prods Baskin for the kind of response that could signify him a pod. Such as why the fro if he's Chinese? She knows pods don't account for cultural differences and fros have gone out with Soul Train back in the 70s, so what's this kid's motivation? Can he be operating as a single life form? Or is this collective he talks about the pod directive?

Baskin hesitates to answer the fro question. He's been through this with me already and who wouldn't resist explaining grooming preferences to every stranger confirming racial prejudice. So he takes a deep breath, gathers his wits, reaches behind and into the back pocket of his distressed jeans from which he pulls a scrunched Yankees baseball cap, slaps it against his other hand to reshape it then forces that hat onto his fro with the attendant result of flattened fro and big smiles from all present. Especially Mrs. V. who says with conviction, "Not a pod. Definitely not a pod."

At this point it's me that's disengaged from this triangle of new friends making history together and that's okay. I have some thinking to do. I disappear awhile behind a deflection smile. They put together their two heads from which words fly out of origin places and trauma confessions. We hear oasis friend's real name which is Chen Adir. He says Chen means "vast and great" in Chinese and that Adir means "strong" in Hebrew. He says his best memory is of a day at the Bronx Zoo, both parents then together, the sun shining, baboons aping the worst faces of humans looking in which made him understand why we fear the other and put him in a cage. His worst memory is of his first day of school. All those bells dissecting the hours, ruining the day. Mrs. V tells of when she first met her husband – go figure – that he was handsome and sensitive and tender. Those, you must know, are her words. I wouldn't of described the SOB anywhere near that spectrum. She breaks down though when it comes to her worst memory. That's when I step in with a migration invite delivered to Chen Adir with good intentions and hopes Mrs. V will forget her husband long enough for a mood adjustment. Who would of thought my AWOL from Poncy would of led me to these after-school playmates. Not in a million. But I can see hesitation building in the silence that follows. I sense they want me to be the glue to better fasten a connection. So, in my best guess from the adult perspective, I offer this: "We need a quest. We need Baskin, I mean Chen, to go down the road together. But, we need a quest."

Chen shakes his head possibly yes, says, "Where we going?"

I say, "South, way deep south."

Chen says, "I have business in south Jersey. Could use the ride, but what's the quest?"

Mrs. V in her magical thinking says, "I thought it was understood. We're looking for a virgin."

After which I say, "What's to understand about that?"

Chen says, "No such animal. Not in Jersey."

Mrs. V says, "How do you know, Chen? Dark matter is never seen but we know it by its effects. Right, Marvin?"

"Well, yeah, I guess."

And she explains in her best poetry meme that young men behave such as unicorns, single-horned beasts (she looks at my crotch), and that unicorns chase after virgins that when found bring unicorns to their laps and tame them.

"We need to find a virgin," she says. "That's the quest. Marvin is right. Every road trip needs a quest, doesn't it?" she says. "You will find a virgin when you fall asleep in her lap. That's mythological fact."

Chen laughs, says, "A virgin? In New Jersey? Seriously?"

Mrs. V says, "Marvin, take me to a mall, buy me a new wardrobe like you promised. Let's find a virgin at the mall and you can catch a nap in her lap."

This will be the most errorist mall trip I've ever done. You'll see.

△

SO CHEN HAS NO VEHICLE and no electronic message connectors at all, only just a backpack stuffed with books. I mean, books? No cell phone, no tablet pc. I wonder how the collective can survive without connection. How will they know what the Kardashians are doing? Chen has no survival essentials beyond a year's bus pass he calls the "people's go-to for getting there" which Mrs. V thinks way cute, but even so asks why he's so retro in his habits. Chen says, "Have you even followed your internet connection to its source?"

"Yeah," I say, "I know where you're going with this. The NSA listening, right?"

"No, dude, not my meaning at all. What you'll find is a single person counting the money. It's a false paradigm, the 'inter' part of the net. There's for sure a net, but it's there for trapping money. You think because it's called 'inter' it's about 'the people' when it's really only about the person ... counting his money."

When Chen's shift replacement arrives, the sun is blazing and the highway traffic singing "Bring it to me, America!" which is a travel song I can get behind. The shift manager is overweight and making that a life choice, eating a pretzel stuffed with cream cheese. Bald as the gerber baby, a day or two unshaved, jazzed on tweak or something else motivational because his words launch out very fast with specks of pretzel in their jet stream. He asks Chen did anything important happen last night. Chen looks at me and winks his nearest sloe-eye but keeps his mouth tight and serious. Chen says, "I'm leaving your employ, Doug. I promise not to say about the unreported food consumption here if you deliver this letter to 'the man' and explain you and me said goodbye as friends."

"Friends, huh?" says manager Doug, then goes off on a confusing smatter of words, chewing and spluttering, which Chen interrupts.

"Yes, Doug, friends. What's the other way?"

We hear rattling and shuffling behind the refrigerator display of liquid goods. Two short-haired scruffy nimrods with Carhartt work pants and yellow construction flagger vests bump in and knock me and Mrs. V nearly off our feet carrying boxes of goods.

Evidence of the damage done by the stealth munching Chen has mentioned. Or at least that's what I figure when Nimrod number one, the anorexical one with face tats all over such as someone has played connect-the-dots with chains and tear drops, he asks Doug to set these boxes of "groceries" behind the counter. He'll come back for them later. Chen pats the other nimrod on the shoulder in a friendly way. He's built such as a smackdown artist on the WWE. He resembles the other two even though his face is distorted from steroids and facial hair. Think Mickey Rourke with a fu manchu.

"It's okay. Doug and his family are part of the collective," Chen says to me while squeezing a shoulder of muscle. "They're from Alaska. Used to fish there. Now their bay is coated in oil. Exxon Mobil agreed to compensate them. That's why they eat here. That's how Doug got this job."

I give Chen a look of wonder.

He says, "I know, right? It's the class action reflex response. Spill over from the Valdez settlement. Dude! The courts work when the collective matters!"

Chen reaches inside a box stuffed with frozen burritos, lifts three then goes to the counter to write a letter of resignation saying the collective appreciates "the man's" generosity but asserts its independence. Further saying Chen is taking personal time to research the collective's needs. He then lifts a few large bills out from the register after saying in the letter no need to send his pay as already compensated, and no address known of where our wheels will eventually stop turning. He doesn't mention the mall destination which is a plan that contradicts everything Chen believes in. But he agrees anyway calling our destination mall a worthy if failed experiment in capitalistic engineering. I can't say I get what he means, unless maybe that malls are as much infrastructure as airports except built entirely for taking our money. Maybe that's it. Chen is hella smart!

Before this all happens, Chen helps me push our Caprice into a disused service bay from when mechanics pumped gas but also handled the wrench for uncomplicated fixes to send motorists back down the road. Me and Mrs. V go to the bathrooms to evacuate tummy trauma of its food remorse and then crash in the cab and dream as Chen tinkers with leftover tools. I'm dreaming about back at Poncy hearing of my AWOL transgressions from a red-faced Langly, old Soc laughing behind me on his pedestal. I awake to Mrs. V's twitching and sad moans, likely running through the Brent Vitello takedown. While we are thus, Chen tweaks under the hood our overheating Caprice, to the end result of no more white smoke when we crank the ignition. Chen says there's nothing can't be done with duct tape and that it comes in designer colors, which is a surprising capitalist statement for him to say which I tell him. Chen smiles, says to always try duct tape first because if that doesn't work, it's a landfill item. I have sad thoughts of the yellow Caprice dumped into a giant pit of cast-off machinery.

Chen says, "Dude, you need to surrender your reliance on material things. They'll let you down."

And people won't? Is what I think but don't say it. And I should be fist bumping Chen for his take on a belief I share of stuff making anchors around our necks. But this time, the stuff is very personal. I'm trying not to feel the impermanence of Ignacio's yellow cab as we drive toward The Garden State Plaza of Paramus, a mega mall Chen leads us to while lecturing the reliability of the collective. Mrs. V is laying down in the back seat of the cab. We're in the slow lane undistracted by the sights because they're minimal and boring, which Chen says is a design scheme of the highway to keep attention on the road and nothing more. I say, haven't they heard of cell phones? Which gets a chuckle from Chen. I ask Chen why he doesn't have one. No answer. Just a twisted smile such as sucking on a Sour Ball. We engage in debate. I tell him I too am of the collective. It's called social media. Try it, I say, share what you know on the cloud. It'll share back. The cloud, Chen says, is a term he's not familiar with. I mean, dude, how can anyone of my generation be so smart and so clueless? Was he homeschooled or something? Yes, he was, and pretty insulted I take that as a negative.

He says home is not always a mindless shelter but confesses blaxploitation films got inside his head with retribution drama, which is what his mom watched forever on video cassette and which she used to reference the ways of the world and what he would likely need to do to prepare. I tell him I don't think the world's that violent. But then I rethink this remembering Mr. V's fists, Mrs. V's frying pan, Rip's Zed aggressions versus aliens and those lax bros at the Dancing Mouse. So I tell Chen, okay, maybe some violence, and say I guess his education at home was not so different from me OD'ing on Survivor reruns which the Mom watched all the time from multiple screens around the house from when I was three-years-old. Wednesday nights sacred because new episodes. But mostly rerun addiction and the Mom punching a TiVo remote for pause and return to feed her cross referencing and analyzing habitude and her need to explain to me the why and what of every contestant's moves and counter moves, triumphs and ejections. At the time, all that lawyer mind of hers going to waste. She's using it now that the Dad's a renegade castaway himself. She's punching the time clock at a lawyer's office that has overload needs.

△

We're in range of the Paramus mall. Can't see it, but I feel it. There's less room for us. Something big has dropped into our space, reshuffled traffic, collapsed the corners. There's a buzz in the air we haven't felt, maybe from planes overhead sucked into the mall's vortex gravity pull, or from orphaned molecules unsure where to bond in a strong pulse of energy lacking surge protectors. Signage becomes more flash aggressive. Siren temptresses on billboards front the latest in eyeglass wear. I point this out to Chen as potential virgin territory. They're not wearing Oaklies. Mrs. V rises from the back seat, shades her eyes, squints, says, "They're not librarians, boys. No virgins there." "Yeah," I say, "never mind the dweeb pose." Chen laughs. But I can see her making calculations off a spring sale advert of Ikea furniture that's, like, mostly just white boxes to sit on and to store stuff. I wonder how she can be doing that? I mean, redecorating? Isn't she running away from all that? Chicks are a mystery. The grown ones especially, motives all torqued out with excess memory load.

Then we see it. The thing that's hogging our space. And I've gotta say, even in the eighth year of the aughts, the death of the mall is much exaggerated. It's as big as the Twin Towers or the Iraq War or maybe even the Great Recession. Poncy Prep could fit inside one wing, or the entire town of Lakeville. Every book Mrs. V has ever read, for sure every book I've ever read, and every song I've heard and every car the Dad has owned or sold, it could all go in there with room still for a lacrosse field.

A skirt of parked cars rings it around, acres of parcel receptacles, noses pointed to the mall such as having found Mecca. From our elevated highway ramp where we wait in line at the toll booth, there's a view maybe a mile away of tiny humans moving together between painted lines invisibly pulled into the faceless behemoth of steel and glass. The mall is cross shaped, or maybe it's x-marks-the-spot for GPS satellite orientation. There's a massive dome of glass in the middle with a chandelier beneath that even in daylight makes a laser light show. Attached is a building I've seen before in New York City. It's a spiral nautilus shell replication many stories high, but this one has cars coming into and out from. The one in New York has only art. Chen sees the cars slide in and right away says, "Dude! That's our first stop. I'll show you where not to look for virgins."

"Yeah?" I say back. "Where at?"

"Top floor of the parking garage," Chen says.

Mrs. V gives Chen a reassessment look and so he says in his polite voice, "In Jersey, it's the place for casual hook up."

Mrs. V looks at us such as we have all entered an awkward elevator moment. I reach for the iPhone, pretend to punch in a text because the battery is dead, must of been for sometime, which explains why Bradley Turcotte has been calling for me at home. Chen rolls down the window, tests the weather with his hand. Mrs. V places more weight on the mood with a stare-down that pretty much collapses our mojo. Her face morphs into ugly adult, a frown pinch twisting those otherwise sweet lips. She pushes deep into the back seat as far away from us as she can get.

I say, "Rubbing parts with a girl in a car is way better than dates as fun as job interviews."

Mrs. V says, "Marvin, sometimes you remind me how young you are."

I say back, "Mrs. V, this is as old as I have been my entire life."

We're near the tollbooth end of the off ramp. We have to pay our portion of the wear and tear, but I don't want to pull a Ben Franklin off the roll and Chen isn't digging into his stash to help out and Mrs. V is carrying nothing but regrets. So it's a Herk decision to press the gas to go through the gate (well, really around it) and the alarm goes off but nothing happens. I mean, not even a bored statey launches out for an easy catch of mellow yellow coughing black smoke from its revved engine. So I figure, what's the big deal about paying tolls anyway? I mean, the whole world is watching Britney Spears cut off her hair from worries over drug testing and being hauled out by a shrink squad because high on Adderall and Red Bull, sleepless and frantic and locked in the bathroom with her kids. Jeeze! Why would anyone give a shit about who jumps tolls?

So we park the cab as near to the mall entrance as possible. I don't drive into the parking garage because after hearing Mrs. V's negative views to that idea. It's a ten-minute walk to the mall. I hand Mrs. V a roll of Presidents to spend whichever way she wants. She's not sure at first how to handle this. But then I tell her we're both criminal. We're on the run. Enjoy the spoils.

Chen gives me a look heavy with eyebrows then says, "Bro, the yellow cab, it's an escape pod?"

"Yeah," I say, "Mrs. V killed her husband. Entirely legit."

"Okay, sure. But, dude, do you think this might have been explained before I quit my job?"

Mrs. V takes Chen's hand, pushes her tongue into the space between her front teeth, lets go his hand, says, "Glad to have you along ... bro." Then nods okay and pockets the money, says once inside she'll split off in her own direction. Says a hair salon first, then maybe a full-body massage, then replace togs with some-thing road worthy but more flattering. She pulls at the bottom of the yellow sweater, gives a pinch to her nose then asks if there's a Monkey Wards? Chen and me, we look to each other for an answer, but there's only silence. She says never mind. Maybe an Ann Taylor. More classy anyway.

But we don't answer because once inside we're slammed with waves of shoppers hauling purchases by the neck such as trophies from sport. We bump along unevenly down hallways. Mrs. V gets dizzy with sensory overload, which I find just enough evidence I'm alive.

She says, twisting her neck and eyes every direction, "The whole zeitgeist, architecturally, the light and vertical space, even the music... it's selling religion."

"Yeah, sure," I say back. "That's what I think too."

Chen gives a WTF lift of his eyebrows then pulls the baseball cap off his head to release the fro. He must think this will keep the crowds off our shins. Maybe so, if his head is a bumper car shock absorber.

"Yes," Chen says taking in the vibe, "I get it." And I guess he does. I mean, shopping is a religion for some. We're standing in a lounge hangout of plush seating under the chandelier glow with four wings of shopping pleasure three stories tall rising up from the central hall.

Mrs. V begins to spin with hands in the air, looks up at the chandelier. "Spend!" she sings. "Indulgences are back! Buy your way to Heaven!" Way embarrassing. I'm thinking she really doesn't get out much. She's getting looks that say we're becoming more spectacle than the advertising. We stand together under the dome, look up through the chandelier at the sky overhead, the music floating us off into expectations of the healing power of buying stuff. All that needs to be done is select one of four directions to wander off into pleasures of excess.

So we begin our mall pilgrimage. As we go farther from the chandelier tunes, we hear a mix of rock-pretention, upbeat generic twang from voices pumped into hallways, every youth-oriented storefront asserting its particular sound disruption when you pass by. And there are pseudo-rebel T-shirt emporiums, a kiosk with an Indian girl reading People magazine where you can exchange gold jewelry for cash, many other kiosks with eccentric functions such as snorg design hoodies and Verizon cell phones and there's a Victoria's Secret already sporting bathing suits and a food court that's more a cattle feed lot with heifer size women dishing calories. Young girls pace the halls in groups wearing spray-on clothing, eyeing me and Chen. They must think Mrs. V the parent because soon as she notices, they giggle behind shy hands and slide away. Windows are dressed in shout-it-out theme messaging, such as why buy one when three will do! Get your glow on here! Post it! Participate in the ultimate Google destination! You have arrived!

$\triangle$

So Mrs. V has gone off on her own adventure. Chen and me, we take a recon diversion up the auto-stairs to the third floor where Mariah Carey sings about her impatience because for so long waitin for it. Waitin for what, we ask? A question that causes me and Chen to discuss the possibilities. I say maybe waitin for a road map. Chen says maybe the next election. Doesn't take long to realize she's promoting the Abercrombie and Fitch agenda, all those beach-side, disease-free, prep-boy and prep-girl youth smiling out from ten-by magnified posters on the windows. Priming the locals to fantasize their own Floridian spring fling of perfect teeth, tight bods in cargo shorts and bikini tops. Wild sex and drugs with perfect strangers.

We go inside. One of the brand representatives comes straight to me because I seem collegiate and quality, mannequin worthy despite the hoodie, chinos ripped and mud stained. I get the look that sees potential in "rebranding." Chen gets the dis look because of his fro, never mind trending distressed jeans ripped by him rather than by tiny Asian elves torturing the denim after run off spools, spun and dyed. The brand rep finally gets that me and Chen are bros. He sidles over to Chen nervously, says he likes Chen's T-shirt, the road construction flagger, if you remember. He directs Chen to a table of T's with controversy slogans. Chen thumbs through the pile, holds up one that says "I had a nightmare I was a brunette," then "Love the Body," then a Chinese laundry with pictogram of two dudes in long braided hair under black caps that says "Wong Brothers Laundry – Two Wongs Can Make it White." Chen says in his offended voice to me, "Yeah, well, I'll be right back, bro." As he's leaving, brand rep talking to me wants to score an easy point so says to Chen, "What are you anyway? Like, the many colors of Benetton?" The manager steps out from behind the counter and says, "Dude! Inappropriate."

So I'm talking lax with corrected brand rep who leads me to the central canoe room away from the nodules modification of Mariah Carey's cords that take her voice seven octaves high. Even modified, her voice can't override the thick scent of Woods Cologne – lavender, vetiver and musk. Brand-rep presents a similar layering of three T's, all very tight, shirttails out with shell necklaces and bead anklets below. He's a Taft School graduate, a football player, which is too much dirt in the mouth for me, but I don't say it. Mostly because he's a ripped 220 pounds. I'm a little impressed. We talk about how much we can bench, what schools we attended. I present myself a Hotchkiss School graduate, a school that brand rep is familiar with because Taft plays in their league, even hangs their school banner on the gym wall with other league teams. He doesn't know Poncy Prep. I'm not surprised. I tell him younger brother goes there and get the bland valuation, which is him saying, "Oh, yeah, right."

So then I confess we're here to find a virgin. He thinks that's cool. We discuss this awhile. Brand rep calls over a brand rep cutie. Dawn is her name. She brings a bad case of sorority voice. Brand rep says in his own prerecorded voice before she arrives that she's a B+, better than most, only just a little light up top and bottom heavy below. Dawn hears my quest, nods a smile, then tells me in her husky over-partied tones where to look. "Oh, yes," she says, "the fat-girl calorie slingers at the food court downstairs." Big surprise is what I think. She says look for the really ugly ones. When she smiles at her own words, she pushes dimples in her cheeks with index fingers. Otherwise, she says, no virgins in this mall, and the food court is "iffy." I have to agree but I don't say it. Most dudes start with the ugly ones before the cuties that might say no.

We talk some of which dating app could best find a virgin, then Chen steps back in with a mojo fix, his hair shaved to stubble. No chance now he'll ever do a shampoo commercial, but that's okay, he's totally rocking the Barack Obama look! That's the long-shot Illinois Senator dissing it up with Hillary for top billing at the big show in November. He'll never get it, but every minority on the planet is taking notice, including Mike Jeffries, CEO of A & F that lost 50 mill to a lawsuit over hiring practices. The manager sees minimal coiffed Chen with me and brand rep and he's right away on the phone with the district manager asking how badly Jeffries wants diversity brand reps in the shop because he's got an Asian Obama lookalike with a big smile, compact bod, fit, very fit, and how much does he want to offer to get this look on the floor? They crunch the numbers, I can see him tapping a calculator, and then the manager pulls Chen aside, makes an offer of a pretty fair salary, then says, "General Motors, General Mills, what the General says to buy, that's what everyone buys. Dude, that don't cut it here. At A & F, we look for the quality. That's how we roll. But first, let's get you some free togs. Just try it out," he says, "see how it feels."

Chen disappears into the dressing booth with manager-selected gear. Comes back out with a jean jacket, a polo with pop-up collars over a fitted T outside a new pair of cargo pants, and two layers of shell beads around his neck, also anklets below. His smile is full on. The manager thinks this kid will send him straight to upper management.

Chen says, thanks for the togs and "You know. All you white dudes look the same to me." Then he walks out. Leaves me to explain our virgin quest to the manager's lip-quiver from sensing he'll now have to engage the long game plan, which is apply again for the MBA. Go third tier this time. Someone has to take him, what with his experience managing at A & F and his quality and collegiate background, and he can bench 106 percent of his body weight even on the day after. He doesn't know it yet, but all he's gonna get is a dead-cat bounce.

△

As the manager walks away I'm left standing awkwardly in meaningless chatter with brand rep who in a tallying frenzy quickly depletes the virgin resource of anyone nearby that might be collegiate and quality, and in frustration advises find a cluster of Pennsylvania Dutch or maybe Hasid Jews in the city. Or maybe try the Saudis where women can't vote or drive cars so don't leave the house. Try there. I say maybe I need to try Craigslist which gets a snicker and a rough slap on the back launching me out into the march of daytrippers where somewhere a pair of hair clippers has given both Chen and Mrs. V a personality adjustment.

I go down the auto-stairs to under the dome chandelier, sit there waiting with the exhausted and overheated citizens of purchase remorse. Then I see them. Three of them drifting down the hall. Chen and some girl and Mrs. V still in the yellow sweater but looking pornoisseur hipster in a red skirt, short and tight, black stiletto ankle-length boots, blonde hair feathered and waved such as a storm cloud formation. When I ask about the hair, she calls it her Farrah Fawcett, pauses, then says, "It's a tribute. Farrah has cancer." Mrs. V has always wanted one of these "dos" because she mainlined Charlie's Angels on TV when a kid. I don't know the show but tell her I remember seeing a Facebook posting of a retro blonde with that hair in a red bathing suit, face all teeth and nipples banging. Mrs. V says, "That's her!"

The girl Mrs. V has in tow nods hello. Chen is watching her with interest. She's maybe Chen's age, that's early 20s, has a pointy, pouty face half seen with hair styled radical bob such as Rihanna, long front locks covering her left eye down to the chin and cut short in back, dyed passion pink. And there's a tattoo message buried deep in the cleavage of a white smock partly unbuttoned. I ask is she a dental assistant. Mrs. V gives me the behave yourself look then says she's a hair stylist and wants to come along with us on a vacation to Atlantic City.

I have no idea I'm going back there. Mrs. V says it's Chen's idea. Chen nods that's right. Mrs. V says Chen wants to crash a conference of Jersey mayors. "He didn't tell you?" is what she says knowing that's the case. Mrs. V says the girl's name is Stacy. She's a virgin. "Right, well," Mrs. V says, "Chen doesn't believe it either." Chen wants to stay out of this. The girl says, "I am. Really. Saving it. Not a religion thing. Just want to wait. Like maybe it's worth something. That okay with you?"

"Yeah, sure," I say, "but what's with the tat? What you hiding?"

"Marry me and maybe you'll find out. Otherwise, pick your dream."

That said Stacy takes off the hairdresser's jacket, tosses it in a trash bin beside one of the plush sofas under the chandelier, looks away and to the side such as sighting a train miles away, places a fist on a wide belt of turquoise plastic, pulls a knee-length black skirt to mid-thigh above the stocking opposite the fist. Her blouse is silver with fluffy white at the neckline. Now she smiles and shit! That runway punk slutty pose just about starts the dreamathon.

But first we have to go to Stacy's car so she can collect some of her things. She's been living in her car, doing tricks on the top floor of the parking garage, but only just HJs and BJs so really a virgin still. Well, okay, and there have been a couple anal hookups at extra charge. She eats at the food court in the mall, bathes in the public rest rooms before they open. The cleaning guy lets her in. He's the one organizing the tricks. She shares an apartment in Paramus with a girl from the hair salon, but sleeps pretty often in the car because works late nights. She has a change of clothes in the trunk and wants to put together a better, higher-class outfit for A-City, maybe to fetch more cash for a hookup is what I think.

We drive Stacy to the top floor of the mall parking garage where even in daylight many of the cars are bouncing. Stacy gets out from the trunk of a roughed-up Corolla a box with clothes folded, looks through, pulls out a selection, then a pocketbook, locks up the car, taps on the window of a black Honda van with tinted windows and four flat tires that's rocking it's shocks, says, "Hey, Glenda, watch my car willya? I'm on vacation."

We hear a soft choking voice say back, "You bet, babe. Keep it casual!" which is a phrase that resonates subliminal until it becomes a contagion of bumper stickers attached to bouncy vehicles. Pink with black lettering that says Keep It Casual! Order the usual! And a website address I can't give without getting Stacy into trouble. Collectives everywhere is what I'm thinking.

As we leave the mall, motor back onto the turnpike for the trip to Atlantic City, me and Mrs. V hear Stacy talking in the back seat of plans to open her own salon somewhere near a back lot for parking a side-line business of bobbing heads. But inside the cab with highway noise leaking in, we can't hear exactly everything she's saying. Only just enough to get the main idea. And it's too smoky from Stacy's cigarettes to see back there, so Mrs. V plays with the radio, dials up the nasal tongue-lashing of Rush Limbaugh laying into politicians for not arming educators to prevent massacre in the classrooms. He's always so pissed-off sounding. He says, "I thought I was the most dangerous man, I mean what with the largest hypothalamus in North America, but not so, listen to this" and plays a broadcast from a local station laying out the details of a shooting at a school in Lakeville, Connecticut, someone wearing a suit of armor as if bullet proof, spraying bullets around hallways with an automatic rifle.

"Oh, shit!" says Mrs. V. "Lakeville."

"Yeah," I say. "It's Willy in reenactment garb."

"You know him?"

"Yeah, I know the dude," I say. "He's my neighbor. He told me he was in kick ass mode. Guess I should of told someone."

Mrs. V turns the volume up more. We hear Rush telling about the "crippling mental tangles of yuppie parents who think the world is going to protect their babies. Well it's not! Arm the educators! And I don't mean give them dictionaries to throw at these nut jobs with a death agenda. I'm talking real guns. Real bullets! Then maybe the liberals will shut the hell up about gun control."

Which leaves me and Mrs. V to guess out loud what must have happened in our hometown. We forget about our passengers in the back seat. Which is just as well because Stacy is a self-talker once you get her started. Chen is just sitting there listening with the strangest smile on his face that Mrs. V notices with a glance behind as Stacy has opened a window to let smoke out. And there's Stacy's left hand in Chen's lap pumping with the same rpm as her lips torquing out words. Mrs. V doesn't say about this little love scene until later, so we consider more the Willy massacre.

We hear Rush say, "A suit of armor? He's wearing a suit of armor! I mean, all you conversationalists out there across the fruited planes, consider, I mean, someone walks into a school with a suit of armor, might as well be wearing a strap-on bomb. Doesn't that just say jihad! Doesn't that just say I have an agenda to kill as many as I can before you kill me. Well, I think so, and because I have talent on loan from ... God ... because I am the man, the legend, the way of life, I say to you, people, shoot that son-of-a-bitch dead the minute he steps foot inside your school. I say..." and this is where Mrs. V turns off the radio.

She says, "The problem with those jihad strap-on suicides, Rush, is not that they have found something to die for. It's that they haven't found anything to live for." I tell her, "Yeah, that's Willy. The SCAdian thing was just about his last try. You could be right. Willy hasn't found anything to live for. Not even the tinfoil hat brigade."

Mrs. V goes silent back into her separate room to fume awhile. Stacy is talking words to fill the space. Nothing I can't tune out. Then comes the Pine Barrens exit and the wheels want to go there, such as fierce electromagnetics pulling from iron in the bog water. I come out of my own separate room of thought when Mrs. V elbows me to pay attention to our passengers in the back seat. I look in the rearview to check their reaction to Willy's meltdown but can't see Chen anywhere. Mrs. V elbows me again, tells me look in Stacy's lap. So I lean back and look behind. There's Chen with his shaved head in Stacy's lap, sleeping. She's stroking his stubble hair while flapping lips over word shapes that float somewhere in the air among clouds of cigarette smoke. Mrs. V says, "He's sleeping in the lap of a virgin. Quest complete."

"Yeah, maybe so. What's next?" I say while passing by the exit to the Pine Barrens and wondering why I know I will return. But I pretend drifting aimless to probe her expectations. "What else is quest worthy?"

"Place your bets in Atlantic City," she says back. I keep thinking the bets are in.

△

WE ROLL INTO TOWN on the Atlantic City Expressway, blow through tolls a couple times more because no one wants to pony up the dollars and, as you know, I don't want to bragcast Ignacio's funding.

Stacy says she has a friend who works for a casino, lives outside the glossy parts of town and will put her up. She gives unsure directions such as turn here, or not here maybe there, which leads us down the backwater streets of A-City. We slide alongside apartment buildings of advanced age. Stacy asserts landmark recognition with a sharp "Here! Stop here!" then "Or ... I don't know," her self-trust blunted because confused by a clump of block-long, look-alike, three-story buildings with bay windows from the second to the third floors, metal grillwork balconies, gas lamp street lights outside on New Orleans artsy ornate metal poles for a once-ago tourist destination that now attracts smut chasers. There's a desperation ATM under the awning of one of these buildings and a front door that opens onto a 25 cent peep show. For big spenders there's live nudes from private booths. And for the advanced, shades are pulled down on third story bay windows so the slag porn junky can bed the baggy knees skeeza mattress grinder for the modest cost of a retirement donation.

Then the views change entirely with a right turn down a neighborhood of duplex rentals, narrow roads, junker cars, dead trees and uncut grass from last fall, trash cans tipped over, stray dogs lapping the litter, one working over a puke discharge. The whole block is aluminum siding coated in dirt but in better shape than the wood trim of faded paint and wood rot around windows no one looks out from. In the distance, over the low profile roofs, somewhere near the water, hotel casinos of glass and stone twinkle and shine. It's the city of Oz with construction cranes bent over such as giant feeding storks the dimension of Godzilla. Despite the streaming sun, everything is black and white and gray. We have invaded the Godzilla meets Oz movie set.

Stacy slows us to a stop outside a no-name eatery where bikers frequent, their locust machines leaning on kickstands beside a fluorescent sign that says "diner," a menu as long as the NY Daily News taped to the window. Someone's raggedy grandfather with the best tan dressed in sweats and sneaks and a patched down jacket trips by pushing found treasure in a grocery cart. Dust and paper trash kicked up in a dervish wind pauses him to shield his eyes. After the bottle-deposit reclamation, he's maybe on his way to under a pier that's nearby I remember from the Dad's symptomatic father/sons outings years back. This lonely grandfather will soon be sliding off to his beach-side lay-down of blanket walls nailed to posts under a pier beneath the fishing lines that me and the Dad and Matt dangled from paying a membership to do so. Beneath on the sand was a village of sleep areas with open pit fires smoking, dogs yapping and voices rising in echo. I thought it was pretty cool. Wanted to have a closer look. The Dad said no. We're here to catch the fish he said and paid good money for that. The underworld beneath the piers is said to have its own citizen dues of membership. These produce scars from territory wars instead of bluefish and herring.

But where Stacy stops us, across the street at the Duck Town Tavern, open 24-7, a sign tacked to a telephone pole says Jimmy Buffett parrot sing-along on Sundays. Another says free parking in the back. There's apartments upstairs for tenants who lean out windows smoking cigarettes in the chill of early spring assessing the inebriation levels of patrons staggering out the door. The motivation of this window loitering becomes clear. It's about curb quotations from the voices of sodden ones who may offer sound bites of investment opportunity. One such drunkelstiltskin sings his retirement package to the bouncer that leads him out the door. He tells that the bookie himself is going to lay it all on Jose Canseco, retired outfielder, for a knockout of another hasbeen succcesslete looking to boxing for a reboot of his recognition status. He tells the bouncer the fix is in. Don't know why that's trusted advice, but at least two sets of ears slip away from upstairs windows with portfolio adjustments to make. Clearly ancientville is reduced to lottery dreams paid for by scraping for quarters left here and forgotten there.

Stacy steps out from the cab, shouts, "Hey, Taggert! That you?"

The dude that answers leans more far out than most, his fugly tummy pouch attached to the sill such as sillyputty squeezed on, a black face covered to the eyes in beard, a round pair of eyeglasses, one hand waving insanely, the other somewhere sleazy inside his pants. He says, "Tracey, girl!"

"What you doing?"

"Sittin here waitin on the view to change."

"Do I count?"

"Baby, you know you do! Where you been? Ain't seen you nor Muffin since when the mayor went missin."

"Yeah, that so? You have anything to do with that?"

"Naw. But I know a cat knows what pills took him there."

"Listen, Taggert, I'm looking for Muffin so's I can crash with her awhile. She there?"

"Naw, girl. She gone. Told you so already. Gone somewhere upscale is what she want. Still workin the city is what I hear. You wanna lay your head at my crib?"

"Thanks, but I'll pass. You hear from Muffin, tell her I'm in town. You doing okay?"

"Jest a little down, girl. The mayor took my pension with him. I'll be aright. Go ahead spin them wheels. I'll be jest here you want me ... me and the monkeys."

"Monkeys?"

"Yeah, they be flyin tonight! You best be watchin out."

"Thanks, Taggert. Bye!" and to me says, "Hit the gas before he airs that hose he's playing with."

Mrs. V says to Stacy, "Honey, never mind the monkeys. You have a unicorn in your lap." Which extracts a way cute nose and eye squint from Stacy in response, like, you're crazy but what do I care?

Mrs.V smiles at her own cleverness then shivers, cozies close to me. She has not purchased the appropriate clothes to warm her in Ignacio's mobile frigidaire. She still wears the yellow sweater, more from fondness memories than anything else. When she scootches closer for body heat, I try to not see, so to stay in the moment. It's those pale thighs exposed, beautiful legs despite bruises gone to green from dark blue, and sharp-heeled ankles linked that jump out the thigh muscle. All this packed into a short red skirt and goddamage! She's a babe. No question.

Then some discharged citizen from the Duck Town Tavern falls off the curb pulling a mangy dog tied to a rope. He's another of advanced age but in a torn suit of gray serge such as Grandpa Herkimer wore to church the few times he was home for holidays with just the cab of his big rig. This old timer has a gray beard close trimmed a week ago with a free-range, brushwood look about it, eyes gray blue, clear as glass if sunk in the folds of skin flap. Hands black with dirt, yellowed with cigarettes which I see clearly from the driver's window because when fallen off the curb, he has fallen onto the cab. How could I not stop for this guy? I feel sorry for him. He straightens, takes a deep breath, adjusts the tweed cap that rides a staticy gray circle of hair, leans down to pat the dog, adjusts eye glasses that slid to the end of his nose, straightens shoulders skinny as a clothes hanger from which his suit sags, says, "You're a cab, are you not? A New

York City cab?" I nod yes. "Well, then, give us a ride." He doesn't wait for an answer. Opens the passenger door. Sees Chen lying there asleep, says, "Oh, I see. Why not let's share. Move over. Hello, beautiful!" he says to Stacy while lifting the mongrel onto the seat, then about Mrs. V says, "Twice blessed. And how much to the Borgata?"

"Pay what you can," I say back.

"Pay what I can? That's lovely. You're a destiny chip, friend. Can't pay much now, but on the way back, generous to a fault."

"Pay what you can," I say again to the man lost in remembrance of things pabst. He smells of cheap beers, talks a combination pulp fiction and what the Mom calls Billy Crystal comedy, which is Klingon to me but is also what she says about the Dad when he uploads the sales pitch. But this dude, he's way more durfy than the Dad. He trips into the cab and lands on the dog whose yelp wakens Chen in an ungenerous way. To excuse himself he says, "Sorry, friend. I'm always bumping things, breaking knickknacks, bruising myself or anyone near. I could start a war with two doves in a nest."

The old dude wipes his nose with a sleeve, pats the dog, lifts it onto his lap then tips his cap to Chen who engages in wonderment to hear that set of words come out this crooked, yellow-toothed grin beneath a gleaming dome of sickly white skin with odd-shaped brown spots under the cap he has removed to nod to Stacy what in his time must of been an elegant gesture.

Stacy looks over at the old gent, tosses her cigarette out the window, says, "Who the fuck is he? Where's he taking us? The Borgata? He can't afford that place."

I say, "Stacy, this cab takes requests."

Chen says, "It's okay, Stacy. Relax. You should drink some milk or something."

△

So we're rolling again, now toward the gleaming casino towers, away from the castaway schemers that spent their lives at the edge of real money but never got past the gate. Except maybe Ardan, he calls himself, the old dude leading us to the business side of town with elaborate verbal selfies that will end with his coronation as "the stud of poker." He tells his first memory ever: kite flying on the beach here in A-City. Then his mother wearing on her shoulders a dead mink he swears she killed herself. She was that fierce. Then cheap, sweet wine and gropes with tourist daughters in bathing suits under the board-walk (a wink at Stacy). Then chased by police down the boardwalk in a stolen rolling chair crashed into the plate glass of a saltwater taffy shop. Mug shots. No chance for legitimate work after that. Then keeping to the shadows with the homeless under piers feasting on roasted pigeon, what the pier colonies call "feathered lobster." Then finally, he says, into the light! He bestirs himself to collect the money casinos owe him. From which exploits with help from the Shylock that friends him he's crowned "stud of poker." He says he's still owed, if not the money at least the title. He says, do we know Borgata is Italian for town? He says this is his town, his family. He says he has taken the oath, bled upon the image of Saint Patrick, and considered it an honor. He shoots two finger guns at us and laughs.

I give Stacy a look in the rearview. She shakes it off.

He tells more memories up until yesterday that he can't remember at all. Ardan lifts a flask from which he drinks a celebra-tion to these words. We don't know if he's toasting forgetfulness or his very full life. He tells us he awoke knowing this is the day to define him for posterity, which leads Chen to say, "Dude, I feel the same. There's some kind of epic vibe happening."

Stacy contorts another WTF pout but this time throws it at Chen, takes her hand out from his lap, rolls down the window, lights another cigarette, says, "That dog smells."

Mrs. V looks back over the seat at Chen, says, "Yes, Chen, I feel it too."

Chen says to Ardan, minus the snide irony that could apply, "She's a poet," like that explains something.

Old dude begins quoting from some obscurd Irish poet about gyres intersecting, history lessons we all could miss if not attuned to the cosmic forces and shit like that. What a load. And so the meanness I have toward older dudes with the wisdom twitch comes to me saying this: "So, Ardan, how did you know? I mean, that this is the day?"

To which he responds first with a silent gathering of answers, then another pull off the flask, another moment of silence, and "All right, I'll say it. I awoke vagitus."

"You did what?" says Stacy.

Chen shakes his head sadly, says, "The dude had a hardon."

Mrs. V giggles, says, "No, he awoke crying, the way a baby comes out from the womb."

Stacy says, "Gimme a break! He's a hundred years old."

Ardan says, "Yes, it was a rise of tears upon waking. They came with a memory, a cottage of white-washed stone by the sea. It feels of home though I've never been. Likely a photograph hanged on the wall of our apartment kitchen. Something of my mother's heritage. Right, Sam? (This he says to the restless dog shifting to find a soft place on the dude's bony lap.) Lately emotions have been as thick about me as chicken broth. Which is to say, I've not felt anything at all. So I take these tears as a sign."

"You believe in signs?" says Mrs. V.

"I believe in moments that define us. And, yes, those are signs. When mother took to the straw, it was already up with me. I was to be a flawed homunculus. The day of my conception, seconds before mother received the spermatozoa that shaped me, she polluted the mix with a question to father. She said, with ire in her voice, 'Did you remember to buy the lottery ticket?' And so, I am become what you see. But, I do believe, some part of us communes with the angels. No matter how broken we are, or maybe when we are most broken."

Stacy says, "I'm a Virgo. What's your sign?"

"I'm a fire sign, darlin'. I am sometimes a spot of brilliance. You may have noticed. Sadly, this fades. Brief interludes. Longer moments of mediocrity. Like the sun, I would say. There are days it's out there doing its job, but not enthusiastically. Then it comes upon us much as a plinian eruption of flatulent gasses. Sunspots. Think of me, today, as a sunspot," Ardan says winking at Stacy, patting Sam.

Chen makes a side-eyed assessment and leans into Stacy who's not so impressed this old dude could be a sunspot. Stacy shakes her head, digs into her purse for a pair of sunglasses, pink with bunny faces framing the lenses, ignores our back-seat philosopher while directing a turn here, no not here, maybe there. Somehow it's working. One of those glass towers is getting closer. It stands out on the swamp landscape miles from the boardwalk casinos that have not been so busy lately, is what Stacy says. This one has. It's at the back-wash end of the ocean, a gleaming comma placed there to convince the eye to make a pause.

Stacy points to the comma, says, "The Borgata. It's a pricey place. Don't see how this old man can buy into a game there, even if he is a sunspot."

She talks as if Ardan has stepped outside the cab to take a piss or something. I'm embarrassed for her behavior, really. Where did she learn her manners? But the old dude, he's unshook, mostly. As we pull into the portico entrance of the Borgata, he looks at her with a squeezed face sending splinters of wrinkles every direction from an eruption of puffed-out lips. One of the funniest faces I've ever seen! I mean very much the look of a disbelieving Sacha Baron Cohen playing Borat from Kazakhstan traveling the USA in an ice-cream truck, thinking he has finally found his Pamela Anderson, and opens his heart to her, and can't be understood.

△

WHAT I EVENTUALLY LEARN from Ardan and from his landlord and a backstabbing Cuban, it makes the best movie, because retro is in again, and Ardan is a known name. He's a deep embed from the days of olden A-City. It should be monochrome, the movie, black and white, because grainy gives dimension. And maybe touches of sepia, as in a faded photo. Bring in Leon the Lion in a circle of light, an iris head shot. Leon the MGM trademark, one big roar, head tilt, a second roar. But Leon in color. Then black and white again. Cue the music. Maybe do the WALL-E soundtrack of Peter Gabriel singing, asking if we feel tricked by the future we picked? Then fade and cue the buzz of a crowd. "Walla walla," the extras say, "peas and carrots, watermelon" if you could hear the words. Whatever. It's the buzz that counts, not the words.

Camera dollies down a sidewalk, focus on the short, fast legs of Ardan in A-City zagging around people between drop zones for bets on earnings you won't claim on the 1040. It's the 70s. He's wearing skin-tight poly bellbottoms with black and white stripes.

He stops, another pair of legs walks into the shot, then off again until another second pair of legs, then pan the vertical for a close up. Ardan's puffy lips beneath the scruff of a Burt Reynolds stash, a favorite movie star of the time. Don't know why. I've seen some of his cassette movies with the Mom when home from school with the flu. Anyway, Ardan's whispering into an ear half covered in side-burns the wonkery done for the benefit of high rolling riffraff, of which there is much, and gets a nod from the Shylock that pockets the mistakes of the high rollers, of which there is also much.

Ardan has been flush and he's been bust. Now switch to the present, and it's all about bust. He knows this is the day he'll break loose. He needs investors. I step into frame, flash Ignacio's roll of hundreds as Ardan steps out from the yellow cab in his old man face and now we're in color. I tell him I'm in, which means I have a bit part. I become a railbird, earn tag-along status in my need to gauge the pay-back percentage of investment booty, which Ardan tells me is "assured up-action, nothing but top kickers." Such as he's got it covered on an insurance policy.

All the hired help of the Borgata know him, even the old Cuban dude that will soon place a satellite location on the yellow cab to Ignacio's contacts, him in the thread-worn service uniform sweeping the front entrance. He's the first to say "my man" to Ardan and so is given a nod in return, which inspires me to pull the Cuban aside to sound him on what he knows of Ardan.

When I ask, he gives me some of Ardan's personal history, then makes an upside down okay hand sign, thumb and index together forming a hole in which he traces more signs with the index of his other hand. I know hand signs, but this one puts me in a flummox. Usually the upside down okay means prepare for a sucker punch, unless you score an index finger through the hole ahead of the punch. But the old Cuban isn't playing that game. He wants me to interpret, not poke my finger through his. He says do I know Ardan's last name?

"Is it Frowny?" I ask as the tracing could have been a frowny face.

"No. Why you say? Is O'Donnell. Understand? 'O' ... Donnell. When Ardan sign name, he put there plus-minus sign in the O. Like this: ± (which he shapes again with his fingers). Every time he make this. Mostly IOU's. I know. I have many. We all forgive what he is owing. A-City ... not the same without Ardan. Understand?"

"Yeah, I guess," I say, "but if he never pays, why the plus?"

"Oh, we know he mean to pay. He just never do. Even when a big win he keep money until he lose again. The Shylock that want vig owed really pissed at Ardan, say is sum-zero he sign in the O of his name."

"What's that?"

"Is mostly same as plus-minus. Means all one way or other bust or flush. You don't know math?"

"Yeah. I mean no. Not so much. I don't get it."

"You with Ardan?"

"I guess."

"You will get it. Just give time. You will get it. Te veo mas tarde," he says and goes off sweeping the entranceway beneath the portico. As an attendant drives away the yellow cab, he's looking down at his feet sniggering. I tell what I've heard of sum-zero to Mrs. V. She says, "Oh ... yeah. Deacon blues." I swear, sometimes there's just too many puzzles to work through.

As Ardan enters the casino, he's given recognition signs from a range of fixture characters behind the bars, seated at the bars and the gaming tables, some looking down officially from above. I start to get that Ardan is more than a tour guide.

A few hours later, when night becomes day, I'll help launch Ardan's Viking funeral. His landlord of 30 years will be there, and some card-player politicians. What I learn from the landlord is Ardan has a bad heart, goes pretty often to a hospital that also knows him well, this after long days and nights of card play then bender amnesia. He once had a wealthy wife, when he was himself flush. They burned through all their together cash in a couple months, she left, and so came a two-year bender landing his bad heart back in the hospital. His landlord keeps a room for him through a cycle of disappearances and illnesses. It's a matter of loyalties is how he explains it.

△

SO WE MAKE OUR WAY deep inside the Borgata that Ardan calls a "whale of a place." That's a Moby Dick reference from Mr. Ralph's class that doesn't have a good ending, so I'm a little worried about my investment. But I'm not that worried. There's still a core roll of Ben Franklins to peel off to meet expenses. I know there must be something paid out for an Ardan education.

As the sun goes down on A-City, it sizzles with treasure seekers. The funny thing is, Ardan's the only one here that's desperate looking. It's not only the way he's dressed but mostly the advanced age of his quest. All the rest punching slot machines, eyeing the croupier spin the roulette wheel, siding up to gaming tables and card tables, they have baseball caps and custom T's and attendant hotties with short skirts that are young and laughing. The most serious are at the card tables. They're intense, attentive to the game. These players don't know Ardan. It's the service help that knows him: the cocktail servers with value-meal glands who have to weigh in before each shift to assure the quality of their presentation, the bartenders that know his Jameson drink preference, the security team that's not sure how well connected he still is. They let Ardan alone no matter what he's wearing or what odors he's contributing. Which becomes a factor as he begins to thaw in the warm drafts of increased human activity and animated chatter and blazing smiles from a staff that lives off tips.

The Borgata is a beast to be tamed. That's what Ardan says. "It's swallowed me whole. Spit me out curbside. Nothing but regrets to shield me from the elements. But not today, my friend. Not today!"

Chen says, "The color would make you think not today. Very Chinese." He says this while otherwise quietly absorbing the sensory input of this place.

In case you don't know, the color inside a whale is red, deep red. In China, says Chen, red is the color of good fortune. But there's also something high-class bordello about the place. Maybe because the female wait staff that stroll the runways of the casino, every color and ethnic preference, they're dripping sex. You have to be careful not to slip because the tile floors are wet with sex. Their dresses black, clingy, very short, held together at the neck with a thin X of ribbon. The material watery over nipples. One of these lanky gazelles stops to give Ardan a hug, a wide smile, a pinch on the behind. Then she's off down the runway with Ardan's flask to refill it Jameson.

Ardan says, "Dylan Thomas and I are of like minds concerning the female breast. Those that have been too early weaned spend their lives finding a way back to the nipple. You agree?"

Oddly, he directs this question to Mrs. V and Stacy.

Stacy says, "Yes, I feel the same," and takes a reassessment look at Ardan.

Mrs. V says, "Poets are often cited as justification for our perversions," and walks away from us such as she did at the Jersey mall with Stacy following after but still looking back at Ardan. Then a very real smile from Stacy and a kiss blown his way. I can't help think there are truth bombs there I'd rather not have to clean up after.

△

IT'S TIME TO INSERT A BOOKMARK and take an assessment of where we've come in our story. This is the place Mrs. V would call the cliff over which the Lemmings fall. It's what Mr. Ralph calls "a necessary plot device: the climax." The first time he said it in the classroom, we hijacked that lesson, because it's so masturbatedly relatable. I mean, the stimulation that comes of making a fantasy in our heads, the beautiful woman obligatory in any story, and then the chase, the complications, the surrender, the stroking, the release.

When we walked into Mr. Ralph's classroom and took our usual seats, those ones with the metal legs attached to desktops and plastic butt pods, it was third period after chapel. Link Rodum and Wayne Peebles were made, as is custom, to turn over their cell phones, which they always make a grumble over. Then we see up on the marker board a diagram in the shape of a pyramid. The base at the left says "exposition" then climbing up that side is written "problem leading to rising action" and at the peak "CLIMAX" after which down the other side is written "falling action" and at the bottom "resolution."

"Mr. Ralph," says Darrell Drummon that blends with the night and stuffs a basketball backwards, "that's no kind of sex ed stimulation. Gimme the marker. I'll draw you something to dream on!"

That's about the most Darrell has ever said in class. We hold in the laughs because Mr. Ralph has gone red in the face but more combustive than embarrassed, such as holding his breath, exasperated, opposite of aspirated (Mrs. V will like that one) and he's looking up at the ceiling before calling us out as the most horn-dawg, ganglia stroking, genderist, self-loving nits he'll ever know. But he laughs. Then one of my lax bros who is most usually a backfield middie, this time he takes the point. He reaches down under his desk with both hands, makes a grab and pull action there with attendant moans. The class sees, ponders, assesses Mr. Ralph's mood then follows. One after the other. Then we go into mass-masturbatory hysteria, making the pud-pulling motion under our desks, laughing the devil's who cares, lifting desks with our knees to the rhythm of the pull, chain-gang grunts timed to that rhythm and Mr. Ralph now uncontrollable in his laughter.

Noise spills out into the hallway beyond our classroom, drawing to our door's porthole window the awed faces of students and then those shooed away and replaced by teachoids with the put-out faces, the contempt faces, especially Mr. Rouse that "shepherds" my dorm, as he says, and lives in a dorm apartment with his uglyfuckasaur wife and complains every minute of his "blessed" life about what we put him through. His face pasty long with a flat nose tickled by a mangy scruff of mustache, a lookalike to the arthritic hound that shares his leash and looks as much ill tempered as him. He's very religious, blesses us every time after he's given us hell. He's now pounding the door so Mr. Ralph waves hello, slides over to that side of the room, blocks the view with his back so we up the action until the room seems about to collapse around us. Then Duff with rock-star dreams, the one inclined to shave words into his scalp and which keeps Mr. Rouse's dog grooming clippers busy taking out those words, he makes an Iron Maiden cum-to Jesus climax wail, which clues us all to do likewise and so we do. Then Duff gets off his seat, rolls up the eyes in his head showing mostly white, says in a whiney, terrified voice, "I'm blind." Others pick up the call, do the same, so we're all out of our seats bumping around, feeling with our hands, slamming into each other, the chairs, even Mr. Ralph, who has melted into tears of joy.

So you are now at the climax of this book. I can't guaranfuck-ingtee you'll feel the joy of a mass-masturbatory tribal groove, but you'll feel something. Of this I'm sure. So now imagine me and my fellow droogs leaving Mr. Ralph's classroom, still blind, feeling our ways down the hall to our next class. Duff stops before leaving Mr. Ralph, says to him in a Mr. Rouse voice, "Have a blessed day," which would maybe have been possible if any of this had ever hap-pened. Never did. Well, some did, up until where Darrell Drummon says, "That's no kind of sex ed stimulation." And because Mr. Ralph has Darrell in the dorms and is tired of his classroom stealth disruptance, such as pulling faces for giggles when Mr. Ralph's back is turned, his after-hours dorm-room evasions, his attention desire disorder, anyway, Mr. Ralph sends Darrell to Headmaster Langly for an adjustment beat down with moody, silent Soc for back-up on his pillar staring from behind. Those empty eye sockets of his pretty disturbing if you think about it.

It's just, I get carried away. And sometimes when I start a telling it becomes gospel. That's a Mr. Rouse word for what's real, which he uses in the biblical way, such as "every word there in the Good Book is gospel." So I figure, if that crazy bible shit can be true? And I've read some Old Testament craziness assigned for English because it's referential significant. Such as the wife of some dude who's killed by God is given to Onan, the brother of the dead guy, to make a baby, but while he's enjoying the shag he changes his mind. And here I'm wondering how he can even have a mind to change? He pulls out and spills on the grass. God kills him for that. Which makes me wonder what he thinks of condoms. Religionists say Onan got what he deserved because he was a masturbator. It gets worse. The father of the two dead sons killed by God (whose real name you can't say), he disses the babe, Tamar, by holding back the third son. Can't say I blame him. Her husbands all end up dead. So she dresses up a prostitute with veil and whatever seduction togs are vogue in her day, gets the Dad to shag her and has his kid. So if that's God's plan, I mean, mass masturbation is pretty tame compared. And I'm thinking, to make a believer of Mr. Rouse, the sightless bros will have to all fall off a cliff. But, yeah, never happened.

Also, Mr. Ralph, he's a pretty cool dude for a teacher, but not so casual as to go tribal with the bros, and if my classmates are, it's the digital rituals they share and not much else. The real climax to this story will not be so orchestrated as my classroom imaginings and not so brotherly. It's a mess, really, the bro drama. There will be no hipster counter-culture proclamation to be made off this climax, but there will be song lyrics to go with the action and bro hoes partying down in spiked hair with frosted tips and kegger laughter. This will all be just ugly, mostly, and but at least more real than imagined even though undocumented digitally because there will be only one brief text, my iPhone battery gone dead soon after me. And this will be more real because, well, words spoken in real time.

△

To BEGIN AGAIN – Ardan must think Chen the most presentable. Tells him to book a room for us and the ladies for the night because he's "going on a rush," is what he says, "until the last dime's played out." He says Chen must do so before the Jersey mayor's convention spillover takes all the rooms. My curious squint at this bit of reasoning finds its answer in a bluster of loud voices from above. Pin-striped card players can be seen greeted at a red door by a bouncer Ardan points to that lights Chen's smile by degrees such as a rheostat boost from which I see his career plans. It's a politician's smile that says join me and both our futures will rise, which places me back at the Hotchkiss boat house where Mrs. V told of the chest of gold in Thoreau's pond that sometimes floats up. Chen's eyes, dark crescents such as two boats on an Egyptian river, they look to the future with expectations of hooking that chest of gold.

As Chen goes to book a room, Ardan leads me to "railbird" the games of poker, which is us leaning in from the sideline railings sifting the field of green-felt tables for "tells," which Ardan says is a player's unintentional movements that give away his hand. The only thing I see is a room of mostly bland MIT grad students looking to bankroll spring break. I tell him so. But he's not listening. Ardan's making mental notes of the smallest gestures from a micro stretch to a scratch to a hesitation or a small aggression and assigning these tells to an outlay of cards and attendant results.

Ardan says winning is winning. There's no wrong way. Which is what the Dad would say, but, I mean, surveillance intel? I look again more closely at Ardan's shabby suit and dingy cap, his long dirt-encrusted fingernails and know that for him winning is not just about the money. He says he's going to start here with these donks and bankroll a seat behind the red door upstairs where the real money floats. Once again, Thoreau's chest of gold. He says there's no one here among these clean-shaved baby faces that's from here, no one recognizable to anyone but next-of-kin and that's a good thing: no repercussion fallout from his sharking. He looks for the chips leaders, places an arm around my shoulder, and for an old dude squeezes hard. Places his whiskery face to my ear. A ghost of cologne soured days ago waters my eyes. He pinches my cheek, says, "Yes, all right, maybe so, jejune college kids, but we can't be too dismissive. There's a nuance, a subtlety to what's happening here." I make a shrug as in sure, guess so, but mostly to get his arm off my shoulder.

"That kid under the white baseball cap with sunglasses bluff inducer ... round face and goatee in a perpetual frown ... he thinks he's giving nothing away. But he's giving it all away. Do you agree?"

What I see is a numbers nerd that keeps the stats on turf warriors only for Fantasy Sports, no beach tan, no babes or psychedelics and who stays up all night in his dorm room with online betting. He's trying his hardest to hide the excitement that wants to pour out from him because he's finally IRL (in real life) making the cards talk. And if they did, he thinks they'd say 'Word up!' But if he ever spoke his mind truly, he'd say "Friend me. Please, friend me!" because no amount of bragcast selfies posted of him at this gaming table is going to generate the Facebook likes he needs to balance a life. But all I say is "Yes, the dude's a pod."

For this I get another cheek pinch. "The advertising is more quiet than I expected from this crowd," he says, "but to a brick and mortar player like myself... an easy tell. These kids started online. Most do now. That one sitting alongside white cap, the one in a green T-shirt, red hair cut short, close trimmed beard, he's the table bully. See his no-nonsense stare meant to intimidate? That big stack of chips says the money doesn't own me. But it does. See the little tug he gives his right sleeve with his left hand every time he's unsure?

"Next to him the Eastern Mountain pullover, wire-rimmed glasses and a rosy hue despite looking sleepless for days, he's the speech player. The chatter he talks, it's called coffee housing. He does this to distract, so he won't give away his hand. He'll call for the floorman every ten minutes. Order a refill, challenge an angle of play that's borderline ethical but still allowed. He'll make the hero call more than anyone. That's calling even with a weak hand, factoring the prevalent bluff. He thinks it's working. It's not. His voice modulated opposite from his true emotion. Real sophisticated that one. Jeeze.

"Maybe I'm wrong about the subtleties of this crowd. Those others in the game at the adult table, the black man in the blue hoodie with the yellow T-shirt and, of course, sunglasses, he's the lag, loose and aggressive. And the Mediterranean wearing his cap backwards, he's the designated mark for this table. The one with the least experience. The raccoon. He thinks it's all about luck. He'll be down the river soon. Along with that spooky older guy, the Cuban with the big mustache and fishing hat. I know him. He's here when not serving rum at the Cuba Libre. He's the nit. He won't take any risks until the play is top range. He'll hold on only until the big play comes his way, and then it's a bust. Ah, very soon. Now in fact. He's been rivered. (The dude throws his hat on the floor, pushes back his chair and walks away.) His landlord won't be happy. And then there's me taking his seat! They'll take me for a grinder."

With that Ardan taps my shoulder farewell, takes Ignacio's cash to the window for chips, walks over to the man Ardan calls the brush. The dude that announces open seats, the one that now looks up at me as Ardan shares a truth nugget with him and seats Ardan after making introductions. The brush looks up at me again, smiles, makes that familiar frowny face sign with his finger, that which is really the zero-sum sign as explained to me earlier and then laughs, changes that to the okay sign. I don't know if that means I'm okay for bankrolling Ardan, or Ardan's a winner, or maybe it's the sign for asshole which could be either me or Ardan. I'm eager to re-enter a world that's easier to read because I have a hard time seeing Ardan as a winner. Until he takes a seat at the table. Then there's a kind of aura around him shines so white he could be radium.

△

So Ardan has handed me the rope to Sam, his bony carcass looped at my feet dreaming chipmunk pursuit. Tongue curled out a toothless mouth, paws twitching. I tie him to the rail and walk over to collect a room key. The desk clerk is a dandelion, weed skinny, stooped from the weight of puffy yellow hair. He assesses my presentation (greasy ripped clothes, juicy underarms, tangled hair) and turns his narrow back such as something behind has tapped the shoulder of his monogrammed body wrap of dark-blue polo tucked into black dress pants slick as oil. Only the belt is not hotel issue. It's Hermes leather I've seen in New York City on a rack of sale items at $600 the Dad seriously considered because of the name Herkimer. There's a big H buckle which in the case of this hotel clerk will be a titanium clasp that automatically locks if he comes within 500 feet of a school.

I see his face hating me reflected ghostly in the glass wall he faces. Behind that I see escalator chrome with belts of black rubber conveying the sweaty hands of ascending customers. His mouth is filled with sour, eyes pretending diversion, lit from above by a glass chandelier of twisty, artsy, orangey orgasmic explosion shards. His needle chin dips to his chest and sticks there. His eyes begin to bounce between my reflection and an electronic gadget he twiddles with cream-softened wacking-off fingers. He's waiting for me to exit, but I root there, lean in, work out a knot in my hair, scratch crotch and smell fingers, pull a face, say, "Dude! I'm here for a room."

This can't be what he wants to hear. But he seems now to have reassessed me as slot-machine zombie come away with bounty and wanting a lie-down with sex-to-order in one of their discretion rooms. His face makes quick adjustment from the sucked-in sour of repulsion to the toothy expanse of programmed greetings. When he turns he's a changed fem dude with hate tamped down and comfort words sticking to his tongue: "Yes ... how ... how may I help? Did you say a room? A room ... for one?

"I'm here with Ardan ... and Sam."

"Who? I don't think I know either" is what he says, raking manicured nails through the dyed, sprayed and sculpted petals of his blonde coiffed hair, the sides shaved to match the hipster, penciled-in stubble of his face. He's a poofter Kim Jong-un with a pharaoh complex, touched by the gods, enthroned here at the Borgata. The Mom would be discussing hair products with this fem dude.

"No, Sam's a dog. You don't know Ardan? All the service help does."

"I am decidedly not service help. I am the front desk manager. A room for two then?"

"No, there's five of us, and a dog."

"You'll want a suite. We don't accommodate pets."

"A suite? I don't know. What did Chen get? Why not pets?"

"You already have a room?"

"Yeah, I told you that. I'm here for a room."

"A room already booked?"

"Yeah, that's right. Aren't you listening? Chen, the dude with the Chinese eyes and the Denzel Washington fro clipped to a fade."

"Oh, him!"

This he says a little too excitement laden, which I wouldn't mind if he was of the quality to share Kerouac's bro affections, but he's not. He's a weed in a seedbed of posers. The migration wants no visitation layover in the land of angry rainbow nation, not if this hostile fem dude is its ambassador. And he thinks he is. If he would only wear a dress and stop the pretend he might feel better about things. I mean, he's no Wheaties box hero that will disappoint because Bruce wants to be Brucilla. I mean, chill!

I make a ceremony of retrieving envelope offered with name printed on, give a wink, offer a fist bump which he retreats from such as my hand carries a dose of unprotected sex. Maybe so. I should have it tested.

But I don't. Instead I go up to the room, fourteen floors, Sam sleeping in my arms. The room sneezy from cleaning products. Chen's backpack lies in a corner. I cozy Sam on the bed and look for the squatting room to squeeze out a tube of body waste off Chen's packaged meals at the Jersey oasis and bring the flavor of the place back to human. I breathe deep the quiet of the "sanctum sanctorum," which is the Dad's term for the porcelain retreat that makes a joke of the soul leaving the body that the Mom dislikes. Such as make a sneeze and bless the soul to retrieve it, such as take a dump and, well, you get the reference.

I notice a seat built into the shower. I take one of the leather sofa pillows in with me, turn on and adjust water to body temp, lean back into the pillow braced by the wall and check out! Best nap ever. No dreams. That's maybe why. I've created my own Zen moment of just being, not trying to be. I feel completely blissed out. The warm, wet massage of pulsing jets and the soft embrace of steam. Then to the sweet liquor in small bottles in the mini-fridg. I spill a couple down the throat and begin to notice a base beat supporting a dance rhythm that's been cranked up and jiggling things in the room. Wall art shaking, bathroom door handle rattling, phone at the bedside table vibrating, glossy pyramid cardboard signage adverting specials at the dining and gambling tables skating down the furniture varnish. I tap out the beat. At least 110 bpm and sounds Aerosmith, which will mean olden farts pretending youth in some obscene hydraulic display of dancing limbs. With all this seismic action, must be next door.

A glance down the hallway and, oh yeah. There's a door revolving balding dudes with girlies attached stepping in and out, and Steve Tyler's thinning voice stretching apart the cords that'll need gel injections later in expand-a-career therapy. Those smiling, shit-faced suits, a spillover of Jersey politicians Ardan seeks to fleece and Chen wants to join. There's no bouncer so I step in behind one of the poodle clipped rent-a-girls that doesn't seem already snatched and try to look connected to her, holding the leash, but of course it looks more her towing me along. My dirty clothes stiff as canvas don't make for suave. She has behind her shimmery, clingy dress a rope of long hair braided and swinging that I have taken hold of on my way in. She doesn't feel the tug until that patch of hair pulls away from the topknot she has mounded as the fakery source of the cascading Rapunzel. She feels behind the missing cord, finds me there staring at that snaky coil limp in my right hand and swings a purse in a wide arch into my nose. Instant blood burst. Then two screams (hers and mine) and one of those freeze-frame moments, all except Aerosmith who wouldn't stop even if the San Andreas was their fault. Attendee dudes pause mid-bragadouche to gawk and I see Chen among them. And I'm ten-years old again.

There's a movie screen in front of me absorbing a majority of my five senses because a blue-faced alien diva sings and moves her eight-feet tall body dancing in a blue rubber dress, tentacles swaying both sides of her horned head reaching to her knees. She's all forehead with long pointy fingers moving through the air such as pushing the notes up to Heaven. She's sad, disappointed in humanity. Has the face of Frankenstein's bride but still hella sexy. It's a sci-fi flick with kickass grandpa Bruce Willis that I remember. Maybe it's the first time I bond with an alien. The first time I begin to think aliens have soul.

And so I'm back in real time. There's Chen trending in his A&F togs linked by the arm to a hotty with neon blue hair, blue stockings, blue eye shadow and a fuzzy blue dress. A blue angora bunny. He's surrounded by those balding dark suits. One still blabbering says, "Yes, an alternative Obama, every minority evident in one, a self-made man, no university brainwashing, which in our remake will... what? Chen, are you listening?" Chen looks at me a sec but then right through me such as owes nothing more to the yellow cab. I see he has found his collective, of which I have no part. So I drop the hairpiece and push out the door. Working-girl obscenities grease my exit.

△

I BOUNCE THE HALL, drop down an elevator that defies its own name. The gods of elevation gift a useful cliché to which Mr. Rouse would add an ibid and religion orthodoxy that suggests whatever goes down can not be expected to go back up. The Lemmings will not be happy to know this. Then back to Ardan who has collapsed the table with a rush win. He's on the ride up. Guess that disproves the Rouse theory. Most players have quietly departed, bruised egos behind pretend smiles. The "nit" MIT players that drifted to his table because Ardan's stack had grown seductively, they fume and gust their violated idiocracy of presumed untouchability, and so must now go online for a cleansing game of whack-a-mole. Ardan rises from his chair, motions me to follow. I tell him, "You must be pretty psyched to of pulled that off."

He says back, "Ah, well, yes, but so far, fairly routine. The real challenge lies behind the red door."

I tell him of the angry fem dude that made an inhospitable scene of hotel accommodation.

He says, "Wouldn't you be mad if you had to romance that thing?" And here Ardan makes the okay sign with his fingers, which I don't get, because probably I'm meant to take this to mean asshole. Or maybe he's saying it's okay to be gay. These hand signs are driving me crazy!

"For sure," I say. "I get it."

"Do you? Do you really?" And he gives me one of those looks that knows I'm full of shit, says, "Ah, I see. You've noted the finger signs."

"What signs?"

"Hey, kid, you think I don't see the recognition gestures that attend my casino appearances? All well deserved. I won't mask a truth."

I give a pretend confused, hurt look that mostly works firewall on the Mom when I'm caught at something sneaky and about to be tongue-lashed for it, then say, "Look, Ardan, I'm in a between place. Not sure what's sense and what's nonsense anymore. When I was a kid, I leaned Zed's way of thinking our planet needs rescuing from invasion aliens. But ... they probably don't exist. Except that I'm beginning to think I may have let one get past that used the yellow cab to advance a political career."

"An alienist are you?"

"I'm Earthling."

He laughs, says, "An alienist is a psychologist. One that makes a study of crazies. Roswell conspiracy theorists by example."

"There it is again!"

"What?"

"Slippery words. Slippery finger signs. Slippery aliens. Nothing's solid."

"Yes, well, I suppose I take your meaning. Where's Sam?"

"Up in the room. Sleeping on the bed."

"Good. Let's grow your investment. Walk me to the red door."

He pinches my cheek. Takes my elbow, leads me away to bank his chips for cash. What would Doctor Westover, the family shrink, say about this guy? About me? Ardan will, I'm sure, be an absent father replacement with me all ADHD on disobedience enactment and goals avoidance. This doesn't help my self-confidence. I tell Ardan, "I don't think I have the right threads. Or at least not enough of them untorn and clean. If you know what I mean."

"Yes. By contrast I will shine with authority and expectations."

"Glad I can help."

We take the escalator one floor up where the red-door card game caters to those living the placebo life. Ardan hasn't been so well protected. I guess maybe I have but for the migration, which has begun to amp up the status reducers. As we get close we hear chatter from inside, the door held a crack open by a Neanderthal breathing deep, peeking out to see trouble before it knocks. I'm guessing we qualify because the giant dude steps into the hallway, closes the door entirely, crosses arms in a Wrestle Mania photo op while awaiting the password. Ardan has it in his two hands. The first goes to the hulk who counts every bill before pocketing the wad. The second hand produces so much cash wilting off the stem of his palm I'm thinking cabbage salad. This is also taken by the large dude but not pocketed who says, "Name?"

"Tell His Honor it's Ardan," says Ardan.

"Wait here." He closes the door. I raise eyebrows at Ardan. He shrugs away the transaction as regulation pay-to-play. He says the money and his name are credentials enough.

The door opens again pushed by a boiler sized black man in a wife-beater T-shirt, a snake head tattooed onto the back of one hand, but with five yellow eyes gleaming, one on each knuckle that say ouch, the squiggly diamond pattern length of it riding arm to elbow, apparent body guard to the decider who motions to open the door more. We step inside walls so gleaming white the room lacks dimension. Could be a closet. Could be the A-City Convention Center. Add to that the ballast hum and buzz of ceiling fluorescence somewhere above a cloud of cigarette smoke. A large table of dark wood floats in the center, the top lacquered over so many times it has the depth of water. His Honor looks to his reflection in the table, adjusts eyeglasses on a mushroom nose that has grown into the black plastic frames such as old tree roots that embrace outcrop rock. He takes a long think dark with suspicion, red tie loosed, knot pushed several buttons down his tidy white dress shirt. Skin an unhealthy gray, which belongs to the wheezing of his lungs, hair sparse and staticy. Then a full-on smile, perfect teeth, and him saying, "Ardan. It is you. Good to see you still in the game."

Ardan says, "Your Honor." Looks around says, "Councilman. Gentlemen."

There's discussion to be had. Ardan pulls me away outside the room, into the hall, tells me the man in the red tie is no kind of titled dude but that he's been for years the one likely to cleanly navigate the next round of indictments. The current mayor is still missing. The City Council President, Big Mac sized, coffee black with coffee-stained, cigarette-stained, prominent rodenture topping the underlip, he's sitting opposite His Honor other end of the table, flicking cigarette ash into the brass ashtray of a naked chick on her back, legs open, supporting a glass bowl for ash. Very enlightened.

Anyway, the City Council President awaits trial for ambushing a rival, a Baptist minister shtupping a prostitute spliced into a live-feed internet video. Both will acquire more fame than punishment, says Ardan. That's how A-City treats political criminals. They're too much part of the system not to benefit from crime. Four of the last eight mayors have been arrested for corruption and have retired off the dividends. Ardan says he knew "His Honor" would be behind the red door or he wouldn't have bothered. His Honor knows Ardan from the Shylock he worked for and from his days running numbers for a 70s Jersey mob boss he won't name. His Honor will vouch for him. Ardan tells me he has a rep as an earner for the organization. He says politicians are useless references because only briefly influential, soon disgraced. Bodyguards come mostly from Paramus so are clueless of Ardan's connections and history. It takes His Honor to apprise the table of Ardan's worth beyond the buy-in cash.

Ardan says it'll be awhile. They're playing out the hand. He leads me to a red leather sofa top of the escalator between two elevator doors. We sit. He looks at me long, says nothing but I see the years fall away from him as he drifts into his past. He tells of a marriage gone bad and more of his early time in A-City. Some of which I have already told. As he ends the story, one of the MIT nits drifts past, gives Ardan the stink eye with earbuds throbbing so loud we can hear the lyrics telling him to pull out his gold teeth and roll them like dice. It's an old song but a good one, says Ardan as he steps in behind the red door with theme song fading down the hall.

What I find out later in the glowing wreckage of Ardan's self-detonation is he wins big at first, starts to drink, gets careless and loses everything. He pushes because feeling dizzy, knows his aggression factor at the table has gone rogue but wants to end quick with a big win. Ignacio will not be pleased.

△

So to find Mrs. V, I walk a concourse of Borgata boutiques and eateries, below which glams in jewel brighteners an indoor pool of aqua with jungle fronds growing beside a wall of floor-to-ceiling glass overlooking the parking lot. The fronds drip from a misting ceiling spray making a tropical canopy through which the sun filters. A mismatched couple below is loving it up. It's Mrs. Robinson and her neighbor's teenage son. He's so unsure what he's doing, won't pounce the fuck-me lounge pose, which is one foot padding the surface of the pool water, arms back of her head exposing her rounds but mostly her angles. He's a better fit for a Nintendo ad. She's a looker, smooth, well-tanned, long wet hair, a nice face, but thin all over, an anorexic cougar. He'll bruise his bones clamping onto that.

I begin to wonder is it too obvious the same with me and Mrs.

V? Well, all but except the anorexia. Chen thought she was my mother. I don't see it, really. I mean, there's a vibe easy to read, right? Rip got it. I need a Mrs. V assurance hug.

I quicken my pace past arcade game machines surrounded by Greek columns of stone, a space more mausoleum than Greek temple, or maybe the home of Vlad the Impaler. Then a steak house of purple décor with art house lighting of shattered gold metal circles tangled, suspended from the ceiling, moving together, chiming, emitting roving beacon light from the shard ends. Reminds me of the mobile of bone on the porch of Big-D and Little-G. Makes you wonder what their steaks are made of. Then slot machines that can be heard long before seen imbedded in another embrace of Greek columns much less elaborate because no carving at the top. Soon farther down the hall a life-size poster advert for Miss Miranda's fan show, a beautiful slinky babe naked but for nipple pasties, hiding her blush behind a fan of pink feathers. This beside a set of black leather doors with massive chrome globe handles that make me think only the well-hung are welcome here.

Then I hear in the distance a DJ blend of EDM that makes me think Deadmau5 will be banging his outsized rodent head to his unique electro house. He's a DJ Bradley Turcotte introduced me to, I mean personally, at a show in Philly where he took me and some others of the lax bros as a birthday gift to himself. The place was banging! I mean, there's Deadmau5 rubbing the remix nobs with passion, elaborate loops patched into new patterns, the lights strobing so bad you're not sure if at times there's anyone there with you, then an entire room of dancers exploding all around, then gone again, and up on stage that huge mouse head swaying with the tunes. I was knocked senseless by it, really.

So the club I go into, it's rocking with tunes. Stepping in, I get the best feeling. This is not a raver's destination but it's classy and low-keyed with the bass throwing out a force field of sound that needs Elvis' pelvis to break through. There's no one here but two girls dancing and the DJ spinning, the girls stepping in and out of the light, then back into the light and it's her, Mrs. V, and I just know she and me are going to boogie down, reboot the migration romance.

Or maybe not. Here's a roadblock. Mrs. V is behind grinding Stacy. Their hips in synch clockwise then the other way, Stacy bending back her head for deep kisses. Mrs. V's hands weaving in the air some kind of Bollywood flutter then down on Stacy's hips twisting in rhythm to the DJ's blend of beat and words from Jet and Fountains of Wayne. The DJ is beatmixing with kick drums lined up, the two bands together making one song of two. The words sung that I hear most searing say Stacy's mom has it going on. Waited a long time for Stacy's mom the song says. Then the DJ spins back a repeat of the Stacy's mom tribute. Then a rip guitar and slamming drums from Jet. Then a pause. Then Jet singing out a question of whether or not the girl can be scored. The DJ leers down at the girls. He must be thinking Stacy has the hots for her own mom. I'm pretty grossed out by it all.

How is this fair? I didn't see this coming. I mean, Stacy and Mrs. V? What are the signs? And I'm at first really freaked, but then I'm thinking, this is kinda sexy. Until Mrs. V sees me amazed but willing, shakes her head no as in stay away, then goes down for a snorkel, and yes, okay, you might think I have kissues. But what I realize ... Mrs. V is the one looking for a virgin. One from her own tribe.

The only thing I can think to do is return to the red door. Find Ardan. But that goes to hell when I turn a corner and crash into the Dad. He's pissed, aggressive, out of breath, dressed unusually casual, a baseball cap pulled low. Must be so he won't be a face on the casino's security cameras. Is this a kidnapping? He takes me by the arm, leads me outside for a talk. We share a spittle bath under the entrance portico. The old Cuban sweeping around curbside pretends to look away, enjoying my embarrassment.

The Dad says with the scrub-down animatronic force of a brillo pad, "Marvin! What the hell you doing here? You're supposed to be in school. What the hell!"

"Dad, you don't pour my cereal anymore!"

"What?"

"You're not the boss of me. How did you find me?"

"From your habit of rolling through toll booths. God damn, Marvin! Did you think that wouldn't catch up with you? Those booths have cameras. Your plates, from a stolen car? Nice move. They have a Sapperstown address."

We're making heads turn. The Dad snags me by the arm, fingers sharp as claws, leads me farther down the sidewalk and deeper into the parking lot away from the voyeuristics eyeballing us and just outside the pool window. We have become no better than poolside exhibitchionist Mrs. Robinson sucking a tropical drink, raking a possession hand through the young dude's hair. The Dad disappears inside a silent stare at this scene, shakes it off, then back at me says, "What are you doing with that married woman?"

"She's not the wife to Eliot Spitzer."

"Meaning what?"

"No paparazzi. What do you care?" is what I say back in like total Dickenese conversation patter, such as here's me out on the streets lifting wallets getting the what's what from snaggletooth Fagan that wants me to give him the dough. But I'm not giving any.

"Look, Marvin," the Dad says, face red with emotion, "you need to take responsibility for your actions. I can't cover for you anymore."

"What cover? There's been a shit storm raining on my head. Or maybe you mean like you covered for Sherman?"

"That's not fair."

I think I see tears pooling in his eyes. I'm not used to emotion pouring out from this hard shell of Detroit engineering. I'm uncomfortable and so less on the defense, more ready to explain, so I say, "Okay, look. Let's say I'm out here logging experience for a better college app essay is all. I mean, better torque stresses to navigate than a Sid Meier action fantasy."

"You're already in college."

"I am?"

"Yes! If you'd answer a text, you'd know. You mom pulled strings, got you into Wesleyan."

"Oh, good. My future is secure."

Two shiny gray vans brake near, disgorge a load of hormone expanded chicks bursting seams of the latest gorilla wear, magnetic signage with IFBB muscle building competition on the van doors. Masculine girlies just off a stint curling in the squat rack, twenty plates a rep. Still wearing the sweat briny headbands. We've become immersed in a throng of comic book she-Hulks. Cool! I make eye contact, say, "So, like, where's the Terminator?" At least the giggles are female.

The Dad shakes his head, says, "You know, Marvin, talking to you is like..., it's like you're a satellite somewhere out there beside Pluto."

"Pluto's not even a planet anymore, just a rock. But so you know, rocks have their uses. I mean, what you don't see, I'm out here turning over rocks. That's what I'm doing if you want to know. And maybe I'm not finding much, but I'm looking, and that is progress, Dad."

"Jesus. Marvin! What a smart mouth. Look, drop the married woman. Return the yellow cab. I'll pay for the miles. Or your mom will. Make a future for yourself besides a homeless jail breaker. Or, maybe better, just go home. Don't you want to visit your high school buddies? Or an old girlfriend?"

"You mean Heidi? (he scowls). And the bros you speak of, they're all in college studying to be baristas."

He opens his mouth to speak but hesitates. Decides not. And that says it all.

△

NEITHER ONE OF US is convinced. The Dad hands me a debit card for Shell gasoline and a set of car keys, points to a corner of the parking lot, says, "Press the locator button. It's a black Cherokee. Please, Marvin, if you won't go home, go back to school."

I say, "A car at school? I'm not allowed," knowing I could be with the right pull.

He says, "It's been worked out with the Headmaster. Go back. He'll find a place off campus to park the car. Show up for exams. Don't get kicked out! Okay? You're in college, Marvin. The car is your graduation gift. Just, please, graduate."

"Okay. Sure," I say back, "Why not," take the keys and ignore his forgiveness hug. He walks away. So what to do with the yellow cab? The heartbeat of America becomes what, swag? Should I just take the Jeep and make an escape with Mrs. V on a better set of wheels? Maybe leave Stacy off at a roadside rest stop for tricks?

Those are the questions most roadworthy that never find an answer because Ignacio and two affiliate thugs are laying for me inside the Borgata. The old Cuban has pointed me out. He raps on the window with his broom handle, gives Ignacio the fingerpoint my direction as I walk into the lobby.

Two thugs doing their best Lil Wayne and T-Pain collaboration box me in, steer me into a fat leather sofa, bookend me there with Ignacio in a matching chair facing us, leaning in. He says, "Look, Ese, I yam not so happy wich you. You know, right? I don't want for you zotzed. I only want stash. I don't care you ganked the hack. But the mazuma, the mesca, they come to me."

I go paralyzed on the outside while my insides roil options.

He says, "These trouble boys, they belong kingpin want stash more. Break you bones. You don want that."

I tell him the weed is still in the cab, the cab is in the parking lot, you can't miss it, and Ardan has the money. See him.

"Who dis punk?"

When I tell Ignacio Ardan's a gambler, he loses it. Shouts at the two thugs in Spanish a reaction to what I've said then goes off on a spiel of insult Spanish meant to take the skin off me, eyes venomous, hands pounding knees. I'm taken up escalator to the red door. I knock and ask politely for Ardan. When the door opens, one of Ignacio's thugs, the big one, pulls the Neanderthal door stopper out by his hair, punches him once in the face, then pushes him inside the room as we follow, closes the door and places a gun to his neck, makes him kneel on the floor hands back of his head. Then Ignacio says, "Which one Ardan?" No one wants to say. One of the two professional skirts screams. The other holds a hand over that screaming mouth, places a shush finger over her own. Ardan stands up. Ignacio says he wants the money. His money. Ardan tries to explain what happened, why he went bust. He says, "I found a pair of kings. I pushed it all in. He called pretty quick and then I knew he had aces and I was in trouble."

Ignacio's Spanish reignites. The spare thug pushes me to the floor then shouts from his metal grill tooth modification a stand-down warning to the bodyguard looming in a corner with the snake tattoo and genie arms folded, every muscle and every knot of his cornrows tense with reaction plans, likely to engage. Ignacio comes at Ardan with a knife. Ardan collapses. The City Councilman shows no emotion whatever. He places his cards down face-up on the table, says he's "all in," looks down at Ardan breathing heavily on the floor, looks sideways at Ignacio says, "My man, you ain't in command here. You just think you is. You ain't come to Disneyfied Vegas. This is Jersey. You know who this is, this man here (nodding to His Honor), this be the man to float your bones in the salt marshes. I suggest you book a private plane fast and make your way gone to your wickiup before he gets a bead on you. You feel me?"

Ignacio isn't sure what to feel. But he knows he's lost the edge. Everyone at the table beams proud to be an associate of His Honor, all but Ardan who is coughing, lying on the floor still, one of the chippies kneeling beside him rubbing his forehead.

Ignacio says, "I never touch wid chiv. You remember dis." And gives a nod to his thug bros to take the money off the table (this is a cash game, remember, no chips). The trouble boy beside me watching all this same as me but also peeking out the door, he sees the Dad running up the escalator with police and a dude in a suit with one hand across his chest pulling at a holstered gun.

The thug at the door says, "Ignacio! Doce bulls. Uno shamus."

All three bust out the red door and run down the up escalator because the Dad and his posse scale the down stairs less crowded with tourists. Those obstacles being pushed aside shout objections that add to the chaos. The Dad in jean jacket, black skinny jeans and Nike cap, the po-po in black uniform, shamus dude doing his best Dark Knight in sunglasses and elegant sharkskin suit with lapels up, Ignatio's sweaty panicky face making Heath Ledger's Joker look almost sane, his trouble boys pulling up their baggie pants, bling jangling and do-rags flapping. Everyone with mouths distorted snarking nonsense words, hands spazzing with guns pointed here and there that don't go off but would have if only one had. Legs and backs twisting from ducking bullets never fired. It's what Taggert said: in the land of Oz, the monkeys be flying tonight!

When the Dad and his posse ascend the auto-stairs, they can only watch as Ignacio flames out the front door. Soon a 911 response adds two ambulance jockeys gone to Ardan with a gurney and canned air. He's taken outside, still breathing, just, the sun rising making a red sky. The driver is told by the old Cuban to see hotel management. "Muy importante," he says. As the driver walks back into the lobby, a crew of homeless seep out from the bushes, from behind parked cars, surround the ambulance, snatch Ardan with the remaining EMT scared shitless to interfere. They place him in a grocery cart cushioned with blankets and wheel sharply away, Ardan wheezing his last words, "I found a pair of Kings ... pushed it all in ... I was on a rush ... in the zone, it was ... beautiful ..." (then coughing and silence).

The Dad's posse, out deep at the edges of the parking lot, still looking for Ignacio, they miss entirely the Ardan abduction, but that's okay, because he's dead now anyway and being taken to under the pier for the Viking funeral that I told you of.

I run back into the Borgata to find Mrs. V but get sidelined by the Dad who grabs my arm again, says, "Don't bother! She's on her way to the bus station. Going back home to work things out with her husband."

"No, she can't!"

"She needs to try," says the Dad in his I-know-better voice.

I give him the look that says he's no expert on this when the elevator dings ending conversation, its door opening slowmo with symphonic flourish from inside that makes all other elevator muzak anemic sounding: it's Coldplay's synthesizer then fuzzbox distortion and a voice asking why his lover left him. Then piano, then a guitar crush, such as what steps out will be the X Factor's nominee of best new act. But what comes out is the old Cuban with Sam in his arms, Ardan's dog. He walks over to us, says, "Do you wish to say to Ardan your goodbye?" I tell him yes, definitely, and give the Dad a look that says do this for me. His eye roll tells me I have depleted his resistance. So both me and the Dad attend Ardan's funeral.

It's, like, surreal. I mean, if you look close at the features of this scene, take them one at a time, it maybe makes sense. The tattered clothes and surrendered dignity of the homeless. Sex for rent on a cigarette break from the back alleys off x-rated Pacific Ave., making relevant the town's motto that says "always turned on." The spiffy suits with stiff poses and stabbing eyes of His Honor's mob bros. And bacon thin drugsters gripping their privates and panning for handouts even now. Olden A-City has gathered under the pier. Altogether, this show is more costume fantasy than the senior prom.

From among Ardan's business connections I meet the landlord that follows beside me and the Dad all the way to the water while telling Ardan's history, most of which I have already told you. He splits off to join other funeral attendees gathered beachside and blends with the one-time mob connections that lived off the numbers games Ardan helped rig back in the days that are well represented by His Honor and members of the old crew with alligator skin and hair loss but that still look threatening and the soon-to-be-arrested Councilman.

The Dad begins to regret this little togetherness session under the pier, maybe because, for once, he's not the one in control. He's off balance and nervous. He says with the voice of concern, "This is maybe something we don't need to see, Marvin."

"Why? It's no worse than Sherman's funeral."

"This is no funeral. Look around. It's a carnival."

"I'll take that over what happened to Sherman. I mean, all you get from Iraq is ashes to bury? A square of ground at Arlington? And then not even a rifle volley, no uniforms saluting, no flag folding, nothing! Just you and me and a backhoe. It's like ... Sherman didn't matter. But look around! Ardan mattered."

Under the pier Ardan is taken out from the grocery cart by an honor guard of retired mobsters and carried to the water beside an aluminum rowboat filled with flattened cardboard and driftwood. Ardan is placed on top. One of the homeless, broad shoulders in a knee-length army coat, long gray beard with the physical bulk and presence of Conan the Barbarian, he brings over a can of barbecue lighter fluid. He addresses the assembled, the sky, says, "Per Ardan's request." Then pours lighter fluid over the body and cardboard and driftwood. Two others in suits and nice shoes, with a nod from His Honor, they remove jackets so you see the gun holsters under their arms, push the boat out into the surf, water to their thighs. One pulls out a silver lighter, flicks it open, turns the wheel and tosses it onto Ardan. Instant flash. Moans from the assembled.

His Honor walks over to the edge of the surf, makes the sign of the cross, but then looks to where the bodyguard with snake tattoo is pointing, off to the right where the pilings of the pier taper into salt water. And I can see, only just, what I would have mistook for trash, one body floating, no, make that two, maybe three. All face down. Ignacio won't be needing his yellow cab.

$$\triangle$$

THE VIKING FUNERAL DOESN'T END WELL. Which is what you'd expect. I mean, overall, it's the most strange funeral ever. So the Dad is right about that. With all the Italian casting of fading stars, their distortion faces, the hardware they're packing, the good guys in black, the down-and-outer townies, the over-the top staging, if this was a movie, it'd be a spaghetti western. I really don't see where the Vikings come in. And Ardan was Irish. Right? But, whatever.

So, this is how it ends. The boat returns to the beach pushed back by waves from which some of the homeless, Conan's orders, shove the boat out again, which comes back in again. One dude gets too close, sets his arms on fire. He's too freaked to know to dump them in the surf. One of the other homeless dudes pushes him over into the water to out the flame. Another brings Ardan's dog Sam over to the boat. He's squealing and kicking, the most life I've seen from him at the final moment of his life, because this dude is intent on throwing Sam onto the barbecue. I'm sure the ASPCA has ruled on this gruesome ritual of a Viking ceremony. But no matter. Conan nixes it. And so the diminished dude with the correction stigma, he comes back to the beach with Sam from which His Honor takes the lead in a rescue. I'm grateful to him for that.

And I'm finally out of there, blending in a mix of homeless dressed such as me in hoodies and ripped pants. I've skipped out on the Dad who walked over to view the bodies in the surf under the pier. Then he's looking around but can't find me. I'm on the boardwalk, disoriented, looking for the bus station and Mrs. V. I see only just a dark casino tower with TRUMP in red that looks of fingernail polish on a giant black finger pointing insult at the sky. Or maybe it's the Tower of Mordor. Seagulls and pigeons are everywhere in the sky and on the ground pecking at litter. Police on the boardwalk look at me as their next hassle task. I ask for directions to the bus station. Two walk away, but a third gives me a series of turns I can't remember. The others of the funeral, the homeless and criminal, have by now bleached back into the debris stains they left behind.

I take a back alley off the boardwalk that feels to me a short cut to the bus station because of the direction the one officer pointed. Then a pimp who thinks I'm homeless pulls a knife to get me gone. I laugh but the pimp is serious, his girlies lined up scowling. I wander off, trash everywhere, the homeless becoming more aggressive, hands out even to me that looks as bad off as them, voices not so much begging as threatening. Then a lesser brand of hookers so programmed they could be sexbots, and some sketchy, trans-genders desperate and angry, right out of Rocky Horror Picture Show.

I find two of Ignacio's big bills left over deep in my pocket and begin to think maybe I should hire a cab. I throw one into a change machine near a liquor store and get counterfeit. I mean, Howard Stern on a twenty? I laugh, toss it all in the air. Even the beggars know to avoid anything that's been changed in that machine. I walk circles around to avoid street life, try to keep TRUMP to my left so as not to walk my same footsteps. This is not working. But then, finally, something familiar: the Borgata rising on the horizon.

So I decide, what the hell. I have two cars waiting for me. And back on the road is where I'll find Mrs. V. I'm sure of it.

As I walk toward that comma in the distance, the highway bridges become familiar, although under one I find families sleeping in cars. A caravan of evicted, mostly fatherless, jobless families. Kids with eyes so vacant they could be zombies. Moms with sleeping bags draped over shoulders heating tin cans on Bunsen burners. The saddest thing I've ever seen. Think of all your glitzy, sexy, speedy, wonky, music-filled car commercials and ask yourself: Is this where the road ends?

When back to the Borgata parking lot, I decide to take the Dad's ride rather than the yellow cab, so to increase the stealth quotient. When I press the locator button the Cherokee sings out. I find myself behind the wheel of a power machine primed to eat asphalt. Major plus: it has a cell phone charger. I can now contact the bros. But as I reconnect, so much back log of digital chatter. Don't know I'll ever get caught up. I decide to take the long way back to Poncy Prep. It's still vacation anyway, a few days more. I find myself itching to penetrate the Pine Barrens.

△

I'M SOON ON THE HIGHWAY north to the Barrens, looking for the road sign I passed on the interstate twice, going north out from A-City and coming back. Once again that exit pulled at the wheels of Ignacio's cab. Or maybe just their rotation made an electric field vector increasing the attraction levels. What makes attraction? Does it come from inside or outside us? One of those times I passed by the Barrens, Limbaugh was recruiting hate-mongers on the radio. I was repelled. Now I'm scrolling the iPhone to find what diversion trivia Bradley sent. This is an attraction. But I'm repelled by and bypassing parental scolds and conditional congrats from Wesleyan College directing me to multiple texts from different concerns at the school: financial aid and the lax coach and even my dorm residence with the tagline "Your roommate wants a shout-out!" I mean, all very user comfy because inducing a "don't-worry-we'll-take- charge" numbness.

Night crashes hard with torrents of rain. The Jeep cruises through battleship steady. No worries. I'll get where I want in this crate. But as I turn off the interstate at the Pine Barrens exit ramp, this time using the E-Z pass lane the Jeep has come equipped to accommodate, I drift into a flat wetlands of small scrub pine. For some reason I want badly to drill deeper into the heart of this place, analyze the attraction dynamics. It's more than Big Foot is what I'm thinking. Rain becomes hail, small at first then large enough to clatter the Jeep's steel plates and send me to shelter under a growth of tall pine. That doesn't last long because limbs start coming down, one very near, and so I adjust to 4x4 to break a path through the ice balls. It's slippery going, and I slide around some, but there are no other cars on the road. No lights anywhere, no towns, houses, anything, but up ahead an old stone arch spanning the road that must once have carried the weight of trains.

I park under there awhile which at first totally creeps me out. In the headlights, a fog of otherworld swirls and light dancing, shadowy figures moving around, particles in the air more sub-stantial than rain drops or dew. I mean, I know fog comes from a collision of opposing temp conveyances. Sky heavy with ice meets warm ground sodden with rain. That kind of thing. But there's something different here. More different than I've felt before. Such as the mist is here to make peace between sky and earth. And I feel something in there welcoming me, recognizing I belong. I mean, how does it feel to belong? It feels good. It feels permanent. I've never felt this before. Even the bros are no substitute.

I stay beneath the stone underpass through the night. Switch off the lights, the engine, go to sleep with windows open, fog drifting in, embracing me, tapping playfully at my lungs as I breathe it in, tumbling around, tickling the bronchia. I'm also taking in the sounds of peepers, large animals cracking through the brush some-where near, then birdsong. No cars sounds. And maybe, faintly, people sounds?

I awake more hungry than ever. Like maybe it does take a "culi-nary synergy" to feed an "awakened spirit." That's what the Mom calls a substantial meal, a culinary synergy that she has labored over for the Dad and us twaddles. Awakened spirits is what she calls us after such a meal where belching and praising and yawning are most often expressed. But that was before she killed her own mom, in this case snuffed the spirit, and then simplified and over-cooked everything after that. Anyway, at this moment, I could eat tree bark, but decide to find a town or a roadside diner. Takes miles of emptiness to find anything. First landmark an old tree split in the middle filled with cement and inscribed "Ong's Hat 1830." Don't see a hat. I look. See only a run-down shack unoccupied such as maybe all the rest of the Pine Barrens and which explains to me the reason for the name "barren."

I drive farther through piles of slag from old mines, brick chim-neys of manufacture attached to nothing, foundations of what might have been a town but now a weed garden, and come to a diner I hope will open soon. No lights. No cars parked. But maybe I arrived before the cook and wait staff. Looks abandoned, but so does everything else in this place all misty and broke down. It's not long before a car pulls in, kind of odd because it first passed by slow, then brake lights in the mist, gnashing gears whining in reverse, backing into the lot. It's an old Ford Torino, once red, pretty much rusted but not from road salt. There's a difference. More from salt air is what it looks. Some of the color still on the sides but hood and roof and trunk, all those places night air settles, they're a ghostly hue of rust and oxidized paint. But what steps out from the car amazes me more. It's a hippie while I'm expecting redneck.

So I'm sitting on the stairs, and this dude, maybe in his 30s, he has shoulder-length hair, light brown and wavy, a sparse beard, black sweat pants, sandals with socks, a loose fitting cardigan Nordic sweater with T-shirt underneath, and black, tight-fitting gloves. Could be Lebowski. Anyway, this dude's face is open and curious of me but strangely out of focus. I rub my eyes, wait until he gets closer to see him better, stretch my legs to ease the effects of stomach trauma from extreme hunger. I rub my eyes again to erase the fatigue of a sleepless night and look again, but it doesn't help. He never does come entirely into focus. The whole place is swirly with mist, out of focus. But it feels good. Like maybe there's no reason to have to look too close. And everything has a soft glow such as light coming from somewhere inside, not from above.

He walks over to me, waves a hand and asks am I waiting for someone. I tell him no, just the people that own the diner. I'm hungry.

He says it will be a while.

I have no idea what time it is. The Jeep has a digital clock radio but for some reason it isn't functioning. I get out my iPhone and open it to check the time and my degree of connectivity, but not only are there no bars of reception, which is no great surprise, the phone itself is dark and dead. I guess the phone charger in the Jeep isn't working either.

He looks at me sadly, says, disconnected?

I say yeah, temporarily, although for a long stretch not long ago.

He asks how that feels, to be disconnected?

I say, I don't know. Feels okay. I kept busy during the long stretch. No time to think about it. I ask does he have a cell phone, does he have reception?

He says never did embrace the digital alternative.

I tell him my name and ask his.

He says J.

I say, oh, as in J-A-Y?

He says, sure, if you want. Just call me J.

Then I ask what's up with the gloves?

He says, disfigured. An accident many years ago.

Oh, I say, sorry.

I'm more sorry, he says and we laugh.

He sits beside me, we shake hands. I'm afraid to squeeze too tight but he isn't. He has a grip such as connectivity for him is this. He smells of resin or camphor or something. Can't imagine he's been using shave cream because he doesn't shave. Whatever. Then we talk some about the Pine Barrens. He says he's been here a long time. Says he's never seen such changes as of late.

I ask what changes? This place seems deserted. What could change?

He says, the migration. I must have heard it last night in the trees.

I say yeah, I guess. Deer? Bear? How does he know where I was last night is what I'm thinking.

He says no, Big Foot.

Yeah, right. You're playing me for a tourist, I say with senses opening and palpitations of the heart muscle.

Big Foot, he says again. Returning home from the northwest. The locals are freaked. Encounters have increased.

Oh, right, I say, could they be aliens? You believe in aliens?

He says, no. There's no aliens. Everything living and breathing is part of the design. Nothing alien out there. Big Foot especially.

Then I get it. Shit! His name is J? He's all invested in the spiritual directive. This guy thinks he's Jesus. So I ask, does he believe in God, have a personal relationship with him? Knowing the answer already and choking off a snicker.

No, he says. There's no God. Only the design.

Now I'm seriously confused. I ask what's the migration about?

He says, you haven't noticed? The hail, the eternal wet. Used to be the Barrens was about brush fires in the spring. Pineys setting fires to make charcoal. But there's so much rain now. No more snow in winter, just rain. And hail as you know. Scrub pines aren't growing but the larger trees are. There's a canopy that hasn't been here a long time. It's what Big Foot likes. Their west coast habitat is drying out, turning to desert, even the far north. So they're coming home.

Yeah, we've baked the Earth.

Yes, as you say. But all part of the design. California gets rain only when Hollywood shoots a night scene on city streets.

Are movies part of the design?

No. I just like movies. But doesn't it tell you something, the fact humans are making it less easy for their own survival?

Well, yeah, I guess. I mean we're stupid, if that's what you mean?

No, I mean it's time for Big Foot.

You really believe in this Big Foot thing?

It's not a thing. It's their time. They are the other swimbot of the gene pool from which humans emerged. They scattered west when their lands were taken by sawmills. There used to be a large growth of cedar. And then glasswork forges tapped the sugar sand, blast furnaces grabbed up the bog iron, big towers of fire everywhere ...

Wait. So, hot liquid glass, liquid iron ore. They're, like, really good conductors of electricity. And so, electromagnetism ...

What?

Physics lab, Lakeville High School. So, all that's here in the Barrens? I mean, that's a strong electric field. Could be screwing with the light here, and the mist. And probably more. Think Bermuda Triangle.

Yeah, I guess. But like I was saying, before all that Big Foot shared this habitat with the Lenape, a native tribe that called them Game Keepers. Every tribe in America has a name for Big Foot. Anyway, they're coming back. Not the tribe, but the white man is leaving. If you don't believe me, ask DARPA. They've been here over fifty years trying to make sense of this fast evolving ecology and its effects. You know. USA readiness. Preparedness they call it.

Sure. I guess. But you're a white man and you're still here.

Yes. I'm part of the design.

△

AND THEN I REALLY AWAKE, the mist still swirling, sun filtering down through the canopy, each individual drop of mist a glass bead drifting one way then the other, shining colors of the rainbow, tiny ecosystems inside each bead – vegetation and sky and horizon. Beautiful. The woods crackling deep inside with noise and activity.

I get out to pee, think I hear people in there, stifled giggles, then something really big expelling air and threatening. I grab a stick, toss it far into the brush, the tall trees moving their tops in the breeze, already in full leaf. I hear Wookiee grunts and the stick crashes back out into the road. Freaks me the hell out!

So quick back into the Jeep. The digital reads past 9 AM. The cell phone vibrates a new message, which I ignore. I'm on the road looking for a place to eat. Doesn't take long before I'm back at the diner, the one of my dream, exact copy, but this time open to a public of ruined cars and bad attitudes. I mean, I walk in, the door slams behind on an over-tight retraction piston, probably to keep flies out. It's not working. They're everywhere. Maybe that door was put there by the flies to keep humans out. Anyway, lots here of interest to the sludge-craving insect world. I mean, how many kinds of grease can you imagine? It's all here, heated, reheated and shining, dripping from the ceiling above the grill, slopped on plates, sliming the wait staff, which is one white-haired lady in a really bad mood and a shiny, dripping, pasty face. There's an over-active fry vat, a margarine-yellow sheen on everything, Crisco grease, pancakes with pretend maple syrup, ranch dressing slick with mayo for dipping French fries and fried chicken. I mean, flies build subdivisions in this stuff. I'm so hungry I order the entire left side of the menu. Seated at the counter, having almost eaten through the butter load, I make the mistake of thinking my passport in Piney land has been stamped, turn on my stool and ask the tables if anyone knows "J," you know, "the dude in the old Ford Torino."

Silence. Then, "Mistuh," the wait staff says, her Airbus A380 nose pocked with zits, eyes rheumy, uglier than a bucket of hairy arm pits, "we for sure know that dude."

"Really?"

"Didn't I say so?" says the waitress, soon understood as wait staff slash owner, then to one of the regulars with gray face deep in a plate of dipping chicken, "Glen, he the one try to git my place closed down? Said I was a health hazard is what. Well, mistuh, that don't make no sense. No one here gives over so much food so cheap. I take food stamps. You on food stamps? I mean, you en't a Piney, but ..."

"No, I have a credit card."

"Oh. We don't take them things."

Glen says, "Wudn him, Sabrina. Hit were a man from upstate gubmint that wanted us to know Pineys hadn't been forgot. He drove a car wid official state plates."

"Oh, right. Got it. I didn't see the places," I say, "and but, sorry. I don't have cash, well, but maybe," and dig deep into the grimy residue of road trip debris that has settled in the pocket of my worn chinos. There crumpled in the mash lay the last of my Ignacio Ben Franklins that survived A-City. I place it down on the table, run a hand over to take out the wrinkles, expect a dentured grin but get instead suspicion, holding the bill up to a greasy light. Well it is pretty soiled, and so I say, "Look, it's real."

"Don't git this bill much."

I say, "Yeah, sorry, but it's real. Look, can you maybe tell me what you know about Big Foot, and, you know, keep the change."

"Why bless me Patsy!" says, Sabrina, "I do believe dis young man intends payin into my secret thoughts. We Pineys cut our own weeds, mistuh, don't share much wid outsiders. That's jest our way. But I'll tell ya dis. They's a lot more motion end noise in the wood dese days. Cain't personally say what that is. But what it en't is normal."

"Yeah, okay. Thanks."

I wipe hard with a wad of napkins to remove grease that hasn't slid down my throat, then pull at the piston torque of the door to get out, which I do, finally, with the kind intention of ignoring Yelp's review ratings. I mean, with China eating dogs and killing their own babies with melamine additives, what's the point? Then Glen shimmies outside his rotund belly wagging a come-hither finger and says, "Son, what dey don't hereabouts want ta say is yer J is very much known. From many years back. Some long hair come here from gubmint to spy inta our woods. Sometime in the 70s."

"He still here?"

"Don't know."

"Was he looking for Big Foot?"

"Never asked."

△

BACK AT PONCY, I'm mildly ripped by Langly and back-up Soc. My defense same as I told the Dad: "On a quest for stellar extra curriculars ... you know ... for college apps." Langly's mouth twists a laugh. "No, really."

He says, "Okay, we'll get you graduated. Your mom has been generous with contributions to the scholarship fund."

I'm told to deliver up the Jeep keys, now to be a conveyance for college visits, or whatever else the parentheticals approve. I'm thinking a pretend Wesleyan College orientation trip to sort out Mrs. V's location, but don't say it. Back in the dorm, I'm online looking for Chen's rise in politics. Nothing yet. But doesn't take long to find Stacy, part-time mall hooker, salon hairdresser virgin who's only done and given oral, both sexes, and posted advert nudies. She must truly be a virgin because the victim of revenge blog from a previous boyfriend. She wouldn't put out. Serious snarky damage intended. And I don't get it. Even after her and Mrs. V sucking lips, I won't bend a knee to the pay-back god. Who will tell the best of Stacy? She's not so bad. I'm saying it.

My dorm room is antiseptic, buffed to raw in the war against microorganisms, even despite having to clean around my left things as I hadn't performed the take-it-home, give-it-away, or store-it Poncy requisite before each major holiday which is thoroughly checked by Dorm Masters during the last Saturday AM chapel snoozefest. But about the cleaning ... I don't see the need. It's bad strategy. Germs come to school to learn how best to infect. Experience suggests, better to just assimilate than fight them off.

There's only a few of us back early from break, mostly the lax bros that I avoid, doors opening, closing, echoes down the hall of voices cranked to outsing iTunes and occasionally shout "Hey!" to returning bros. I turn a corner into the washroom, gorge rising from chemical assault. Better the smell of poor aim at the latrine, scum in the shower, turd slime and puke residue at the throne. I hawk a loogie and wash it down the sink. I did this once in English class. Well, not the sink part. I have permanent sinus complications. So I'm looking for a place to deposit the goo and see Mr. Ralph looking and so swallowed it down. Should maybe have also swallowed a shot of Drano along with to clear the pipes, but maybe not as I think of Big-D and Little-G's mom.

That was Mr. Ralph early in the school year, first weeks of September. Even then wearing the usual dark pea coat and a Greek fisherman's hat, driving a vintage Chevy pickup, which is way cool because he comes from oil money out from Pennsylvania. Quaker Oil. Which is lots of dead Quakers buried since the early colonies that have leaked their juices and over the years become oily. Who would of known? He told us he was just out from grad school, a philosophy major, such as Langly, which didn't win many points. It was his first year teaching. We would soon break him of the habit. He said he wanted to help us discover answers. But first wanted to show us the books to read to find the important questions. He said he got very psyched about this when during his interview with Langly they mostly talked ideas, the abstract ones that never factor into account ledgers. Unless, he said, when the "big guy up there," finger pointing up, factors the end effects of a life. But we didn't take this as religionist rant, no hashtag for conversion ethics. It was more, like, the biggest idea of all: what's up there? I used to think aliens. Mr. Ralph said that on his way out the door from the Langly interview, he took a big chance and planted a wet kiss on top of Socrates's cold, stone head, then said, "Maybe it's not too much to hope there's still room in the hearts of men for Socrates?" "And," said Langly, "the occasional boy or two."

Mr. Ralph said the cornerstone to his enthusiasm shattered when the department chair nixed two thirds of his assigned reading. Also, he confessed he was despairing of the suicide of one of his favorite writers, David Foster Wallace. Then he found the Xerox copier and we were given to read some Wallace essays said to be off-the-charts profound that made no sense whatever. Maybe if your brain works off the sonar ping of a whale. Whatever. Mr. Ralph wouldn't give it up. He was on a mission. Kept going over this dude's message such as it would save our lives from inconsequence.

He called Wallace the voice of our generation. Mr. Ralph said Wallace was a Gen Xer, which is also the Dad, but that he spoke for us Millennials. He was looking for a better place. Such as, if there's nothing for us here, why are we still here? "His work was so much himself," Mr. Ralph said, "so self-aware and, beyond that, lacking in defenses needed to keep the vulnerable essentials of himself a secret. Imagine that. A clear view into the human soul. Never been done before," said Mr. Ralph. We didn't know what he was talking about, but he was genuinely moved and so we were too. Most of us.

One of our proudest thought vacuums wanted to make his mark, sharpen his steelo, legs stretched out under his desk pushing forward the desk in front of him with lesser dude scared to call him out because every one of the 100 billion nerve cells in thought vacuum's small brain was engaged in motoring around muscle mass twice his size. And then thought vacuum saying, "So, Mr. Ralph, you're saying our generation is all about suicide?" Then laughing, "Niugh, niugh, niugh."

"No, not what I said," Mr. Ralph said. "Wallace had many accomplishments. He was a serious tennis player, a ranked player, and he could quote lyrics from bands I don't know but should. He had an incredible education, really smart parents, and I mean, he would be just the coolest one in the room. He was the voice inside our heads, but in him, it was too loud, too demanding."

"Yeah. Know what you mean. I hear voices all the time. Like, Leonard, get to the corner store and bring back a quart of milk, or Leonard, get your homework done. Football will not be your future. That's my mom. Notice I'm here on a football scholarship? Those voices, they ain't so smart. Niugh, niugh, niugh."

I told Mr. Ralph I know a famous poet myself, personally. Sunneva Vitello, published in an ezine, which he said was like, no, not famous, more sitting the bench, leaning in, looking good, but not exactly in the game. The real players get printed in ink. Once again, Mrs. V and me, we're the same.

△

WHEN MR. ROUSE, my dorm master, gives me a welcome from scripture, I want to tell him I know Jesus personally, but instead hold my tongue. Not as in engage the censorship filters, but like, use my fingers. Mr. Rouse says, what's wrong? You okay? That's when I tell him what he needs to know about Jesus with my tongue held, speaking in tongue, which he will cipher if he's truly touched by the spirit. Sounds something like this: "whad j us wannds frrum u isss dissscunnectivitee." Mr. Rouse shakes his head and walks away.

I don't know the extent of my popularity until the first lacrosse practice that afternoon. It's a raw day. Gray and windy with streams of yellow pollen aggravators blowing off trees and bushes. Allergies kick in. I crash into the locker room sneezing and even so mobbed by the bros with questions appropriate and not so much, such as how did I break out of jail? what did I do with Ignacio's cab? is he coming after me? why'd I return to Poncy? snatched in Atlantic City? cool! the Sapperstown Gazette said so. did I see the highway pic taken when I ran the toll booth? it was in the Gazette. who were those mystery babes in the cab? did I bag em? how come I'm not answering their texts?

I'm still not answering. I'm skipping off to evacuate the ooze, wiping it off with fingers on the way to the john for tissue, hands patting my back, fists poised for bumps I ignore so dissolving into fadeaway finger sparkles diminished by my rudeness. I'm desperate to peel off a wad of TP in the squat box but instead find it empty of paper wipes. I panic, close the door as if to make booty waste, take the T-shirt out from my cinched pants and blow into that. Sneeze. Blow again. Repeat. Disgusting! I can't stop.

It's Invasion of the Body Thrashers. It's like full-on spasmatic lung evacuation of tiny alien space nodules making colonies in my branchia, deep convulsions and mindlessness. It's Nicole Kidman, wife of Scientology, and blue-eyed 007 making a stand for humanity in another rip-off flick. When recovered from this shattering exorcism, abs tighter than 20 reps of weighted crunches, I flush the T and its alien slime residue down to a sunless certainty of sewer companionship with discarded goldfish and turtles, alligators and turds. But something of this makes me feel bad. I remember J said there's nothing alien. It's all part of the design. And I remember the mist I breathed deep from the Pine Barrens. So then I think, maybe I should be a better host.

When I return, humbled and dazed, I don't do a great job fielding questions. Blame it on my handlers. They haven't prepared me well enough for the fame that comes from outlawry.

But I do reveal a Jeep Cherokee escape pod parked temporarily behind the maintenance building on campus and morph boldly into brag-a-dude, saying, "Yeah, what the Dad gifted me for maneuvers on-road and off. Comes with 3.7 liter V6, 5 speed, 210 hp, heated leather seats, HID headlamps to bore into the night, tire pressure display, SIRIUS digital satellite radio, interface module for the iPod, 4x4 Trail Rated with hill assist, and what the Dad wanted most, ESP sensors to keep me on track. All this at maximum emissions and 15 mpg. I mean, with this bad boy, bet your ass, I'm road worthy! If I can get a set of keys, which I forget to mention.

After which I'm volunteered to shuttle the Poncy bros to a party off campus at one of the acropolis homes evacuated for the weekend by its parents, Charles Squire III and glittery spouse. Hosted improbably by geeky son Danny Squire known by us as Squirrel. Many local babes invited. A pharmacy of drugs, good tunes, an indoor pool, pizza delivery, comfy sofas if too woozy for a Mr. Rouse sobriety test, as the host parents have sent a letter to the Headmaster inviting the bros to a sleepover pool party in celebration of Squirrel's birthday, which is also the Vernal Equinox. Very pagan. Mr. Rouse will not approve. And the letter, forged, of course, written by Mr. Ralph with what he calls "gravitas," so very effective as a Headmaster end run. Mr. Ralph? There's a development mote worth pondering.

Coach Greerson is much against this overnight of his "boys" as the Pontificate Invitational LAX Tourney, a pre-season display of East Coast teams, begins next morning, Sunday, and runs three days into the school week, with teachers of lax bros expected to go light on attendance and homework. Headmaster Langly is reluctant to say no to the overnight because the Squires are a prominent family with two boys to educate at Pontificate at full pay. And with Mr. Squire's seat on the Board of Trustees for investment advice, the Jeep keys appear in my student mailbox.

What I learn is Danny Squire, early admit to Yale, he's the one tasked Mr. Ralph the letter to Headmaster Langly. And Mr. Ralph agreed because Squire senior fitted Mr. Ralph in his job at Poncy, new money greasing the way for old money, and Squire junior, Squirrel as we call him, he knows something about Mr. Ralph that would pull down the mask if told. But that's not why he wrote the letter.

Squirrel has way over much black curly hair spilling down his forehead, the teeth of SpongeBob, a skinny face busy adjusting angles of unsure, poking here and there, chattering, blinking, short legs, eyes shoegazy. Derpy. Creepy. And now even more so because of carmel-colored hair on top with pink frosted tips that make him look more voodoo doll than rodent. But whatever.

You might think this is where I drink the koolaid, that everything goes cattywampus and I return suicidal to my dorm room. Not so, my droogs. It goes down like this: I run the shuttle from school to Squirrel's party. Same as Ignacio, I meet the bros in small groups in the black-out secrecy of the gym parking lot. Much before-party prep in that Cherokee. Coke in the back seat, nuzzling the high school chicks invited along that sneaked on campus and waited for the Cherokee in a giggle scrum behind a pair of dumpsters. Should of told them not to expect their Facebook likes to go up from this bromance spectacle, especially with Squirrel asserting status as Bromancer in Chief. But then, Squirrel will become for me the most happening pilgrim of the twenty-first century. I know. Right? All the emoticon faces in under twenty seconds expressed here.

After all the shuttle trips, I step inside Squirrel's house intending to forget about Mrs. V, readjust my dopamine dependencies, and bro-hug the best friends Poncy has to offer. After the crazy of the road, I'm ready to feel the inertia of college student with Jeep Cherokee, credit card, and four more years sleeping in class.

First thing opening the door, a wall of sound, then flashing pixels on a big screen HDTV of Flo Rida singing "Elevator", meeting his man needs with ripe apple bottoms grinding up against him one floor after another, surprises every time the elevator door opens, dancing girls and hoodrats giving hand signs, Rida singing about diamonds on her wrists and how she pimps Bugs Bunny, and another girl steps in, and another, all riding his elevator.

Except for the wall-sized video display, all else verging dark. Strategic points of light here and there such as a black-light poster shop with everything in the UV spectrum of blue with chrome reflections. When I focus, I see partiers with moshing mojos engaged seething in the dining room, a case of Robitussin on the glass and chrome dining table, bros and guests invited to snap a cap and toast with Squirrel a trippy DMX high. I'm told one of the lax bros, a day student from Philly, he comes from pharmacy funding. I walk in on the scene as Squirrel stands on a chair and extends above his head a bottle of red syrup, below that a pyramid of quivering bodies, each moving to its own headsplinter. In a bold celebration launch, Squirrel says in a voice borrowed of Vin Diesel, "Fuck my birthday! And fuck America! It's a rotting corpse." Then a deep drink of the thick syrup. Then, "We do the danse macabre on her rotting corpse."

Way cool! More than I would expect from Squirrel, but then no one until now has much listened to anything he has to say. No one but the teachoids. I'm listening now. I should have before. I mean, to live in this place that looks more bomb shelter than house, thick walls of poured concrete, except more inviting inside with clusters and loops of blue leather sofas, chrome tables, spot lit from above, and facing the river windows two-stories tall probably bullet proof and altogether everything packed tight and perched on a bluff of red stone overlooking the Delaware River. The lights of Philly twinkling other side of Jersey. I mean, to have all this and to know, maybe even be sensitive enough to smell the rot it's built on ... that's way cool. Doesn't the child of the one percent just call it? I mean, Squirrel knows he's gifted this life from sucking dry what's left of America's fading heartbeat. And tonight we're all sucking off the same tit.

When the doorbell rings it's pizza delivery which seems low class for a cement palace except, when boxes are taken to the Robitussin table and opened, there's cocaine and weed and a note from Bradley Turcotte saying "party on down," and beyond that

Squirrel points to a bowl of prescription pills mixed together sitting on one of the sofa end tables with directions written in Squirrel's handwriting (all cramped and squiggly at the same time with cross-strokes and hooks) that say something about go ask Alice in the back bedroom. Which we come to learn is a working girl Squirrel calls a party favor. This too Bradley Turcotte gifted us as a goodbye gesture. Brad never came back from spring break. But, says Squirrel's sign, you can't see Alice until you've swallowed pills.

Dennis Wilson is the first to attend this cornubropia of psychedelics and read the sign. He says, "Dude! That's messed up!" Dennis has been expelled but he's here by special invite of Squirrel. Dennis swallows a handful, runs up the stairs to open the "assignation door," as Squirrel calls it, all eyes on Dennis who looks back and says, "420 has come again! And this girlie," he looks inside, looks again down the stairs at us, "she's hot! She's my future ex-wife."

"She'll make a great wife if your career's military," says Squirrel in an almost whisper, head bobbing. "She's seen more helmets than Hitler."

△

THIS IS THE NIGHT OF ONE-LINERS. No one hanging long enough to converse a topic, or maybe just long enough to zing a devastating, arresting, quotable, self-defining statement sharper than a butterfly knife cufflink. Such as Trevor Isley, bench sitter and resident barfoon who has something unexpert to say on everything, saying to Duff, the dude with words carved into the side of his head, saying that Squirrel suffers from Dissociative Facebook Identity Disorder.

And word head saying back, "Yeah, I've seen it before. Oversharing on Facebook. Too many selves out there. I mean, dude, just pick a self!" "Like, totally," says Trevor. And a third voice satelliting the conversation leans in says, "Friend me. Please friend me!" then spins away.

At the bottom of the stairs, a knot of anticipatious Alice askers debrief Wayne Peebles, a fifteen-minute receiver tumbling down the stairs. One such curious one with two pair of glasses, one to see and another of Oaklies on his forehead, asking, "Apocalypse sex or what?"

And the answer from Wayne Peebles that found a reason to set down his iPod, "No, more like aggressively mediocre."

"Dude! Dish the deets," which gets the wonk of intercourse doing a mimic of grabbing ass that's grabbing his own ankles and blowing air out his mouth such as Darth Breather, then standing back up saying, "Plebe porn, only just that. Plebe porn. But you'll get off."

And from the leather sofas facing out onto the lights of Philly over across the river, the girlies I brought in the Dad's gift Jeep huddle in a scrum of sorority support making conversation over the thump and hiphop of HDTV tunes. One is going all loser gesture on one of the bros strutting by frontin, now badly in need of a mojo fix judging by the girlies with put-down hands to their foreheads, index fingers up, thumbs sideways, other hand pointing at the insulted one, all laughing.

Another of the lesser dudes because not really a lax bro, Tripp Matthews, him of the granite face but liquid lips that move all over even when not speaking, a hockey player with NHL dreams but a laxer in the spring by default, he stops, leans into the most blonde with the most hotness quotient, says, "Queenie, can I score your digits?" Queenie says, "Why not? The whole world is binary. You know that, right?" Then Poncy dude saying, "Cool, what's your number?" Then Queenie saying, "Dude, since we agree, life is like, 1s and 0's. First tell me, which are you? A one or a ZERO?" Poncy dude slinks away to a flurry of fist bumps, impolite middle fingers, finger guns, high fives, more loser gestures, the shocker, the wanker, even a Vulcan salute. I am once again having to look beyond words to make sense of things. But I mean, since words can't be trusted ... whatever.

Then Darrell Drummon from inner city Philly that stuffs a basketball backwards does the truckin stroll that on him becomes a prowl while smoking a fatty which he offers to Queenie who looks into those shining dark eyes while taking a drag. He says with quiet, self-assured steelo, "I conversate best when I'm relaxed." She says, "It's working." "Discover to me," he says, "what you want of this party?" She says, "Maybe you." That's when I drift away into the kitchen where the geeks have gathered, plastic cups in hand, around the one lone keg, way low class for this gathering, but these are Squirrel's only true friends, one saying, "Yeah, so, the clock of the long now, like, its real! Deep inside some mountain in Texas. One tick every hundred years. And a cuckoo that sings out once every thousand. Designed for ten thousand years!" Which for reply another geek says, "Yeah, well, I mean, probably no one left alive on this planet even to hear the first cuckoo." After which the clock geek says, "Real genius doesn't try real hard for happy."

"Word up! Who needs happy?" is what I say peeking in, which gets frowns and one geeky dude pushing up his glasses (no, really, he did) then saying, "Clearly, a citizen of the idiocracy."

"Yes," says another, "and so we hear from the hipster tsunami of whinging."

"Friggin keyboard warriors," I say back and bounce out of there. What I see is the line to Bradley's orgasmic delight going all braggsmack intentional on THC laced testosterone, and the lights suddenly bright other side of what was black glass that is now an indoor pool with splashes from Queenie and Darrell Drummon. Others from the sorority scrum fake pleasure at the sight, and some of my bros bend their noses back in place because how could a black basketball player from inner Philly score the Queen? And the geeks in the kitchen still engaging in thesaurus geekalogue. And I suddenly feel very alone even though I've had so many bro hands patting my back. I make an emergency visit to the WC to find a mirror and see if there's a sign someone taped there saying, Hands here! Guess not. I don't want this much contact. I thought I did, but I don't. I look for an escape at the edges of the party. I see a door part open, mostly darkness inside, an unused room, but with one significant beam of light compared to pin lights above everywhere else. Well, except for the swimming pool. Anyway, I step inside that room. I'm alone basking in a triangle of light that gets me thinking of Mrs. V. It's her sign I'm surrounded in.

It's also Squire the III's study. There's wall-to-wall book shelves and investment reports in graph paper littering a desk so big it could float the Delaware as a ferry boat. If Langly's room is all about the punishing head trips of psych drama layed on students with dead philosopher in cahoots, this place is all about bullying numbers into projecting half-truths. Somehow it's even more cold in here. And it's dark but for that triangle of light I spoke of coming in from a spotlight outside directed mainly on the circular drive. I look closely at my hands because they're starting to shake. I don't any longer feel they belong to me. Or maybe this skin receptacle of what I am inside needs to be replaced. Maybe become a tree, a pebble, a house cat. I don't know. I just don't feel it's me I'm looking at on the outside. That's when Squirrel steps in, asks am I all right? Asks is it the drugs?

I haven't taken any. I tell him.

He says him neither, although I do remember a bottle of cough suppressant which I don't say. Maybe he's got a cold. I tell him what I'm feeling. I don't know why, but it seems he might get it. He does ... I think.

He says, "Ever read Ovid's Metamorphosis?"

I tell him not on my list.

He says, "Great stories. Lots of violence. Victims become constellations to escape, or swans, or grape vines. Stuff like that."

"Yeah," I say. "That's pretty much how I feel. I'm ready to be something else."

"Yeah," says Squirrel. "Me too, though I think I already was once. I remember what it's like to live on Venus. You ever feel that? Part of me wants to go back there."

"But," I say, "no one lives on Venus."

"How do you know? You been there?"

"Okay. I get it. I guess I'm ready for college, ready to get the fuck out of here!"

"Yeah, me too, but fuck college. What makes you think that'll be different from here? You think your skin will fit you better there?"

"I don't know. Maybe."

"Why did you give up the road?"

I have no answer.

"Look, I don't know you. I shouldn't be saying this stuff, but me and Mr. Ralph, we're going off together. Soon after graduation. Oh, he's coming ... wait ... (a vintage pickup pulls into the circular drive, it's headlights illuminating the top rows of leather book spines). That's him."

I look out and see a man sized to fit a Mr. Ralph in a Mr. Ralph blue pea coat and faded jeans and worker boots but obscured in an anonymous mask. He walks up to the study window, knocks, raises a hand with fingers signaling hook-'em-horns. How did he know we were here? Is he really an Anon? Did he hack Scientology? If so, Mr. Ralph is way more cool than a word wonk. Squirrel is very animated, or nervous, or going epileptic, twisting every which way, looking hard at the books of his father's study, raking with fingers an eruption of stiff, dyed hair, releasing, pushing it down, then piling it high, then raking it back down again, now looking at his feet. He has become all octopoid tentacles reaching out from the center of his over-revved brain.

I ask, "Where you going?"

He says, "I don't know. East? West? It's Ralph's idea."

"You call him Ralph?"

"Yeah, well, he told me to."

"Isn't he kinda old for you to hang with?"

"He says we're age appropriate. Ralph says I'm the same age as Aristotle that attended Plato's academy. And he's the same age as Plato that left Athens when Socrates drank the hemlock. He says he thought Langly was his Socrates, until he showed he's not. He wishes he could get Langly to drink the hemlock, but we're out of here no matter."

Soon Mr. Ralph is at the study door, knocking, entering, takes off the mask, looks at me with shy eyes I've never seen before, goes over to Squirrel and gives a hug expressive of relations beyond mentoring, says, "Did Squire Senior agree to the terms?"

"Yeah, sure. I sold it as the grand tour, like you said. And also agreed I'd cut the hair after and go straight (he looks awkwardly at me) ... straight to college after. The trip will be my graduation present." Eyes now on his feet.

"Okay, good," then, "Hi, Marvin. I hear you've been Mad Maxing the road."

"Not anymore. I'm in college. Where you two going?"

Mr. Ralph hesitates, looks to Squirrel for confirmation of my security clearance, gets a nod okay then says, "We're off to travel the world. Visit nation capitals. Find the right questions to ask. Otherwise, answers don't count. You know this. We've talked about this. We're going to find a place that suits us better than ... here."

"What here? Sapperstown? Poncy?"

"Just," says Mr. Ralph with arms spread gathering in the here, "just here."

I wish them well together down the silk road. They're good together.

△

AFTER THE PARTY, the lacrosse game, first match of the round-robin tourney, early morning. Way, way early. Every one of the bros a post-party grump. Our first opponent is Hotchkiss School. Go figure. I was too distracted to even notice. Two of Poncy's starters, PGs both, have got into college and haven't returned from spring break. Bradley Turcotte is especially badly needed. Even with Coach Greerson desperate on the phone lines Saturday night, they aren't expected back. That means I get the nod to start.

We jog from the locker room onto the field. I'm feeling some of the old adrenaline pull. Same with the bros. They wear smiles of anticipation. Because of the scent of grass and dirt and briny chin straps, the juicy squelch of the mouth guards. And laxaholic fans lined up on the sidelines with dogs on leashes, little lax rats running on the field with baby sticks dragged off squealing by parents. And coaches shouting words that can't be understood.

And the heat under helmets and under jerseys that says midsummer when it's only 50 degrees outside. And also shouts of encouragement from teammates, taunts from the other team (mostly bench sitters). Until we're on the field stretching. Then we see the red and white colors of Hotchkiss School. I quick put on the helmet. But it's too late. I hear voices rising other side of the field, fingers pointing. Shit! They've got my jersey number. It's the enemy bros that Mrs. V brought low back home at the Dancing Mouse.

So because so many starters are missing, and because the other coach won't agree to Coach Greerson's suggestion we play with only seven on a team, I'm a starting midfielder. This means I'm doing a lot of running upfield to score and backfield to defend. I'm all over the place. And with Hotchkiss, I know what I'm in for. Many players trash talk, but Hotchkiss players take it way far. There's cheap shots here and there at opponents, often when coming through the midfield substitution box where no one expects to be hit.

But mostly, Hotchkiss is known for its distraction penalty strategy. At least whenever they play Lakeville High School. We're all onto it, as are the refs, but not so here at Poncy. What they do is create a diversion minor penalty that everyone notices when the whistle blows, even if just seconds, which is enough for a major penalty to occur somewhere else unnoticed that injures a player or shakes him up or at least puts the fear of injury in his head every time a whistle blows. If he complains, his paranoia fantasy is blamed on turf monsters. Usually a single player is targeted, the best on the field. This time, it's me, for other reasons.

When the first minor infraction occurs, a trip with holding coming out of a scrum, when the whistle blows, I see a hit coming at me from behind, dodge and slash at his head with my stick. This happens again twice. The second time, I spin around and cross-check the hitman. Third time, the offending dude sees me see him and refuses to engage. Now I get heated and a little too sure of myself. Verging on mary gait, I take a run upfield cradling the ball, knowing most Hotchkiss players are a little in awe of my stealth detection skills. I plant the drive leg and make a vertical jump, crank back my stick and follow through with mustard on a perfect pass to a Poncy attacker that pulls the Hotchkiss point off balance away from the crease and blinds the goalie and score! The ball rolls in with embarrassment slo-mo between his legs.

I do a little victory dance in front of the Hotchkiss bench that really pisses them off. And when I turn around to join my teammates in a celebration scrum, Dieter Vollander, hook nose, him that's still limping from Mrs. V's hammer and hasn't yet seen play on the field, he comes off the bench and collapses my legs with a full-body take-down check. My teammates notice and go crazy, shout out to Coach Greerson who brings along the dude with bandages. I'm laying on the ground, trying not to make much noise. I'm pretty near the Hotchkiss bench as they remove my helmet. Then it's "Hell, yeah, that's the dude!" coming from the enemy bro with the flask and braces I remember from the Mouse, while Dieter that took me down is getting a correction from his own coach and two refs, but I'm hurt pretty bad. "Hey, that dude," he's saying to his coach, "he's the reason I'm riding the bench. Shit! That's him." Two other Hotchkiss players on the field hear his remarks, come over to have a look, take off their helmets, one smashes it on the turf near my head, the other smashes his stick on the turf, and both curse me with anger appropriate to laxers who could never got a response from an NCAA Division III coach to a game video posted online. They too are taken off field and told to quiet down by their coach. But they won't. They are ejected for unsportsmanlike conduct that only makes them more mad and more noisy. I'm hoping someone posts a video.

I'm helped off the field by a very nervous Poncy coach, as he has no idea what has escalated the bad feelings. Then it's the half-time buzzer and D.O.F. (dogs on the field) – which is an actual lacrosse statistic Baltimore refs keep, you know, goldens and labs escaping the leash or given puppy freedom, running and barking, shitting and pissing for us to step in. I'm taken to the locker room by the dude with first aid. But, and despite the pain of my knee, I tell him I'm okay but should maybe go get looked at by the campus nurse. I dress quick and get to the dorms soon after the band-aid box has clattered back to the field.

I send a text message to Brad:

> Bradley dude like I dont know where
> Im at anymore or what Ill be 2moro.
> feel like outside the cloud, totally
> nowhere

And he comes right back with:

> Marvin dude, u be on my phone, in
> the cloud, whats 2moro? whatever.
> rock on

I strip down, get into the shower, make it really, really hot, watch the steam fill the room, fog the mirrors. I leave the bathroom door open, watch the steam spill out into the hall and into my dorm room which is near, put on blue and gray Poncy formal wear, get onto the top bunk, watch the light change to an energy source inside the mist making the room dimensionless, and I'm thinking, what's the best question I learned from on the road? And then I know. It's this. How much can you take with you? And the answer, if you care to know, is that you can take with you only as much as your heart will carry. And that's so right. I take a deep breath of mist, and see a white house by the sea, and feel the white legs of Mrs. V pulling me in, and see an old trunk floating in a lake, it opens and in it a beating heart. So I knot to the bed frame the "tail," which is the thin part of the tie, and the "blade," which is the thick part of the tie (terms I learned by Mr. Gainer of his how-to-tie-a-tie chapel talk at Poncy that I told you of, which maybe says Chapel is not so much a waste of time), and from the white mist ... hands pulling me in, familiar hands ... I lean out beyond, way out beyond, and it feels right. I feel infinite.

Back on the field, before the game resumes, some of the benched Hotchkiss players start a chant: "Mrs. V, Mrs. V, she gave good head. Too bad she's dead!"

A Poncy bro shouts back, "What the fuck you talking about." Even with the Hotchkiss coach getting in the face of the obnoxious, poor sports on his bench, the evil bro from Marvin's failed beatdown under the bleachers, and from Mrs. V's leveling at the Mouse, he shouts back, "Killed by her husband! Beat to death. Deserves every bruise. Check the papers you don't believe me!" This is an event that's tailspin worthy if I was a bird. But I'm not. I'm not that bird I saw at the Hotchkiss boathouse that couldn't find its way out. I'm not that feather spinning down. I have become part of the design.

Fomite

About Fomite

A fomite is a medium capable of transmitting infectious organisms from one individual to another.

"The activity of art is based on the capacity of people to be infected by the feelings of others." Tolstoy, *What Is Art?*

Writing a review on Amazon, Good Reads, Shelfari, Library Thing or other social media sites for readers will help the progress of independent publishing. To submit a review, go to the book page on any of the sites and follow the links for reviews. Books from independent presses rely on reader to reader communications.

For more information or to order any of our books, visit
http://www.fomitepress.com/FOMITE/Our_Books.html

More Titles from Fomite...

Novels

Joshua Amses — *During This, Our Nadir*
Joshua Amses — *Raven or Crow*
Joshua Amses — *The Moment Before an Injury*
Jaysinh Birjepatel — *The Good Muslim of Jackson Heights*
Jaysinh Birjepatel — *Nothing Beside Remains*
David Brizer — *Victor Rand*
Paula Closson Buck — *Summer on the Cold War Planet*
Dan Chodorkoff — *Loisaida*
David Adams Cleveland — *Time's Betrayal*
Jaimee Wriston Colbert — *Vanishing Acts*
Roger Coleman — *Skywreck Afternoons*
Marc Estrin — *Hyde*
Marc Estrin — *Kafka's Roach*
Marc Estrin — *Speckled Vanities*
Zdravka Evtimova — *In the Town of Joy and Peace*

Fomite

Zdravka Evtimova — *Sinfonia Bulgarica*

Daniel Forbes — *Derail This Train Wreck*

Greg Guma — *Dons of Time*

Richard Hawley — *The Three Lives of Jonathan Force*

Lamar Herrin — *Father Figure*

Michael Horner — *Damage Control*

Ron Jacobs — *All the Sinners Saints*

Ron Jacobs — *Short Order Frame Up*

Ron Jacobs — *The Co-conspirator's Tale*

Scott Archer Jones — *A Rising Tide of People Swept Away*

Julie Justicz — *A Boy Called Home*

Maggie Kast — *A Free Unsullied Land*

Darrell Kastin — *Shadowboxing with Bukowski*

Coleen Kearon — *Feminist on Fire*

Coleen Kearon — *#triggerwarning*

Jan Englis Leary — *Thicker Than Blood*

Diane Lefer — *Confessions of a Carnivore*

Rob Lenihan — *Born Speaking Lies*

Colin Mitchell — *Roadman*

Ilan Mochari — *Zinsky the Obscure*

Peter Nash — *Parsimony*

Peter Nash — *The Perfection of Things*

Gregory Papadoyiannis — *The Baby Jazz*

Andy Potok — *My Father's Keeper*

Kathryn Roberts — *Companion Plants*

Robert Rosenberg — *Isles of the Blind*

Fred Russell — *Rafi's World*

Ron Savage — *Voyeur in Tangier*

David Schein — *The Adoption*

Lynn Sloan — *Principles of Navigation*

L.E. Smith — *The Consequence of Gesture*

L.E. Smith — *Travers' Inferno*

L.E. Smith — *Untimely RIPped*

Bob Sommer — *A Great Fullness*

Tom Walker — *A Day in the Life*

Susan V. Weiss —*My God, What Have We Done?*

Peter M. Wheelwright — *As It Is On Earth*
Suzie Wizowaty — *The Return of Jason Green*

Poetry

Anna Blackmer — *Hexagrams*
Antonello Borra — *Alfabestiario*
Antonello Borra — *AlphaBetaBestiaro*
David Cavanag*h*— *Cycling in Plato's Cave*
James Connolly — *Picking Up the Bodies*
Greg Delanty — *Loosestrife*
Mason Drukman — *Drawing on Life*
J. C. Ellefson — *Foreign Tales of Exemplum and Woe*
Tina Escaja — *Caida Libre/Free Fall*
Anna Faktorovich — *Improvisational Arguments*
Barry Goldensohn — *Snake in the Spine, Wolf in the Heart*
Barry Goldensohn — *The Hundred Yard Dash Man*
Barry Goldensohn — *The Listener Aspires to the Condition of Music*
R. L. Green — When — *You Remember Deir Yassin*
Kate Magill — *Roadworthy Creature, Roadworthy Craft*
Tony Magistrale — *Entanglements*
Andreas Nolte — *Mascha: The Poems of Mascha Kaléko*
Sherry Olson — *Four-Way Stop*
David Polk — *Drinking the River*
Janice Miller Potter — *Meanwell*
Joseph D. Reich — *Connecting the Dots to Shangrila*
Joseph D. Reich — *The Hole That Runs Through Utopia*
Joseph D. Reich — *The Housing Market*
Joseph D. Reich — *The Derivation of Cowboys and Indians*
Kennet Rosen and Richard Wilson — *Gomorrah*
Fred Rosnblum — *Vietnumb*
David Schein — *My Murder and Other Local News*
Harold Schweizer — *Miriam's Book*
Scott T. Starbuck — *Industrial Oz*
Scott T. Starbuck — *Hawk on Wire*

Fomite

Stories

Fomite

Susan Thomas — *Among Angelic Orders*
Tom Walker — *Signed Confessions*
Silas Dent Zobal — *The Inconvenience of the Wings*

Odd Birds

Micheal Breiner — *the way none of this happened*
J. C. Ellefson — *Under the Influence*
David Ross Gunn — *Cautionary Chronicles*
Andrei Guriuanu — *The Darkest City*
Gail Holst-Warhaft — *The Fall of Athens*
Roger Leboitz — *A Guide to the Western Slopes and the Outlying Area*
dug Nap— *Artsy Fartsy*
Delia Bell Robinson — *A Shirtwaist Story*
Peter Schumann — *Bread & Sentences*
Peter Schumann — *Charlotte Salomon*
Peter Schumann — *Faust 3*
Peter Schumann — *Planet Kasper, Volumes One and Two*
Peter Schumann — *We*

Plays

Stephen Goldberg — *Screwed and Other Plays*
Michele Markarian — *Unborn Children of America*

Essays

Robert Sommer — *Losing Francis*